The Christopher Quimby Chronicles

Kaden K. Schrock

Copyright © 2023 Kaden K. Schrock

All rights reserved. This book or any portion thereof may not be reproduced or used in any manner whatsoever without the express written permission of the publisher except for the use of brief quotations in a book review.

This story, all names, characters, and incidents portrayed in this production are fictitious. No identification with actual persons (living or deceased), places, buildings, and products is intended or should be inferred.

To Mom,
who told me I was worth listening to.
And to Jenna,
Who never let me believe otherwise.

Part I

Blue Velvet Blazer

My Vans slapped the cold pavement of the empty street. I sucked cold air in heavy breaths as a chilling wind blew against my face, my throat growing sore. Looking over my shoulder, I saw no sign of my pursuers, but I kept on at a full sprint until I knew I was completely safe. Glancing at my watch, I saw that it was well past midnight. Somebody at home had to be wondering about me by now, but at this point they were used to me being out at all hours of the night.

Where was Nolan? He'd been with me up until Justin and his buddies came upon us, and in the confusion of bailing out of the place we got split up. I hadn't cared much at the moment, all I'd cared about was getting myself out of there before Justin Hobbes and his crew of weightlifters got a hold of me. I knew it was a bad idea to try to mess with Justin's truck, but nothing is fun unless it's a bad idea.

When we found the pickup alone in the school parking lot, it seemed almost imperative that we tamper with it. We'd planned to rewire the truck's brake light wires with a bridge wire so that the horn would sound every time Justin hit the brakes, but he'd caught us in the act. Whatever he assumed we were doing to his truck, he didn't approve, so he and his three goons had taken off after us. I'd been on the run for about ten minutes, but I'd lost them about five minutes ago and hadn't seen a sign of them since.

Suddenly I worried that they'd caught Nolan and were beating the daylights out of him, so I pulled out my cell phone to check if he'd tried to get a hold of me. There were no texts from him nor anyone else, so I slipped it back into my pocket. I wanted to find a safe spot to catch my breath and call him.

As I came onto Main Street, bright headlights shined directly in my eyes and it took a few seconds for me to recognize the vehicle, but I heard the hollering first. It was Justin's truck, with Dalton Stevens hanging out the passenger side window with a baseball bat. Burning out in my worn out Vans, I turned a corner before they reached me and ducked into a wide alley. I heard tires screech as he backed up and turned into the alley behind me. I sprinted across 3rd Street and into an alley on the other side, this one didn't seem big enough to fit Justin's truck.

I glanced over my shoulder and saw him swerve down 3rd Street after seeing that he couldn't fit this way. As the truck passed the alley, Dalton made an expected gesture with his right hand and whooped like a crazed warrior.

I grabbed a hold of a fire escape ladder and pulled myself up to the landing, and from there I shimmied up a small metal chimney to the roof of the two story building. I crouch-walked to the center of the roof and crouched behind an A/C duct. Pulling my phone from my pocket, I called Nolan. He picked up before the second ring.

"Hey, Chris," he answered casually. "Where y'at?"

"I'm on the roof of the pharmacy building," I answered. "Where might *you* be?"

"I got to your car and peeled out. I was about to call you and ask where you were so I could come pick you up before Justin and his buddies tear you apart."

"Like I said, the roof of the Meyer Pharmacy." I heard tires rolling to a stop on the street below me and all four doors of Justin's truck opened and shut. "Justin's here," I hissed. "Hurry up." I hung up and laid flat on my stomach and listened to the voices below me. All four of them split in opposite directions and I heard them scanning the entire area. Within my anxiety and fear I felt a serious pain in my bladder that told me I was in need of a restroom or a dark corner.

"Think he could'a got on the roof?" I heard Dalton Stevens' whiny voice say.

"Yeah, yeah, look!" Jacob Montgomery shouted. "The ladder on the fire escape is pulled down." The rusted ladder creaked as the four thugs climbed up it and then grunted their way to the roof. I saw four sets of feet spreading out around me as I made myself as small as possible betweens the air ducts.

Like a sound from heaven, I heard the rumble of my Mustang speeding down 3rd Street. Nolan came to a halt with it, attracting the attention of my pursuers. I watched them walk to the edge of the roof and peer down, then mumble amongst themselves. Nolan was in perfect position, except for the fact that four athletes stood between me and my escape.

"Where's Chris?" Justin yelled down.

"Good question," I heard Nolan reply. "I was wondering the same thing."

Knowing this was my chance, I leaped to my feet and sprinted towards the edge of the roof. Justin and his friends whirled toward me a second too late, as I jumped through them, saying, "Right here, fellas." I dropped off the edge of the building and onto the canvas awning on the front door of the pharmacy. Nolan whipped the car onto the sidewalk and I slid from the awning into the passenger seat of the convertible. Much less graciously than I'd planned, my foot catching on the seat and my forehead hitting the dash. The tires screeched as Nolan sped the car down the street and away from our imminent beating. Between my awkward landing and Nolan's upshifts, it took a moment for me to find my seat.

Laughing and hollering, Nolan said, "That was almost the death of Chris Quimby."

"Quite the save," I said. "But this doesn't mean you can drive my car whenever you want." He laughed, his dark, wavy hair fluttering in the wind that blew over the windshield. Nolan had been my best friend since elementary school, and oftentimes I forgot that we weren't blood related. To the naked eye, we'd seem like polar opposites. I was what some called a trust fund baby, he was a preppy genius, the child of two lawyers, and shaping up to be a talented one himself. But there was something that made the two of us fit together well, we didn't quite know what. He was my best friend and I'd take a bullet for him, as I knew he would for me.

I sat on the front steps of the house the next morning, tying my shoes. It was a sunny October day, a cool breeze common to central Virginia. The front lawn of the property was freshly cut and looked as neat as the rest of the place. It was a classical, old-fashioned mansion with sandstone pillars and a gravel driveway, purchased by my father at the age of thirty, the year I was born.

My father, Henry Quimby, was a hotel proprietor whose wealth and holdings accumulated every year, and the specific trust that held my name grew in assets with it. My brother, Jared, the eldest of three, was already three years through business school preparing to take over my father's company after his retirement. My older sister, Olivia, the middle child, was studying cosmetology.

As for me, the youngest child, two months into my senior year in high school, my career was yet to be decided. Of course, you could say it was a bit irresponsible for the almost-eighteen-year old son of Henry Quimby to not have a career picked out, but the way I saw it, it wasn't my concern. Money was about the last thing I'd ever have to worry about.

Nolan Bragg came out the front door and sat next to me. He dressed more presentable than I, as usual. His family was wealthy as well, but not as openly and obnoxiously as mine. Nolan was extremely intelligent, he always had been. Although it was just the beginning of his senior year of high school, he was already taking several classes at the Virginia School of Law during his free periods. I, on the other hand, had very few classes of any kind. I had selected the bare minimum amount of school time in order to receive my credits to graduate.

It's not that I couldn't go to college, because I could. Tuition obviously wasn't a problem, and it would seem fitting of Henry Quimby's child to attend a prestigious school, but if there was anything in the world that I found unnecessary, it was college. I knew dozens of college dropouts that made six-digit salaries with ease, and none of it came from knowledge they'd learned in a lecture hall.

The thing that most people didn't know was that my own father, the wealthiest man in Dixon, Virginia, had never set foot on a college campus. He and my mother, Valerie, had been married at the age of twenty and had started their own bed and breakfast while working side jobs to bring in extra cash, which had blossomed into a chain of bed and breakfasts, which had eventually brought them to constructing their very first Quimby Suites hotel at the age of twenty-eight, and were now nearing fifty destinations on the east coast.

My father had never pressured me to attend college, because he knew that someone like me didn't belong there. He was a rolled-sleeved dirty-handed hard worker that had the natural intelligence that it takes to be an entrepreneur. He lived through toughness and faith, and he'd made it out of the hard times.

So sure, a college degree might be a good idea, but my heart was destined for different things than a high-rise office building. I was a dreamer, a "tragic romantic". Nolan liked to tell me I looked like something straight out of a 60's greaser movie. My wardrobe consisted almost exclusively of Vans, worn out denim, and album cover t-shirts. I drove a loud Mustang. I read novels for fun. Although people knew me and loved my family, I was still known as the black sheep of the Quimby empire.

"Let's head down to The Grind," Nolan suggested. "I need coffee on a Saturday morning."

"There's coffee in the kitchen," I said.

"That's never stopped us before."

We strolled down the walkway to the garage and hopped in my dark blue '67 Mustang. It had been a gift for my seventeenth birthday, a year ago. She was about the only real love I'd ever known. Sure, I got attention from girls at school, and I had my fair share of circumstances with them, but I had yet to be in a serious relationship, and wasn't interested in starting one any time soon.

We drove into Dixon, watching heads turn every time they saw the vehicle. But most citizens of my hometown were accustomed to seeing the convertible around, and it was usually followed by a pleasant smile or wave. I was indebted to my father for making the

Quimby name a good one in the mouths of Dixon's citizens. He was a generous philanthropist and a steadfast promoter of the growing community.

I found a parallel parking spot near the least amount of cars, trying to save my pride and joy from the most common result of parallel parking, then crossed the street to The Grind coffee shop. As I stepped inside, the tiny bell above the door jingled, attracting the attention of the barista at the front counter.

She'd also attracted my attention.

I'd never seen her before, even though Nolan and I made an appearance at The Grind a good five times a week. And believe me, had I seen her before, I would've remembered. She was short and blonde, with the build of a volleyball player, and her hair was pulled in a tight ponytail falling out the back of her hat, which matched her apron. Her name tag read "Jennifer".

Nolan voiced my thoughts: "Oh my."

"Back off," I said, casually shoving past him. He grabbed me hard by the bicep and I tried not to wince in pain. Gently pulling me back, he stepped ahead of me and walked nonchalantly to the counter.

The barista laughed and said, "Take it easy there, boys."

"Sorry," Nolan apologized, gesturing toward me. "He's a little clumsy."

She grinned widely at Nolan, "What can I get started for ya?"

I started speaking, but Nolan interrupted. "I'll have my usual, but I guess you're new here so you don't know what that is." The two of them laughed. I was irked at how charming Nolan was coming across, and how foolish he was making me look. The roles were usually switched. "A Kahlua macchiato, and Chris gets a regular vanilla iced coffee."

"Alrighty," she said. "Can I get a name for the order?"

"Nolan."

"Nolan," she repeated in a weird tone, exaggerating the syllables with her tongue. I watched her make eye contact with Nolan and then laugh shyly. I was dumbfounded at what was happening in front of me, so much so that Nolan had to grab me by the shoulder to snap me from my trance and lead me back to our corner booth. He was in an unusually good mood, for obvious reasons, and it drove me crazy. Every five seconds he took a glance up the front counter, and then looked back, smiling.

"Whoops, she caught me staring," he whispered once, holding in a weird laugh. When I showed little interest, he tilted his head. "You alright, bud?"

I threw my head back dramatically and used a feminine voice. *"Oh! She caught me staring! How absolutely stunning she is!"*

"You're jealous," he accused me. Before I could say I wasn't, he shot me down. "Yes you are. You're always getting the girls and they're always all over you and I'm always just there in the background. 'Oh sure I'll bring someone for your friend.' No, Chris. No more pity dates, no more third-wheel. She likes me, not you, and I'm not trying to be a jerk, but politely back off. It's my turn."

I couldn't help but smile at his outburst. He was right, she liked him, not me. Nolan was a good-looking dude, and he deserved love. I was being immature about it, and I decided that even though it was going to suck, it was my turn to be the wing-man. Brotherhood was a two-way street, so it was my responsibility to not only support Nolan in this affair, but to help him in any way I could. Had it been a girl I'd previously had my eye on, it would've been different, but she was new, so I had no reason to claim her as mine.

A thought came to my mind, and although it hurt, I brought it up to Nolan. "You still lookin' for a date to my dad's anniversary gala?"

Nolan's hands shot in the air out of praise. "I love you," he wheezed. But he quickly brought his arms down as he noticed the barista staring at him with a curious glance. She checked the front door for customers, then came to hand deliver our drinks instead of calling Nolan's name.

"Kahlua macchiato and an iced coffee." She handed us our drinks, then added, "Sure seemed like something interesting was going on over here."

"Well, you've been working so hard, why don't you take a break and we'll talk about it?" I couldn't believe Nolan's sudden charm. He was quiet around most people, especially girls, but I'd come to learn that a person who brought out unique characteristics in someone was a unique person themselves, especially to whom they had the effect on.

Her name was indeed Jennifer, and she'd just been working three-day weeks for about a month, but those three days were mostly weekday mornings, times that Nolan and I didn't come for coffee. She had graduated high school about twenty minutes south of Dixon a year ago, which made her somewhere like a year older than us. After graduating, the best apartment and job she could find was in Dixon, which was how she ended up here. She was taking online classes at William & Mary and working towards a degree in physical therapy. Once Nolan had described his future career in a law field, she seemed even more interested. After ten minutes, the two of them couldn't get enough of each other, and it was getting a little too comfortable.

"You know, Jennifer," I interrupted as they both laughed at something that wouldn't have been funny if they hadn't been head over heels for each other. "Nolan was talking about something earlier and I think he had a great idea." I gestured to Nolan with a smile.

"Uh, yeah," Nolan stuttered. "As you know, Chris' dad owns Quimby Suites, and they're hosting a twenty year Quimby Suites Anniversary Gala at their, uh, house next Saturday, and obviously, being Chris' best friend, I have to be there. That also means I should probably have a date. . ." He paused, apparently hoping that she would catch on. ". . .and I decided that you were quite a dazzling candidate."

She smiled shyly and her face grew red. "You know, I think you're right. I would be delighted to be your date." Before they could fall even deeper in love, a few customers began filing through the door, which made her hastily stand up. "I have to go back to work, but if you write your number down on this napkin I'll shoot you a text later." She smiled and handed him a napkin from her apron, and then a pen. He quickly scribbled down his number and gave it to her, then said a sappy goodbye.

I shook my head in disbelief at my responsibility. "Alright, buddy. Looks like we're gonna have to get you ready for a date."

Wednesday afternoon, Nolan and I worked out in the top floor of my garage, as was a weekly custom. We were both naturally fit people, so the main goal of our workouts were to put on weight in the form of muscle, for the benefit of our health and, let's be honest, the benefit of the ladies. Usually, we went out for a high-protein dinner after this, and then finished the night hanging out and talking over coffee. Tonight, we skipped the caffeine and went straight from *South Main Bistro* to the strip mall on the eastern side of town, the closest businesses to the interstate exit. There was a small tailor shop run by guys who looked like they belonged in New York or California.

"Chris, I told you I already have a suit," he tried to argue.

"You have one black suit and like three ties," I said. "She's not gonna dig that. You gotta stick out, look flashy."

We looked around for a minute, finding a size section that was closest to Nolan's physique. Normally, we would have gotten one tailored, but it took about a month for a tailored suit to be made. It was hard for me not to get tempted into buying something for myself, but I had plenty of suits and jackets. This mission was for Nolan.

"This is it!" I pulled out a blue velvet jacket with a black lapel and presented it to him. He bit his lip and considered it. "Come on, just try it on," I urged him. He slipped it around his shoulders and looked at himself in the mirror. His lips pursed and a smile grew on his face.

Looking more like Daniel Craig every second, he gave me a satisfied nod. "This'll do."

I had a much louder closet than most, as per my personality. On Saturday, we dressed in my bedroom, and I selected a maroon plaid double-breasted suit. I tied my shiny black dress shoes and buttoned a pair of silver cufflinks to my white shirt. Nolan looked equally dapper, his velvet jacket matching nicely with black pants and shoes. I was almost jealous of the blazer, it complimented him perfectly.

As the time neared seven o'clock, Nolan left to pick up Jennifer from her apartment downtown. Dozens of guests arrived every minute, and I stood outside with my mother and father, greeting everyone as they handed their keys to the valet, and then directing them down the hall to the ballroom.

"Where's Nolan?" my father asked me. He was in a pleasant mood, as he always was at parties and events like these. He wasn't a boastful man–satisfied was a more fitting word. He often said his goal was to live "comfortably", but he'd reached that and was still climbing.

"He went to pick up his date," I replied, absentmindedly shaking the hand of my father's Chief Operating Officer and his wife.

"Date?" my mother asked. "I thought you were the one getting all the dates." Both my parents laughed, but it was true, and I felt a tad guilty about it. I'd gotten somewhat of a reputation at school for it, and it was embarrassing, and a little shameful. I wasn't trying to "get around", it just seemed like whatever situation I'd find myself in with a girl hardly lasted long enough for me to get to know them, and it frustrated me. Plus, as much as the attention flattered me, the paranoia always remained that they were most likely just courting me because of my wealth. In the back of my mind I always came to wonder if I was unpleasant to be around, or worse, perhaps I was simply a bore.

"Speaking of which," my father said. "This is just about the first gala we've had that you don't have a date to. Something wrong?"

"No," I mumbled, but I hadn't really thought of it that way. As Nolan pulled in the driveway with his gorgeous date in the passenger seat, a flushed awkward feeling came over me, but I pushed it off. I could still be my suave, debonair self with or without a date.

Jennifer was even more attractive in her red gown than she was working at The Grind. Her hair and makeup looked professionally done, but I knew that was something her best friend must've spent all afternoon doing for her. Nolan's smile never faded for a second as he accompanied her into the ballroom.

The two of them sat with us at my family's table, as Nolan always did. He was a third son to my father, they talked often about business and law, enjoying having someone to have a real intelligent conversation with. I tried to keep up, but I was eventually as lost as a first-grader playing *Jeopardy!*, every now and then throwing in comments that I hoped were relevant, just trying to remind them of my presence. But my parents spent little time at our table, as they had to make toasts and entertain. My brother, Jared, and sister, Olivia, were both present. Olivia had a new boyfriend, as she did often. He was alright, but the earring and permed hair didn't appeal to me. Although, his attire was nearly as sharp as mine, which I respected.

Nolan was talking to Jared, who was even more of a business fanatic than my father, so between that conversation and Jennifer, his attention was taken up. As I listened to the background piano music being almost drowned out by nearly a hundred voices, I took a moment to look about the guests. I recognized most of them. All of my fathers executives and corporate officers were there, along with many hotel managers and those higher-ups. Then there were the family friends, and some of the more sophisticated citizens of Dixon that my father had business dealings with.

It's a peculiar thing the way certain strangers can seem so familiar. Like every feature of their appearance adds together flawlessly, something so irregularly perfect that you feel comfortable staring at them, because everyone else certainly must be. A certain guest with this particular ambience had caught my attention in the far corner of the room. Her long legs were crossed in a long black ball gown, similar to what every other woman was wearing. Her hair was blacker than her dress, the lights from the chandelier dazzling off of it.

The dark mascara around her eyes gave her the look of a beguiling witch of some sort. Whatever it was, it drew me in like a siren.

She sat with a woman and a man at her table, but there was very little conversation between them. I watched her for quite some time, even as I made rounds about the room, saying hello to my father's friends and putting a good face on the family, but she never left her seat. She scanned the room, then looked back at her glass of chardonnay, which she hardly seemed old enough to be drinking.

Even as I walked nearly right in front of her, she seemed to almost avoid me, as if she wanted nothing to do with me. Undeterred, I decided I had to dive right in. Gathering myself and acting like the fine businessman's heir that I was, I approached the table.

"Everyone having a nice evening?" I asked politely.

"Yes, absolutely," she said softly, elegant whilst being forced into a conversation. Her voice seemed to have the slightest British accent, but it may have just been the graceful way in which she spoke. Her tablemates replied much the same.

"I'm Christopher Quimby, Henry Quimby is my father."

"Veronica Teague," the woman answered. Her companions also gave their names, which hardly broke the atmosphere before depleting from my memory. I was mesmerized. The other woman was dressed just as perfect, but Miss Teague looked like she was born in the dress she wore now.

"What brings you all to tonight's gala?" I asked, trying to stimulate conversation.

"Oh, I'm the hotel manager in Hilton Head," the man replied. I glanced at him and nodded to show acknowledgement, but I was hoping that Veronica would speak up. She didn't.

Her disinterest made me stumble, so I simply ended the conversation with, "Well, it was nice speaking to you all. Have a nice evening." When I was somewhat out of her eye line, I watched her for a few seconds. She looked around the room again, casually, until her eyes stopped halfway around. Following her gaze, my eyes landed on who else but Nolan.

This was beginning to feel like some sort of mind game, like a cruel test against me. What was I doing wrong, and what was Nolan doing so right? Sure I was happy for him, and gave myself plenty of credit for his social upbringing, but it was beginning to feel as though something was wrong with me. I worked my way back to my table, feeling rather defeated, just as Nolan was getting up.

"Where you going?" I asked him.

"To the little boys' room, if you must know," he said with a smirk.

"Do hurry back," I said sarcastically. "We mustn't waste this pleasant evening."

But he didn't hurry back. After fifteen minutes, I was somewhat embarrassed that he'd become so sick on his date with Jennifer, and I could tell she felt a bit awkward as well, but neither of us said anything. Bored, I wondered whether or not my new interest had moved since the last time I'd snuck a glance at her. When I looked, she was nowhere around. Scanning the room, I couldn't find her.

By twenty minutes, when Nolan still wasn't back, I was afraid something was wrong, so I texted him. At thirty minutes, when he hadn't answered, I *knew* something was wrong.

"Do you think something happened?" Jennifer asked awkwardly.

"I'm not sure," I said. "I'll be right back." I stood and strolled to the hall. The guest bathroom was extravagant and pleasantly-designed. Old-fashioned and elegant, like the rest of the house, so much so that it almost seemed necessary to hire a restroom attendant like matinees.

I meekly knocked on the closed door, but there came no answer. When I checked, the door was unlocked, so I pushed it open, fully expecting to ruin the night of an innocent guest. But it was empty. Puzzled, I checked my phone again, but he hadn't even read my message. This time I called him. I leaned against the sink and listened as it rang. From somewhere in the room, I heard a faint buzzing.

Wait, what?

I followed the sound to the silver trash can in the corner of the room. Peering through the pile of paper towels, I saw a lit up screen. Carefully reaching into the trash can, I pulled out Nolan's cell phone, with a missed call from "Trust Fund", his sweet nickname for me.

That was peculiar.

After I'd spoken to his parents on the phone, I decided that had been a serious mistake. Stewart and Estelle Bragg were frantic as soon as I told them of his disappearance, and it made me a bit more panicky than I had been to start.

Geez, this might be serious.

Jennifer was almost the worst. The fact that she knew nothing about any of us made her head spin even more, so she just sat there, hands on her cheeks, not speaking, but breathing heavily.

By midnight, every guest was gone, and all that was left were caterers and servers. My family, Nolan's parents, and Jennifer sat anxiously in the foyer, trying desperately to figure out where he could have gone. We'd searched just about every app in his phone to find any clues or messages or hints as to where he might've run off to. So far, nothing. We'd questioned everyone that he talked to on a regular basis: nothing. We searched his car, which was in the same place he'd parked it: nothing. As the night progressed, we grew more fearful and less calm, and by 2 a.m., we decided there was nothing left to do but call the police. When told by the 911 operator that protocol was to wait around 24 hours before filing a missing person's report, Estelle promptly cussed and chewed the woman out for three minutes, explaining the confusing evidence and circumstances. After a few minutes of convincing, the operator said that she would send someone out.

After hours of answering the police officer's questions, and more police showing up, and then answering the same questions, and crying, and stress-induced fits of rage, we'd come to a conclusion.

Nolan had officially gone missing.

It was early the next morning, the sun was just barely peering out from behind the usually beautiful hills of Dixon. But this morning, they were ugly, gray, dead. Mornings were colder now, as October grew closer to November. I wore an old hoodie with sweatpants and tennis shoes, not my normal going-out attire. I'd felt guilty about not going to church with my parents, but my mind was just too jumbled. I'd eventually regret it, as church was exactly what I needed right then, but I didn't go. This morning, I only had one thing on my mind: Nolan.

The police were still working. They'd closed down the scene, from the ballroom to the bathroom to his car. They hadn't concluded whether or not it was a kidnapping or just some random irresponsible act by a typical teenager, but I was sure it wasn't the latter. Nolan wasn't stupid. He enjoyed a thrill and a good time, but he wouldn't leave so abruptly, ditch his phone, and not tell anyone where he was going, while on a date, no less.

I put the top up on the Mustang, the air was just too cold this morning, as was my mood. My coffee fogging up the windshield, I sped down my road and a few more to reach that of the Braggs' residence. As expected, Stewart and Estelle were wide awake, and looked as if they hadn't slept, which they most likely hadn't. They welcomed me in, saying they'd just been praying, and anxiously waited for me to share any kind of good news that I had, but I had none.

"I just thought we'd try to figure some of this out ourselves," I explained. So for fifteen minutes we threw out every single thing that any of us had seen Nolan do in the past week; where he was when he wasn't at school, what he ate, who he'd been texting, anything we could possibly remember. Still, we came up empty handed.

"I just don't think–" Stewart was abruptly cut off by someone honking in front of their elegantly secluded two-story home. He rushed to open the door, but we saw nothing in front of the house. Whoever had honked had sped off, obviously wishing to not be seen.

"Sunday's an odd day to send out mail," I mentioned to them, nodding towards the flag sticking up on their black mailbox. Their puzzled expressions didn't surprise me one bit. They didn't have any outgoing mail, the flag was put up by whoever had just driven past, in order to attract their attention. Hustling down the front steps in sock-feet, Stewart opened the mailbox door, and from the front porch we watched his face turn even more sober than it had been. His hand trembling, he reached into the mailbox and pulled out a torn piece of a pink note card, folded once. I watched him unfold it, his normally stern face now one covered in anxiety.

After a two-second glance, Mr. Bragg leaned against the mailbox and held his hand to his forehead. I rushed to him, grabbing onto him before he passed out, and helped him back into the house. Setting him down at the kitchen table, I let him catch his breath. Once he'd recovered, Estelle reached over and gently grabbed the note card, unfolding it for the two of us to see.

Pinned to it was a square of blue velvet fabric. Written in neat, untraceable capital letters, were the words: *DROP THE CASE.*

The fabric was from Nolan's jacket, the one we'd bought just a few days before the gala, the one I'd picked out for him, the one I had coveted as he'd stolen the glance of everyone in the ballroom. Estelle felt it in between her slender fingers, tears streaming down her face. I watched her read the sentence once more, and her hand shot to her mouth. Both the Braggs were lawyers, Stewart a prosecutor, and Estelle a defense attorney.

"My God," she hissed, looking at her husband. "Neil Trace."

Neil Trace, I learned, was a middle-aged man on trial for the murders of an elderly Italian barber and his wife. The evidence said that Trace murdered the man, Mateo Barbieri, after he'd "cheated" him on an investment. Witnesses from nearby stores stated that they watched and/or heard Trace enter the store in a rage, shouting and accusing Barbieri of dishonesty. Next, they heard two gunshots, followed by the deafening screams of Mateo's wife, Elena, followed by another gunshot. Mr. Bragg was to be the prosecuting attorney against Trace.

"Sounds like a pretty cut and dry case," I said after hearing the summary.

"That's what you'd think," Stewart said. "But the main witness, the one who'd had a partial view from across the street, is getting cold feet, afraid to testify, and I'm beginning to understand why.

"They want you to drop the case so Trace has a better chance to walk," I concluded. "They probably used a similar tactic on the eyewitness in order to keep them off the stand."

"Should we tell the police?" Mrs. Trace asked.

I pondered it for a moment. "I'm not sure. If the kidnap–or, if these people find out that the police know about it, they might, you know, hurt Nolan."

Estelle gasped again, and Stewart rubbed his distressed forehead. "It's simple," he said. "I have to drop the case."

"And risk a murderer going free?" I asked before consideration.

"This is my son you're talking about!" Stewart said powerfully. A bit frightened, I sat back in my chair. He immediately apologized. "I'm sorry, Chris, I'm just so riled up about all of this. But let's be honest here, is there really any way to get Nolan back without dropping this case? We don't have any idea who it was that was waiting for Nolan in the restroom. There were hundreds of people at that gala, it could've been anyone. We just don't have a single lead."

Suddenly there was a knock from the front door, and Estelle hurried over to answer it, wiping her eyes and trying to look presentable. There was an old woman on the front porch, wearing slippers and pink pajamas.

"Mrs. Lent, what's the matter?" Estelle asked the woman.

"Honey, I was just sitting in my kitchen, watching the birds on the feeder in my front yard," Mrs. Lent began. "And I saw a car pull up to your mailbox. I thought maybe it was just the mailman using a different vehicle, you know, but it suddenly blared on the horn and went squealing away. I saw you come out to the mailbox, so I figured I'd come over to tell you that I saw it."

Mr. Bragg and I rushed to the door. "Did you see what kind of car it was? Or the license plate?" I asked desperately.

"Well, I don't recall there being a license plate," the woman feebly said. "But I know it was a black sedan, a Ford, I think. Black body, black wheels, everything. Seemed a bit obnoxious to me, but I guess I'm a bit old-fashioned."

Stewart and I looked at each other and I said, "There's our lead."

I drove through town for about an hour, looking for a blacked out Ford sedan, but I saw none, which made sense. Had I kidnapped someone, I would've also made an attempt to hide the getaway vehicle. My next plan was to check the footage of the security camera posted on the driveway pillars from Saturday night, to try to find the car that Mrs. Lent had identified. By now my parents and Jared were gone to church, and Olivia had headed back to school, so I was alone.

I double-stepped up the staircase to my father's study and swung into his desk chair. Quickly, I made my way to the live security camera footage. A copy of the previous night's tape was already with the police, but I simply rewound the live feed to seven o'clock of that evening. Doubling the video speed, I watched every vehicle that pulled into the driveway.

There it was. Around seven thirty, probably the thirtieth car to pull in, the blacked out sedan rolled past the pillars and up the driveway. Quickly switching to the angle from the garage, I could see every car as its passengers stepped out and handed their keys to the valet, who drove the vehicle around to the open space at the side of the house where cars were parked.

From the sedan emerged three people. The driver was a large man, who opened the back door for two younger-looking women. I felt my face grow hot and my palms clam up as I came to recognize the second woman. Her long, slim legs and black dress were unmistakable. It was Miss Veronica Teague.

Running my hands down my face in anxiety, I mumbled to myself, "It just had to be her, didn't it?"

As soon as my father entered the door, I was grilling him. He held me off until he was on the sofa in the foyer, removing his shoes. Again, I asked him who Veronica Teague was.

"Well, it was that young lady you were talking to at the gala," he said.

"I know, but who *is* she? Like what kind of hotel exec is she? Why'd she get a table? And who were the other two that were with her?"

My father spoke as he led me up the steps to the study. "Teague is the concierge at the Myrtle Beach Quimby Suites, one of our nicest destinations, but she's a new hire, so Friday was my first time meeting her." He checked the guest list from his desk drawer. "The two with her were Linda Sykes and Michael White. White is the manager in Hilton Head, Sykes is his assistant. They're all new hires, so I'd yet to meet any of them, probably why you didn't recognize them either."

I tried to put this together. It made no sense that a Quimby Suites hotel manager from South Carolina would be involved with Neil Trace. There had to be some kind of connection here. There was no way that it would be mere coincidence. Plus, I knew someone linked to Trace would have a hard time getting a job as a hotel manager without being background checked, referenced from other jobs, etc.

Finally an idea came to me. Grabbing my cell phone, I typed into the search bar, "Michael White Quimby Suites". Tapping on "Images", the first picture I saw was indeed the man that had been with Veronica, the image coming from the Quimby Suites website. He was well built, with short buzzed hair and a rather large nose. Right next to it was a picture of a different man, with an identical background and image format, also with the name Michael White. Confused, I tapped on the image and was taken to the Quimby Suites website, to the picture of the Michael White that I'd met.

I showed it to my father and watched his brow lower in confusion. "It almost looks like Michael White lost about twenty years and gained about fifty pounds," he said, comparing the two of them.

"Well, for this image to be on the internet, it must've been on our website at one time," I thought aloud.

"So somebody changed it?" my father voiced both our thoughts.

"There's only one explanation," I said. I looked at the two Michael Whites, the old one and the one I had met. Tapping my finger on the one that had been at the gala, I said, "That's not Michael White."

The next day was Monday, but the idea of a school classroom seemed so ridiculously unimportant at the time that I wondered why I ever bothered with it. I had much more pressing matters at hand, and my mother's protests were hushed by my father. My mom was a gentle woman, almost to a fault. She was so non confrontational that even the idea of her child getting involved in something like this made her anxious. I had searched through the images that the hired photographer had taken the night of the gala, and though they'd done their best to hide themselves, I found three decent pictures of our three suspects. Uploading them onto a hard drive, I dressed in black jeans and a black hooded sweatshirt, laced up an old pair of Vans, and headed for my car.

I flew down the country road that led into the heart of Dixon. I avoided Main Street, not for any specific reason, but I was beginning to be more cautious about the moves I made. The top stayed up on my car, and the hood of my sweatshirt was always over my head. Of course, this was all for naught due to the fact that I was driving the most noticeable car in town. Either way, I remained wary.

I pulled into an apartment complex that I passed rarely, only on my way to a cheap Chinese restaurant a block down. I parked and tried to slow my gait as I headed for the steps, and eventually found apartment 27. I knocked twice, and the door opened before I could get in another. Gabriel McDowell stood at the door, all six feet, three inches, and two hundred twenty-five pounds of him. He wasn't overweight, but he wasn't athletic. He'd been born extra large, and he'd been that way his whole life. There wasn't a coordinated bone in his body. No matter how many coaches in high school tried to get him to try out a sport, God just hadn't given poor Gabe the athleticism of a goose.

"Hey, Chris," he said, showing genuine delight. "Come on in. I don't get a whole lot of visitors, especially not old buddies like you." His apartment wasn't disgusting, but it could've used the loving touch of a mother. From the vanilla candle on the counter and cushions on the sofa, it was obvious his mother had made an attempt to make the place appear more homey, but at the end of the day, it was still just the apartment of a single twenty-one year old freelance computer technician.

That was why I was here. I knew if there was anyone in the world that could help me identify who the three suspects really were, it was Gabe. He was the smartest person I knew when it came to computers and other devices of technological innovation. He had already earned an associates degree in Computer Science from Lynchburg, and from what I understood, he was preparing to go to Virginia to get his Bachelor's.

"I'm kind of in a hurry, Gabe," I explained. I pulled the hard drive of the photos out of my pocket. "I have three pictures of people I need to identify. I knew if anyone could do it, it'd be you."

Flattered, he took the drive from my hand and smiled. "You've come to the right place. It'll take less than a minute. Well, not actually, but you get the point. Follow me." He led me into one of the two bedrooms in his apartment, unveiling an entire world of computers, monitors, gaming setups, and devices too advanced for my layman's eye. Sitting down at the biggest monitor, he stuck my drive into the computer box next to it and let it download. Meanwhile, he opened an icon from his home screen that read "Facial Recognition".

"I downloaded this program when my cousin was trying to figure out if his girlfriend was cheating, and I didn't think I would use it again, but here we are. Basically, it can scan a two-dimensional image and, if I filter off a few possibilities, it can narrow it down to one or two people." Now downloaded, I watched Gabe take the images and insert them one by one into the program, and the computer immediately began scanning and dissecting the pictures.

"I'm guessing this is for Nolan?" Gabe asked me. It startled me, for I had thought no one knew about Nolan's disappearance besides my family, his, and the police. "Don't worry, I didn't tell anyone. I have a channel of the police radio scanner, and I was listening to it the other night. I pieced it together that it was Nolan. I'm sorry about it, but if there's any way I can help, please just give me the word."

I smiled and put my hand on his large shoulder. "You're already helping. If you can do this for me, it'll put me three steps ahead." As I said it, the computer program let out two buzzing noises that left an uncomfortable feeling in my ears, and the three faces were projected on the screen.

"Alright, this says that young lady number one is either Linda Sykes, age forty-three, or Miranda Blaine, age thirty-one. Wow, that's either the best-looking forty-three year old I've ever seen, or it's an average thirty-one year old."

"The latter," I told him. "Sykes was her alias. The name's listed there because her picture was listed by the name of the Quimby Suites website. The other two will probably be the same case."

"I think you're right. Our man here is either fifty-six year old Michael White, or forty year old Soloman Payne. I'm guessing Payne?" I nodded, staring at the third suspect, eager to find out who this enchantress was.

"Who's the last one?" I asked urgently. "Her alias is Veronica Teague."

"Well there's an extra option on this one, although if she's 'Kate Sanders', she is deceased. If that's the case, this is starting to seem like a *Ghost Hunters* episode. If we cross off that possibility, this stunning deviant turns out to be twenty year old Blaire Devereaux. That's a mouthful, but she sure makes it look good." He was staring somewhat intimately.

"Gabe, she kidnapped Nolan," I said, snapping him from his trance.

"Oh–no, yeah, you're right," he said. "Sorry."

"Can you run a background check on the three of them? Do the same for Neil Trace while you're at it."

"Will do." With that, Gabe searched names, keywords, and bios to find all the information possible for our suspects. He rattled off criminal histories, which were small or nonexistent for most, known associates, and known family.

"Miranda Blaine has a meager criminal history. She was picked up on a few auto theft charges, which she served a total of six months for. She has a child, but from the look of it, she hasn't seen much of it since the baby's father married another woman and the two of them took custody of the child. That's kind of sad, but if she's mixed up in kidnapping, I'm sure she doesn't have a care in the world for that poor kid.

"Soloman Payne has been inactive since he was released from prison two years ago on a series of illegal merchandise marketing charges. Local guy, though. His sister, Launa, owns a club near Virginia Beach. His brother, Dominic, runs a small storage facility right near the West Virginia border. That's something to keep in mind.

"Wow, there is pretty much nothing to speak of for Miss Devereaux. One DUI at the age of nineteen, but no immediate family to speak of. Of course, that doesn't mean she has no extended family, but this database couldn't find me anything. I'll go ahead and print this out for you, but hey, explain to me why you shouldn't tell the police about all this?"

"If those guys find out that the police are picking up clues," I explained. "They'll start using Nolan. And you know what that means. . ."

Gabe's gaze looked distant, and he turned slightly pale and sad-looking. "I guess you're right."

"I'm getting close," I said. "I'm getting into something serious here, and I can't go into the finale without some help. Can I count on you to do some recon and provide some technology?"

"Absolutely," he answered. "What do you need me to do?"

"Keep finding information, however you possibly can, and if you find anything significant, let me know. I might need some sort of technology when it comes to the endgame, so if any of your little devices here would be beneficial, I'll be willing to pay for anything I use. Just notify me if you have anything else. I really appreciate all this, and I know Nolan will too."

I discreetly left the complex and cruised through town. My mind was racing with all this new information, desperately trying to piece things together. In spite of myself, I couldn't keep my thoughts away from Veronica, or Blaire Devereaux, rather. She seemed to be one of the least significant in this case, yet there was something that I felt like I was missing.

The thing that was bothering me most was that note left in the Braggs' mailbox the day before. I realized I had left it too soon and hadn't stopped to make a thorough examination of the note and the jacket fragment. Making a left at a stoplight, I made my way back to the quiet neighborhood of the distraught Mr. and Mrs. Bragg.

I knocked on the back door and was let in by Estelle, wide-eyed, awaiting my news.

"Anything?" she asked me as Stewart hustled into the room. This time, I was glad to share whatever I could. I knew after leaving the day before that I ought not return without some sort of progress.

I went over what I'd put together in the past day, trying to be overly hopeful and confident about everything, and it seemed to brighten their spirits somewhat. My intentions weren't to give them false hope, but I myself was confident, and eager to check out the threatening note.

It was laying in the same place they'd left it the day before, sitting on the kitchen table. The cloth from Nolan's new jacket, the jagged piece of paper, the words "DROP THE CASE" etched on it, and the silver pin that had been stuck through the cloth and the folded paper. Setting down in front of it, I stared at it from afar, then up close, trying desperately to pick something up from it. The handwriting was square and untraceable, the cloth was clean.

Leaning forward, I took a deep sniff of the three items. The strongest smell I got was from the new cloth, which still smelled of the tailor shop. Pushing it aside, I smelled again. This time my nose quivered slightly at a sour smell. Sniffing again several more times, I picked up the same scent. I tried the paper, but it wasn't it. It was the pin, the thick, metal pin with a ring on top. Taking a strong whiff, my eyes nearly watered as I discovered what I was smelling.

"Alcohol," I said aloud.

I handed the pin carefully to the Braggs and they came up with the same conclusion. As Stewart held it, he suddenly held it up and examined it. "This isn't a pin. It's a martini pick."

"Like the ones they stick olives on to put in drinks?" I inquired.

"Exactly, like at bars."

I nearly shouted as I came to a realization. Solomon Payne's sister owned a club near Virginia Beach. I desperately ran over the other evidence, trying to find something more incriminating. The cloth didn't hold a single hair, fuzz, or fleck of dirt. Taking the paper, I held it up to the lamp, but it showed nothing. I ran my fingers along the rip line and examined it closely. My eyes stopped in the rounded corner, where the pattern changed. There was a distinct ninety degree angle jagging into the paper. It was a dark blue point, barely large enough to see. It had been the very corner of a larger dark blue shape. It was barely a millimeter in length, but it was definitely there.

I pulled out my phone and quickly called Gabe, whose number was luckily saved in my contacts from years before. "Hey, Chris," he answered.

"Gabe, you said Soloman Payne's sister owned a club in Virginia Beach, right?"

"That's right," he said. "It's called *Rêverie*."

"Can you get me a picture of the logo?"

"Sure, I've got it right here. Stay on the line." I listened to him click and drag a few times, until he finally said, "Okay I emailed it to you. Check it out."

I pulled up my email and felt my heart skip a beat. The word *"Rêverie"* was scripted in calligraphy, with a sharp, ninety degree, dark blue border. I put the phone back to my ear and looked into the eyes of Estelle Bragg, speaking to them both. It came out in a whisper. "I think I know where he is."

"I need your driver's license."

My brother Jared sat on a barstool on our back patio sipping mimosa. My father had gone off to the bathroom, and I leapt at the opportunity to get him alone. "Why?" he asked me, confused.

"I think Nolan is at the *Rêverie* club in Virginia Beach," I explained. "We figured it out from the threat they put in the Braggs' mailbox. Obviously, they won't let a seventeen year old kid into a club, which is why I need your ID. People have asked if we're twins before, Jared. It'll work."

After a few seconds of consideration, Jared pulled his wallet from his pocket and handed me his driver's license. "I can't believe I'm doing this. You should call the police about it, but I know you're too stubborn to use common sense. I'm doing it for Nolan. I would come if I could, but we can't pretend to be the same person. But if you're wrong, or you get caught, or if I get in trouble, I'll kill you." He slapped me on the arm. "Good luck."

I thanked him and ran to my bedroom. There was a holstered handgun bolted to the back of my headboard, in perfect position for me to grab while lying on my bed. I'd put it there myself after watching too many episodes of *Forensic Files*. Now, I shoved the gun in my waistband and put my hoodie over it. I walked gently, trying not to blow off my rear end, and left the house unannounced.

The sun was setting on Dixon as I pulled out of my driveway and drove to Gabe McDowell's apartment. He opened the door before I could knock. Leading me into his tech room, he showed me a few things he'd put together.

"I figured it would be necessary to have communication between the two of us, so here's the smallest bluetooth earpiece I could find, it's hardly visible. Just call me when you get there and we'll be in touch the whole time. Other than that, I have this fake coin, which can record audio for a radius of about fifty unblocked feet. I'll turn it on if you give me the word, but you may not need it. What do you have?"

I pulled the pistol from my waistband and Gabe nearly fell from his chair, covering his face. "Okay, different approach," he said. "But equally effective."

I showed him Jared's license and said, "Also, from now on, I'm Jared Quimby. It's the only way I can get into that club."

"Understood," he said, swiveling to his computer. "I found the construction plans for the club, and I decided that these two rooms would be the most likely locations to hold Nolan. This storage room and a janitor's closet are the only rooms in the basement. Either of them would be a reasonable spot. If it's not that, there's a few private rooms on the top floor above the bar."

"Alright. . ." I said quietly. "Thanks for everything. I won't forget this. I know Nolan will be more than grateful for all that you've done. I'll be sure to repay you whenever you need."

"You want to repay me?" Gabe said seriously. "Bring Nolan back here and let him thank me himself."

I shook his hand. "You got a deal. Keep us in your prayers." With that, I took what he'd given me and left. After a nervous vomiting session in the trash can behind the complex, I hopped in my car and headed east, toward Virginia Beach.

The parking lot was quite full, as full as could be expected on a weeknight. I parked at the grocery store parking lot down the street, out of view of anyone who'd be watching for me. Taking deep breaths and mumbling prayers for five minutes, I worked up the courage and stepped out of the Mustang. In fear of a pat-down, I tried to figure out a place to conceal my pistol. Realizing it was the only place they wouldn't touch, I shoved the gun down the crotch of my pants, in a way that it didn't bulge irregularly. Now I was sweating even more profusely, due to the fact that I had a bullet aimed at the most important part of my body. I tried to walk as normal as possible, under the circumstances.

The bouncer immediately asked for my ID, which I showed him, acting as if I used it every day. He examined it a minute, then asked me to take off my hat, which I did. His eyes narrowed, he asked, "Growin' ya hair out?"

"Sure am," I said confidently. "Still got that sun bleached look, too." My enthusiasm was an attempt at annoying him, which appeared to work.

"Mm, hm," he mumbled. I breathed a sigh of relief as he handed me the ID and let me inside. I made a beeline for the bathroom, locked myself in a stall, and put the gun back in its original place, then made sure it wasn't visible. It spited me that I'd almost blown myself away for no reason, he hadn't even patted me down. I was seventeen, how should I know what to expect? Finally, I headed out to the bar. I knew they'd be suspicious if I sat there without buying a drink, so I ordered a martini. Finding an empty table, I examined the pick that the olive was stuck on. It matched perfectly to the one that had been stuck through Nolan's jacket.

I called Gabe and placed the earpiece in my ear. "Hey, Gabe, you there?"

"I'm here. You make it in?"

"Sure did. Stand by until I'm ready to make a move."

I sat around for a while, scanning the place for cameras, but I found none. There was a winding staircase that led to a balcony, where the second-floor private rooms were. I saw no sign of the basement, so I asked Gabe.

"From the layout, it looks like the door to the basement is through the kitchen. I don't know how you'll make it back there."

Suddenly an answer came down the staircase. I whispered to Gabe, "On second thought, I won't have to."

I recognized Blaire Devereaux's legs before I saw her face. She came down the metal steps in a pair of black jeans and a dressy top of the same color, normal apparel for a club of this class. She looked exhausted, like she hadn't slept in days, which was most likely true. In fact, I probably looked the same. Still, she looked over every patron in the establishment. Stepping over to the bar, she ordered a drink, then took it to a table in the opposite corner of the room, where she could keep an eye on everyone. I kept my face as casually hidden as possible, while stealing glances at her. One hand was on the table, fingering the stem of her glass. The other was hidden beneath it. She seemed out of tune, not the elegant deviant that she'd been at the gala.

She was smart, though. There was no way I could approach her without her recognizing me before I got there. I thought it over, then decided there was only one way to get there. "Gabe," I whispered. "You ready to hear some high-caliber acting?"

"Oh, boy," he said back. "This should be interesting."

I stood somewhat loudly, picked up the drink that I hadn't touched, and sauntered toward her table. Purposely stubbing my foot on the leg of someone's chair, I said, "My apologies, sir. I was just on my way to speak to the young lady."

Now there were several sets of eyes on me as I strolled over to her table, giving her no opportunity to dash or make a call of any kind. Her eyes were narrow as I sat down and the other customers turned back to their table. I'd made a nonchalant glance at her ears and had seen no communication device, and she carried no purse or bag of any kind, so I figured I was clear to talk.

"I'm sure there's a gun pointed at my stomach," I whispered. "But there's another one pointed right back at yours."

She smirked, but wore an otherwise sad expression. She slowly pulled her second hand up and set it on the table, empty. "That's not a very attractive way to say hello, Christopher."

The hair on my neck stood up at having been called by my first name by this bewitching criminal. Her stare made me feel vulnerable, as if she'd known every move I'd made in the past forty-eight hours.

Through gritted teeth I hissed, "You've got about three seconds—"

"Until what? Are you gonna blow me away?" she asked. Shaking her head sorrowfully, she mumbled, "Too late. You slipped up."

"You sure did," came a voice directly behind me. I heard Gabe cuss in my ear. Next, I felt a jab in my spine. "Hand your gun to the girl and stand up, real casual."

As I stood and turned, I realized my fatal mistake. The man I'd "accidentally" bumped into happened to be Mr. Soloman Payne himself, and he wore a devilish grin as he told me to head upstairs. Blaire stayed at the table, looking disappointed, although I didn't know why. I walked up the stairs, Payne hiding the gun in hands large enough to break my neck in a second. Holding the gun on me, he unlocked room 4 and opened the door. "Get in."

The first sight I saw was the back of Nolan Bragg, slumped over in a chair facing the wall, his hands bound.

"Well, isn't this sweet?" Miranda Blaine said as she sat on the bed, holding a suppressed pistol on me as I walked in. "Best friend coming to save the day. Too bad you barely made it inside. Good effort, though, little fella." Her condescending and mocking attitude drove me insane with hatred.

Nolan craned his neck to see me. His cheek was bloody, his sweaty hair covering his forehead, and his eyes sagging. "Chris," he said, barely loud enough to hear.

"To be honest," Payne said, closing the door. "I'm surprised you made it this far. I don't know how to managed to find us here, and actually," he clenched his teeth like he was mad in the head. "It makes me really unhappy." Putting his large shoe in my chest, he sent me coughing to the floor.

"Surely now that prosecutor will have enough sense to drop Trace's court case. If he would've done it in the first place, this would've ended days ago. Maybe if you people would *do as we say*," Payne yelled in my face. "You wouldn't be here right now. You've got me in quite a predicament, now. You know as well as me, Quimby, you can't leave here knowing what you know."

"Chris," came Gabe's voice in my ear. "Cough if I should call the police."

I did so, then heard Gabe frantically dialing on a separate phone. Just as he did, Payne grabbed me and emptied my pockets. The ID, the listening device, and my cell phone, which showed an active call to Gabe McDowell.

"He's talking to someone!" he yelled. Cussing, he grabbed the bluetooth from my ear and smashed it on the ground. "Whoever it was will have the police here in a minute. We have to get out of here."

"Okay, get the other kid," Blaine said, raising her gun. "But we don't need this brat alive."

I stared down the barrel of my death as my life flashed before my eyes. I heard the expression said before, read it in novels, but now I learned it was true. In the few short seconds, I saw years worth of memories, images I'd long forgotten but were stored somewhere in my brain. I couldn't possibly believe that every thought, word, move from my life had led up to this ending, but still, here it was. I heard the shot and awaited the hit, my eyes falling shut and body chilled, but none came. Instead, Miranda Blaine fell to the ground, screaming, blood flowing between her fingers as she grasped her thigh.

There was a splintered hole in the door, which Payne now aimed his gun at. Without thinking, I leapt at him, tackling him full force and slamming into the wall. He slammed the butt of his gun against my head, which dazed me, but I sent my fist into his chin. Falling back, he scrambled to aim his gun at me, but I had a hold of his arm, and I slammed it against my knee. Screaming, he lost his grasp on the pistol and it fell to the floor. I leapt on it and whirled, aiming it at his head and stopping him in his tracks.

"Chris!" Nolan yelled with what little strength he had. "Everyone must've heard that shot, we have to go. You know there'll be more of Payne's goons downstairs."

He was right. It was his sister's bar, she must've been in touch with them. I found a knife in Payne's pocket and cut the binds from Nolan's wrists and ankles. They were raw and bloody. Putting my arm around him, I helped him to his feet. "My legs are numb," he said. "I haven't stood up in two days."

"I got you," I said. "I got you."

Blaine was on the ground, a bullet in her leg, and Payne was gripping his arm, which seemed definitely broken. Nolan put his fist across the big man's jaw, sending him to the floor. We scrambled out the door, finding no one in the hallway. There was an exit sign at the end of the hall, which we raced to, to find a back staircase leading into an alley. Nolan was slowly gaining feeling in his legs, and if he was dehydrated or malnourished, he didn't show it.

We crossed the street, nearly getting slammed onto the hood of a minivan, whose driver gestured at us with disdain. We made it to my car before we said a word, and I sent gravel flying across the parking lot as I sped out of it. Nolan had burst into hysterical tears by the time I made the on-ramp and merged onto the interstate, headed back to Dixon at ninety miles an hour.

I couldn't stop looking at Nolan, holding tears deep in my throat. He was sobbing out of relief, sadness, and joy, from one to the next, and he constantly hugged me from his seat. He was alive and safe, it took me a moment to comprehend. I slapped myself across the face several times to make sure this night was real, and every time I did, I still found my best friend sitting in the passenger seat.

Solomon Payne and Miranda Blaine were arrested on kidnapping charges. Launa Payne, the club owner and Soloman's sister, told everything she knew after being threatened with accomplice charges and potential seizing of her establishment.

After a very emotional reunion with his parents, Nolan ate for an hour straight, everything that Estelle could fit in him. At some point, Jennifer burst in the front door and Nolan still had the strength to pick her up in a powerful embrace.

Wednesday afternoon, Nolan, myself, Jennifer, and Gabe McDowell found ourselves at The Grind, talking about anything that didn't bring us to tears. Nolan had finished crying sometime during the night before when he'd run out of tears and put himself to sleep. Now, he looked decently refreshed, and although not as bright as his former self, he was a healthy step up from the way he'd looked when I'd first seen him at the *Rêverie*. He had a raw scar on his cheekbone now, which only made him appear more suave.

"There's a lot I can't remember," he said. "But there's one thing I've been thinking about all day: I can't figure out who shot through the door. The one that hit Blaine. I didn't see anyone when we ran out."

I looked at Nolan, then at Gabe. "I can think of one person that it could've been. The last person that had my gun, the one that had stayed behind when Payne took me upstairs, with an especially regretful look on her face."

And that was the reason that the three of us, when questioned by police, never mentioned the name of Blaire Devereaux.

Part II

From the Water Tower

"You know, Chris, I think this is the first time *you've* ever been the one getting set up with 'the friend'." Nolan Bragg was all smiles as he sat on my bed, watching me struggle to find something to wear. "Usually I'm the third wheel that gets matched up with the other third wheel, but this time, it's you."

"Not an overly encouraging pep talk," I commented, holding up a light blue t-shirt to see if it gained his approval.

"It's January," he said. "Light blue makes me think you've got a tee time Sunday afternoon. Pick something that sets the mood. Jenn said Heidi's got a saucy attitude, so you need to dress like that suave trust fund baby that you are. How about that dark olive one? The long-sleeve, yeah."

"Since when did you become my wardrobe designer?" I asked, slipping the shirt over my head. "All this coaching makes me feel like I've never been on a date before. I'm *Chris Quimby*, for Pete's sake. This should come natural to me."

"Well, if I recall, the last person you used your devilishly debonair charms on happened to be the same drop-dead gorgeous young misfit that held a gun to my head and threw me in the trunk of a car that same night. I'm correct, am I not?"

"Give her some credit," I said. "That same misfit is the very person who saved your life just a few days later."

The joke had passed, and Nolan had a bit of a distant look in his eyes. The incident had been over two months ago now, and he was completely physically healed, but there were some psychological scars that I knew he'd battle with for years to come.

Pushing it away, his dashing smile returned to his face. "Of course, there was that waitress at Olive Garden last week, when we went out for your birthday, but that hardly got past hello before she pulled out the 'my-boyfriend-is-six-inches-taller-than-you' look. . .Sorry, I didn't mean to hurt your feelings. But hey, speaking of birthdays, you're a big ol' eighteen year old now. An adult, ready to face the world's most unconquerable mystery: women."

"You got that right," I said jokingly. I pulled a classy silver watch from my swiveling rack, a new one that had been a birthday present from my older brother, Jared, a week ago. Making one final full-body check, I deemed my outfit adequate and we headed downstairs. Throwing on a black bomber jacket and suede Chelsea boots to help me appear taller, we bid farewell to my parents and hustled to the garage.

"Okay, I'll give it to you," Nolan chuckled. "You've got the unfair advantage of an absolute girl magnet of a car." He slid his hand along the hood of my 1967 dark blue Mustang convertible.

"Yeah," I said despondently. "I think that's the reason girls want to hang out with me. Sometimes it feels like they're on a date with the car, and I'm just the chauffeur."

"Oh, give yourself a break. You're a good-looking kid and you know it. I don't know what's gotten into you lately, all heartbroken and despairful when it comes to the ladies. You gotta get your swagger back."

I gotta get my swagger back.

We pulled up to Buffalo Wild Wings around six o'clock and parked next to Jennifer's Honda. They stepped out of their car as we did and Nolan and Jennifer indulged in their odd couple's moment, which put me in an awkward position when Jennifer's friend, Heidi, came around the car. I said a casual polite hello to her and the four of us headed inside.

It had been the girls' idea to come here tonight, although it's common sense to most that a Buffalo Wild Wings isn't the number one place to go on a date, especially not a night that Virginia's basketball team was playing. Either way, Nolan and I had decided that we would do our best to control ourselves, even whenever the rest of the restaurant was getting rowdy and into the game.

We'd never really established that this was a "date" between Heidi and I, but it was kind of an unsaid knowledge between us. Personally, I wasn't looking for a girl-type-friend of any kind, but Nolan had desperately wanted to go on a double-date of sorts, so I gave in and told him I'd go, even if I secretly loathed it. Heidi was attractive, I'd seen pictures of her a few times before, but I just couldn't bring myself to be interested in her. She was fun and polite, but I sensed that she was a bit of a good-time girl. She spoke very freely, at some points a bit too freely. I didn't have a terrible time, but I hoped that Nolan would let me off the hook after tonight. I did feel obligated to repay him for all the times before this, whenever he'd been the one who'd been forced into the double-date with someone he wasn't interested in.

My dating life, my whole social life, really, had been off-kilter lately, ever since Nolan's kidnapping, but I couldn't put together why. Inversely, Nolan had been the one who'd gone headlong into dating life with Jennifer, his athletic high school graduate girlfriend. He'd also gained more friends at school, whether that was because he'd just become a more likable person or if he'd thrived in the attention of being a former hostage. My senior year, on the other hand, was the same old mediocre classes with the people whom I cared little for. But hey, I was eighteen now, the day-after-New Years baby, so I had a tad bit more freedom.

"Well, Chris sure goes to town on his wings," Heidi joked as we ate, which I laughed at, but her amorous expression made me shrink back. I was somewhat frightened by her advances, flattered of course, but frightened nonetheless. My trust-fund lifestyle had given me a bit of a playboy reputation, which was filthily untrue, although it still caused some bizarre overtures made by some of the young ladies at Dixon High School.

"Chris," Jennifer said with a pleading expression. "We have yet to use your patio and hot tub. . ." Jennifer was my friend, she had been as soon as we'd met her at The Grind, a coffee hotspot of Nolan and I's. Nolan was the only person that I'd hung out with on our newly installed patio and hot tub spa, so I decided she was right. The warm jets would feel good on a cold night like this. It was around 8 o'clock by the time we left the place, and thirty minutes later, after letting the girls pick up swimsuits, we headed out my backdoor and into the bubbling hot tub.

It was a peaceful place, the hot water steaming into the cold air so thick it was almost hard to breathe. I was sore from working out with Nolan and some other baseball players earlier that day, trying to get a head start on our senior season. The jets and hot water soothed my aching muscles.

I could tell by now that Heidi had some funny ideas going on in her mind, which I wasn't one bit interested in, but I tried not to let it ruin my night. We sipped orange juice, which gave a euphoric contrasting sensation as it trickled down my throat, which was warm from the water around me. As I relaxed next to Nolan, the stress and memory of recent events were somewhat melting away.

That feeling was short-lived.

I'd noticed her five minutes ago, standing still in the stand of pines that lined the eastern edge of the property. She hadn't moved, but I could tell from the silhouette that it was her. I wouldn't have seen her unless I'd been looking, but a hawk had flown into the branches overhead, which caused me to look in her direction. I said nothing to my companions, but instead waited a few minutes, watching out of the corner of my eye. I couldn't understand the reason for her visit, and I contemplated the safety of going out to see her. She had no reason to have it out for me, I didn't think, but I was still cautious.

Standing, I announced that I was going to use the restroom, and as I stepped out, I whispered in Nolan's ear, "If I'm not back in thirty minutes, call the police." At first he chuckled, but upon seeing my sober expression, he became serious as well, and nodded.

I snatched a towel and wrapped it about my shoulders as I walked in the basement door. As I rounded the corner of the hallway and was out of sight of my guests, I charged in a full sprint, up the basement steps, then to the grand staircase and up to my bedroom, drying myself as I went. I seized my pistol from its holster behind my headboard, newly replaced, and ran downstairs.

She had no view of the front door, so I exited there, then walked flat against the side of the house, holding my pistol in front of me. I'd forgotten how cold it was, and I was still only clad in swim trunks, but my adrenaline was flowing and my heart thumping through my chest, keeping me plenty warm, or oblivious to the cold, rather. Working my way to the corner of the house, I peered around, but she wasn't visible from my vantage point. Normally, this would mean she couldn't see me either, but knowing her, she probably had eyes on me at that very moment.

The chimney from the main sitting room jutted out from the pale bricks, giving a perfect view of where I'd seen her. Of course, there was about ten feet of bare wall between my current position and the crevice of the chimney. Mentally crossing my fingers, I slipped around the corner and took three long steps, then slammed my body flat against the chimney. When there was no reaction from anyone or anything in my surroundings, I held my gun near my face and peeked out once more.

Just as I did, a voice behind me whispered, "Good effort." It was so close to the back of my head, my heart shuddered and I nearly fired a wild shot into the darkness. Whirling, my gun aimed in front of me, I faced the very person I'd come out here looking for:

Blaire Devereaux.

She also held a gun to my head, so we stood for ten seconds, barrels to foreheads, waiting for the other to speak. The only difference between us was that she was cool and collected, almost nonchalant, while I was almost trembling in anticipation and fear. Also, she was wearing an adequate amount of clothing for the current weather conditions, while I was not. That also may have had something to do with the trembling.

"Surprised you made yourself so easy to see," I said coolly. "I would've expected better."

"You think I'd stand out in the open like that if I didn't want you to see me?" she said, almost mockingly. I slightly dropped my guard while understanding what she'd said, and she took this moment as an opportunity to jab her palm into my forearm and promptly snatch my pistol from my hand, which she did all before I realized what happened. "Relax," she said, and lowered the guns. "I'm not here on a revenge mission. I'm the one who bailed you out the last time we met, anyway."

"I knew that was you," I declared. "When the ballistics came back from the bullet in Miranda Blaine's leg, it matched to my pistol, so the police took it as a given that I'd fired the shot, then lost the gun, but I knew that you were the last one that had my gun whenever–"

"Oh, shut up. Anybody could've put that together, especially the guy who owned the gun."

My pride faltered a bit. "Well, if you didn't come here to whack me, why'd you bring a gun?"

"Same reason you brought one," she stated. She looked me over. I suddenly felt a bit awkward, standing here nearly naked, not to mention getting frostbit by the second. I felt jealous of her, warmly wrapped in her black outfit of leggings and a sweatshirt. She was as gorgeous as ever.

"Why don't you tell me what you want?" I asked, growing anxious. "I've got company."

"From the looks of it, you weren't enjoying that get-together any more than I was enjoying watching. You're right, though. That new girl isn't much. Seems like kind of a ditz, if you ask me."

"Okay, why don't you lay off the whole spy-detective act and tell me why you're here?"

Her face grew serious. "Your life is in danger, Chris, and so is Nolan's. Putting Neil Trace and the two kidnappers in prison didn't go over well, and you're to blame. Trace is a powerful man, more than you know, and you've gotten yourself into something way bigger than you thought."

"Alright, hold on a second," I said. "First of all, *you* were one of those kidnappers, and just because you had a little change of heart or something at the last minute doesn't mean I'm going to trust the very person who abducted my best friend."

She was frustrated. "You either trust me now or you never get the chance."

My heart thumping painfully once again, I managed an answer, "Okay."

"I'll be back here tomorrow. Make sure Nolan is around, and we'll talk this through. And Chris, don't say a word about this to *anyone*." She turned to sneak away.

"Okay, you can't keep stealing my guns," I mentioned, gesturing to my pistol still in her hand. Smirking, she tossed it back to me, then faded into the darkness.

Nolan slept at my house that Friday night, as he usually did. We woke early in the morning, both of us restless after our visit from Blaire. So I brewed a pot of coffee and we sat on the front porch, watching the frost twinkle against the Virginia countryside. My hometown of Dixon was invisible from here, so our entire view was of the elegant rolling hills surrounded by stands of trees. An occasional cow wandered into view in the open pasture that lined the road. This was one of the similarities between Nolan and I, that we were both staunch morning people. We spent lots of mornings just like this, except most mornings we didn't have a panging fear that our lives were in danger.

I had no idea when she was planning on being here, or where she'd be, but I decided it was Saturday, we had nowhere to be. Usually, on days like these, we'd make at least one trip to The Grind to sip coffee and watch people. But today, we sat in anxious silence, waiting.

Luckily, the signal came sooner than expected. It was half-past seven a.m. when I heard a car horn. Looking down the road, I saw no vehicles, but I soon realized the sound had come from my own garage.

"That's our queue," I said, taking my mug and strolling down the front steps. I tried to act casual, since I knew our front porch security camera was aimed right at me. Nolan followed suit and we made our way to the garage. Cautiously opening the door, I deemed it safe and stepped inside. Nobody was near my car, but I crept slowly around, still trying to make sure this wasn't some kind of a trap. Suddenly, the lights flicked on above us. Nolan swore, and I nearly jumped out of my skin.

Blaire stood with a gloved hand on the lightswitch. She wore her normal attire of all black, which she managed to do with stunning attractivity every time. Her jet black hair only added to the elegance of her person. She was dauntingly prepossessing, her deft and stealthy attitude making her features all the more appealing.

"Don't you think it'd seem somewhat suspicious to anyone watching if you two came in here without turning the lights on? Gotta use your head, Quimby."

Nolan was staring at her, seeming somewhat frightened, but she ignored it. She led the way up the ladder to Nolan and I's weightroom, knowing exactly how to hit the trapdoor to make it fly open. It made me a bit uncomfortable that she was so familiar with the place, but knowing her, it didn't surprise me. She probably knew what color my toothbrush was.

I pulled up a workout bench, Nolan sat on the mini fridge, and Blaire remained standing. "First things first," she said, gesturing towards me. "You have no need for a gun, so take it out of your pants before you blow yourself away."

Annoyed, I pulled the pistol from the backside of my waistband and set it on the floor.

"Why don't you tell me why you find it so necessary to be here trying to help us?" Nolan asked accusingly. "What's your interest in us?"

"Because I was instrumental in the arrest of Neil Trace's hired guns, and you aren't the only ones that know I'm the one that shot Miranda Blaine. To add to that, me running around free with all that I know about them is a hundred-foot red flag. I've been in hiding ever since, because I know I'm their main priority. My life is just as much on the line here, if not more so. So I figured it would make sense for the three of us to join forces on this."

"Tell us about Trace," I said. "What's so special about him?"

"Neil Trace does anything and everything, but his main areas of business are in drugs and guns," she explained. "He runs coastal Virginia and Washington D.C. He's built up his drug game over the years and grown a lot more powerful. He's also exported hundreds of thousands of illegal guns, mostly military grade, and millions of rounds of ammunition to various organizations around the world, bad organizations, willing to pay top dollar for anything they can get their hands on. He met Soloman Payne during that business. He's also dealt with stolen automobiles, that's where he met Miranda Blaine."

"Where'd he meet you?" Nolan interrupted.

She gave him an annoyed glance and ignored his question. "Trace has dozens of hoods under his payroll, and I'm sure ever since he's been given two life sentences, he's eager to get his hands on us, figuratively of course, since he's in the state penitentiary, but he's got plenty of people to do it for him. I've been following a certain group of them for the last couple weeks, and I've tracked them to Dixon."

Nolan spent a minute throwing up in the trash can. I felt like doing so myself.

"Well," I said flatly. "I'm going to have a heart attack."

"Do you understand now why it's so important for us to act on this?"

"The last time I saw you, you tied my hands behind my back and threw me in a corner for three days!" Nolan said accusingly, abruptly standing and pointing his finger. "If you think I'm stupid enough to trust you with my life–"

"I *saved* your life, you idiot!" Blaire shot back.

"*Why!*" Nolan yelled. I'd been wondering the same thing myself.

She didn't answer. Her frustrated expression melted, and she was calm again. Her straight black hair settled back on her shoulders, and she sat on another workout bench, crossing her long, athletic legs. "It's not important why. What's important is that we do something about them before they do something about us. I met with you guys because I think we'll do better together than we would apart. Three guns is better than one."

"Even when two of the guns are high schoolers with only one previous encounter with anything to do with a gun, which we were most likely going to die from?" I asked cynically.

"Well, that's true," she admitted. "But that's exactly why I need you. What's less daunting than a trust fund baby who's never had a struggle in his life?"

"Why is it a good thing that my profile isn't 'daunting'?"

"Because an incompetent prey is the perfect bait."

"Did you say bait?" I asked.

"Did you say bait?" Nolan repeated.

55

"Indeed, I said bait."

I was concerned about my parents. I knew they'd worry if they knew what was going on, but Blaire assured me that she'd ease their minds if anything were to happen. I was also slightly worried about the prospect of them being in danger themselves, but my uneasiness was once again soothed by Blaire's confident words. It was Monday now, the day set for our plan to take action. I vomited throughout the morning and focused very little on my schoolwork. Finishing my final class at a quarter till two, I tried to act nonchalant as I strolled out to my car in the student parking lot. Once inside my car, I put my head against the steering wheel and tears seeped on to the leather.

    This was simply a nightmare. To think, a few months ago I was a care-free rich brat with all the securities and luxuries I could ask for, and now, my life was at stake. Sure, my mother had warned me of the dangers of being the child of two wealthy parents, and how I'd be "of interest to some people", but I'd taken it with a grain of salt, tossing it to the corner with that "it'll never happen to *me*" belief. Well, it was happening to me, and I was deep in the middle of it before I'd even realized it. Now all I had was my best friend, as incompetent in an engagement as I, and a twenty year old woman with a ghost of a background but skill and experience in this field. The three of us, up against countless criminal ruffians, whose sole purpose was to end us.

    Just another day in the life, huh?

    I played with the clutch as I drove through town, making my presence known to anyone who may have been interested. After driving obnoxiously down Main Street, I parallel parked in front of The Grind and sat for a few minutes, watching my surroundings. Down the street, I saw Nolan and Blaire sitting in a blue sedan, watching. I was sure I'd been noticed by Trace's men, that is, if they were indeed around. Blaire had said the last time she saw any sign of them was two days ago coming off of the interstate, so once again, I shut my mouth and trusted her.

After five minutes, I casually stepped out the door, stepped onto the sidewalk and leaned against the lamp post, scrolling on my cell phone. As expected, out of the corner of my eye, I saw two equally imposing men exit an SUV across the street. They'd made an attempt not to look obvious, but it was still apparent that they were the fellows I was baiting. Unless my heart was visibly beating out of my chest, I did my best to hold in my fear. After a few seconds, I slipped my phone into my pocket and walked down the sidewalk toward Nolan and Blaire in the sedan.

I was startled to see a third man walking head-on towards me on the sidewalk. The three men were closing in on me, and I knew if they got close enough they'd be able to discreetly hold me at gunpoint. Frantic, I abandoned the plan and turned into the first door I passed, which happened to be a family-owned retail store. The place was fairly old, and based on the layout of the it, I was quite sure that there'd be a back door. I knew there was an alley that lined the back of this strip of buildings, some built with loading docks, some with fire escapes hanging from second-story rooms. Still doing my best to act calm, I made sure I was out of sight of the cashier before I slipped down the restricted hallway and searched for the back door. After rounding one corner, I found only a janitor's closet. Quickly, I retreated back the way I'd come.

Coming back into the opening, I nearly ran into two of the goons that were after me. I startled them as much as they startled me. No longer trying to disguise my fear, I broke into a sprint down the other end of the hallway, praying aloud that the door would be on this side. I could hear them thumping the floor not far behind me. To my relief, I found a commercial push door with a glowing "Exit" sign above it. Shoving through it, I found myself on a shallow cement staircase in the alley.

My eyes saw him before my mind was able to process it. In the corner of my eye, my third pursuer stood, wielding something in his hand. As I prematurely leapt from the staircase, I learned this was a pistol. I heard the bullet zip through the suppressor and enter my thigh in midair. My body went limp and I landed hard on the asphalt, gripping my bloody leg. I writhed as the bullet sat lodged in my muscle. I could hardly see straight as the three thugs stood around. I swore and cried and thrashed on the cold pavement for several seconds before I began to lose consciousness. I heard one of the men mumble, "Easier if he's unconscious, anyway."

I didn't see nor hear any sign of Nolan or Blaire. As my world turned to black, I knew that this was very likely my end.

To my surprise, I woke up, unaware of how long it had been since I'd been in the alley. I had faint memories of being thrown into the backseat of a vehicle, which was where I was now. Suddenly I became aware of the searing pain in my right leg and I remembered the shot that had taken me down. Jolting, I grabbed my right leg with zip-tied hands, but my head was instantly shoved into the seat and a strong pair of hands gripped me by the shoulders and held me still. I realized that my sudden movement had been somewhat foolish. There were two men on either side of me, the two that had originally been tailing me through town. Glancing toward the driver's seat, I recognized the fellow at the wheel as the third man, the one who'd shot me.

As I slowly regained consciousness, I glanced around the interior of the vehicle from my point of view against the seat. It was a blacked out leather interior, wide and spacious, seemingly a large SUV. I decided it must've been the silver full-size Chevrolet I'd seen these two yahoos get out of.

I had a pounding headache, but it unfortunately didn't distract me from the bullet lodged in my thigh. It felt like a hot torch being pressed against my skin, and the more I looked at it, the more it hurt. My jeans were stuck to the wound, some of the torn threads agitating the raw hole. My body was cold, but I was sweating profusely.

"I gotta get this bullet out of me," I complained.

The driver whirled with a pistol pointed at my forehead. "If you so much as breathe loud again," he yelled. "I'll finish the job right here. Shut up!"

I did so.

I had little idea as to how long we'd been driving, but it was another long while that we drove at a steady speed before we slowed. Seeing green road signs on our right side, I deduced the fact that we were heading down an off-ramp, which meant we'd been on the freeway that entire time. But I saw the signs somewhat upside down for half a second, so it was impossible to make out what they said, what town we were in or what exit we were taking. We were a good ways from Dixon, I knew that much. My adrenaline, still somewhat high, was keeping me focused. We drove slowly, making several stop sign turns. Rusty sheet metal and battered roofs passed through the windows as we traveled slowly through the ugly neighborhood.

After twenty minutes of the same speed and monotonous driving, it seemed as though we weren't going in any direction. A few times, I thought I recognized a lightning-struck tree and a warped metal roof, like we'd passed it a couple minutes before. We were going in circles.

Bored and exhausted, I was about to pass out once more when the driver cussed and yanked on the steering wheel. A half second later, an ear-splitting collision occurred against the hood on the driver's side and we spun, slamming into some large object on the side of the road. I went flying into the lap of the man on my left, screaming in pain. The driver was also a mix of screams and swears, fighting to get back on the road, but the car was unable.

The man whom I'd fallen onto threw me back onto the seat and I hollered in pain once more. He jumped over me and jumped out the right-side door, along with the two other men. I tried to do the same, but I stopped when the shooting began. I'd fallen to the floor of the backseat, which was where I stayed. Trace's men fired dozens of shots, but I only heard a few from whoever they were shooting at, but those few were usually followed by swears and yelps from the thugs.

The most relieving voice I'd heard all day suddenly came from the front of the car. It was Blaire, yelling at the men to lie face down on the ground. I heard constant husky groans. Still, I remained where I was.

The backseat door opened. Bracing myself, I looked up and burst into tears of relief upon seeing Nolan's face. He was haggard, his brown hair sweaty and his face red. He nearly cried as well as he helped me from the floor of the car and out onto the ground. Blaire stood, holding two of the men at gunpoint. The driver was also on the ground, unmoving. I nearly vomited, but I was too weak to do so. I only sat on the ground, dazed.

"He dead?" I asked.

"No, he's not dead," Blaire answered, scoffing at my idiotic remark. "But he might be in a little while. I'll let Big Guy here take care of him, but this one's coming with us." She gestured to the shorter of my two guards. He gave her a nasty glance, but slowly stood, hands raised. I didn't know what had gone on outside of this vehicle, but from the looks of these men, they knew that our female companion meant business.

I realized that the sedan that Nolan and Blaire had been driving was nowhere near. Instead, the vehicle that they'd rammed Trace's men's car with was a lifted Ram pickup, with a wide grille guard that showed very little damage after destroying the front end of the Chevy SUV. I had no idea where the truck had come from, but I realized that it was much more logical of a ramming device than the small car they'd been in before.

As the other guard took the driver and fled down the street, Nolan held his gun on our captive and directed him into the backseat of our vehicle. I limped painfully to the passenger seat of the truck and pulled myself up, wincing as I did so. Blaire looked out of place in the driver's seat of the extra large truck, but she handled it well, down a few blocks through the junkyard of a neighborhood that we were in. It was right off the highway, and I didn't recognize any of it, so I knew we must've indeed been a good distance from Dixon.

Blaire pulled into a gravel driveway, where a man in a tank top smoking a cigarette stood next to our blue Mazda sedan, looking quite flustered. He eyed the new scratch marks on his grill guard, then looked through the windshield at Blaire, dumbfounded. We hopped from the truck and hurried to switch to our vehicle. Blaire pulled a large wad of bills from her waist and slapped it into the scruffy man's hand. His expression quickly changed to one of delight as he held the cash in his hands, waving off Blaire's apology for the inconvenience.

Blaire slid into the driver's seat of the Mazda and laid her hand on my arm. "We'll get that bullet out of you, don't worry, but we have to get a few miles down the road before we can take a breath." With that, she threw the car into reverse and sped out of the dusty driveway, then weaved through the neighborhood until she worked her way into the middle of the little off-ramp town. A few seconds later, we were speeding back onto the interstate, headed back toward Dixon.

Blaire had pulled into a desolate Walmart parking lot, far away from the nearest vehicle, whenever I woke from my second episode. The wound was throbbing painfully. I'd pressed my undershirt onto it for most of the ride, but it was now stuck to the wound, and I bit my lip as I gingerly peeled it off.

"Okay," Blaire said, looking to the backseat. Nolan sat, gun resting on his knee, pointed at Trace's man that we captured. The man looked annoyed and irked at us, but my partners paid his feelings no mind. "You two, come up here. I need to get that bullet out of Chris."

I nearly fainted again, but Blaire rushed me out of my seat. I winced as I crawled to the backseat and laid longways, her coming in behind me and kneeling in the cramped space. She reached into the console and retrieved a small black bag, which she unzipped, revealing several metal tools, like a dentist office, but worse. Right away, she flicked open a wide knife and went towards my leg.

"Hold on!" I yelled.

"Relax, I'm just cutting your pants." She sliced a large portion of my jeans off and pulled the denim that she could from the bullet wound. She folded up a piece of it that wasn't overly bloody and shoved it in my mouth. "Bite."

Without further warning, she grabbed a pair of forceps from the bag and went to work. I cried and screamed, desperately wanting to get away. For a moment, I contemplated if death would be the less miserable scenario. I could hardly breathe between screams and cries and a mouthful of denim, slammed my fist against the door of the car. I could feel her tool inside my leg, digging around, searching for something.

Images of my life flashed across the back of my eyelids, memories from the joyful care-free times before these. Before Nolan was kidnapped, before I'd ever handled a gun, before I'd known Blaire or any of Trace's thugs, before my life was in grave danger. To think, that was only a few months ago, but look at me now.

After a minute, I was shaking and couldn't keep myself from trying to get away. Blaire sat up, her hand covered in blood, frustrated at me and at my leg. "Nolan, come here!" Nolan came around the car, still pointing the gun at our prisoner in the front seat. She whispered to him, he seemed to not want to follow her order, but upon her threatening gaze, he took her forceps and knelt down by my leg.

"He doesn't know how!" I protested, but she told me to shut up and hold still. She put a knee on my waist, and Nolan put his on my shin. Blaire held me by my shoulders. I couldn't budge.

"Do it," she told Nolan, and he went to work. I screamed, eyes wide. "Gentle," she said softly.

This time, as I struggled to get away, the numerous limbs on top of me prevented me from doing so. Still, I couldn't stop from shaking my leg. Blaire, holding a gun to the front seat, was becoming angry at me. "Chris," she said through gritted teeth. "You have to hold still."

I could hardly hear her through my groans and the pounding in my ears. She tried slapping me, but that only made me more frantic. Finally, she let out a sigh, yanked the denim from my teeth, and kissed me. I froze, somewhat enjoying it, but also fighting a miserable need to scream. After about three seconds I felt a sudden opening in my leg, and I head-butted Blaire as I led out a groan.

"Geez, I just met you," I painfully joked.

"Even with a gunshot wound in your leg, you can't lay off the jokes," Blaire said. "It was the only way to get you to shut up and stop acting like a child." She wiped her mouth with the back of her hand, which I took offense to.

Nolan was drained as he held the brass bullet in his forceps. "I got it," he said to himself.

I had a small bit of relief, now that he was done digging around, but everything still burned and ached and throbbed. Blaire handed the gun back to Nolan and thanked him, then worked on dressing the wound. She used gauze and bandages from her bag, pulling my skin together and making sure the wound was sealed. She covered it all with Nolan's t-shirt, which she tied painfully tightly around the wound, applying a lot of pressure.

Exhaling, she asked, "You alright, Quimby?"

"I think I'm still breathin'," I said with a weak smile. "At least, this definitely isn't how I pictured Heaven."

Patting my chest, Nolan smiled. "Atta boy."

.

It turned out we were roughly an hour from Dixon. As we drove, I took pain medication and drank half a gallon of water while Blaire drove and Nolan sat in the backseat with our POW, trying not to fall asleep. That was my job, Blaire said, to make sure Nolan didn't fall asleep and we all didn't end up with a bullet in our heads.

My partners had picked up my phone when the thugs had dumped it in the alley, and I'd had time to ease the minds of my worried parents. I told them Nolan and I had an urgent meeting with a friend, and that we'd explain when we returned home. Nolan's parents and mine had been much more protective since Nolan's kidnapping, rightfully so, of course.

"So, what happened?" I broke the silence.

"What do you mean?"

"Uh, for starters," I said sarcastically. "Why'd you let me get *shot* and *abducted*?"

"Oh, calm down," Blaire said with her usual glance that told me she was annoyed by my ignorance. "Things worked exactly as planned."

"The plan was to get me shot?" I exclaimed.

"Can you relax?" she hissed. "No, the plan was obviously not to get you shot, but things happen. It's all in a day's work. We got what we wanted: somebody from their side to tell us what's going on, willingly or not. We also got a general direction of where they're hid out."

"Why didn't you follow them all the way to their spot?" I questioned. "They were already off the exit."

"That little runaround was just a ruse to get us off their tail once they knew we were behind them. That's when I knew they weren't going to lead us any further, so I made my move."

"Yeah." I rolled my eyes. "Your move was ramming a car that your gunshot partner was in and almost killing them."

"I'm not gonna listen to any of your stupid accusations and butthurt complaints anymore," she said, frustrated. "I could stop saving your ass whenever I wanted and you'd be dead within the hour!"

"Awh, guys," came the mocking voice of our captive. "Please don't fight. You're so cute together."

His forehead met the butt of Nolan's gun and he took the message to shut up.

We were back in Dixon within the hour, where we put up our prisoner in the weight room, zip-tying him to a squat rack and moving any weaponizable objects out of his reach. My leg was brutally sore, I'd taken about ten pain pills in the last two hours. While Nolan and Blaire went into town to pick up my car, I stayed to guard our man, giving him a half-drank bottle of water, although he wasn't able to drink it. He'd had nothing with him, no cell phone or ID.

We sat in silence as minutes passed. He was a younger guy, less than thirty, and no taller than me. He was well-built and athletic, but not a generally attractive guy. He didn't seem very worried, which irked me, and made me somewhat paranoid as well. Annoyed by his confidence, I decided to try to get to him a bit.

"Either you know something that I don't," I said. "Or you're just stupid. Because you seem pretty undisturbed by the fact that you're the prisoner of the people you're trying to kill. If I were in your position—"

"If you were in my position we would've killed you already," he said sharply.

"Then why didn't you?"

"We wanted to use you to get closer to the other two, and it almost worked out perfectly. Now you're just making it easy on us, all three of you packed close together."

"Don't you mean all four of us?" I asked. "You're here too. And we both know that those killers don't have a care in the world whether you live or die, and I highly doubt they'll go out of their way to save you. So while you're so confident that your comrades will come right up here and blow us away, just remember that it won't be hard for you to get caught in the crossfire. I doubt they'll go for the whole hostage bit and give up anything just to keep you alive, so we're the only ones that you have hope in. We're the only ones that'll keep you alive, depending on your cooperation."

He seemed unphased.

"And believe me," I added. "You've seen my female partner in action, and you know she won't be as conversational as me."

His confident expression faded.

I smiled. "We can start with your name."

He didn't answer. I heard the rumble of my Mustang as it crept up the driveway.

"Sounds like my partners are back. Better get to talkin'."

He didn't answer, but his lips tightened. We heard the car pull into the garage.

"She'll be mad to find out you haven't told me anything yet," I said warningly.

He didn't answer, but his forehead was perspiring as we listened to the car door shut and two sets of footsteps approaching the ladder.

"Last chance," I said.

Blaire punched the trapdoor open, and climbed out, saying, "If he hasn't talked yet–"

"Okay!" the hostage said. "Just relax! Let me talk."

"Wow," Blaire said. "That was easy."

"I had him worked up," I said.

"Oh, yeah, sure you did, Deputy Fife," Blaire said sarcastically. I bit my lip to keep from firing back at her, and focused on our prisoner. "Go ahead," Blaire said to him, arms crossed.

"Yeah, okay, it was Neil Trace that hired us, I'm sure you know. I was just a hired gun, that's all. I don't have any real connection to him. My name's Rosen, I'm just– I was just partners with Smith and Francis. Smith was my step-dad's ex-wife's brother-in-law. He was in charge of this, but he didn't come along. He knew I was hard up for cash, so he offered me this job, and I got my head in too deep. It was just for the money. I got nothing against you."

Blaire grabbed him by the hair and pointed his face toward hers. "I don't care. Tell me what they're planning and where they're hid out."

"Well, Smith was my–"

"Step-dad's ex-wife's brother-in-law," Blaire finished. "What about it?"

"Well, he's been in this business for a while, and he's got, like, a bunch of different places that he hides out at."

"All around here?"

"Everywhere. Richmond, Virginia Beach, D.C., even a few places in the Carolinas, just in case."

"Where were you taking Chris? You were on 64 going west."

"I don't know. . ."

Blaire bent over and grabbed him by his hair again. "I've made it extremely easy on you so far. You said you'd talk, so talk."

"Smith didn't tell us for sure, but I'm guessing Charlottesville," he said. "He spends a lot of time there."

"Any other possibility?"

"Uh, I don't know. He's mentioned Gordonsville before, and that's close by," the captive said.

Blaire released her grip and threw his head aside. "Settled, then. We'll go after them before they come after us. Charlottesville. If they're not there, Gordonsville." She bent down to him and whispered, "And if they're not there, you won't leave the place alive, so you better hope you're right." She stood and addressed Nolan and I. "We'll go in two days, once you've rested that leg and things have settled down around here. The police were already investigating around the alley where you got shot. Let's go."

We shut the light off and left our captive in darkness, through the trapdoor and down the ladder. Before we stepped out the side door, Blaire turned to me and whispered, "Is your car locked?"

"No," I replied. "But the garage door always is so no one can get in, so what's the point?"

"Because the one that wants to steal it is already in the garage. When he makes his escape, he's going to want a car."

I stared blankly.

She sighed at our stupidity once more. "What do you think I did when I bent down to talk to him? Didn't you see me cut a notch in his zip-ties? They're hanging on by a thread now, one good yank and they'd break."

My gun had been in my hand the whole night, it'd grown comfortable. Now I gripped it tensely, waiting for her to elaborate.

"Oh, relax, Chris, I did it on purpose. Lock your car and come outside so we can talk without him hearing. We have one more place to go tonight." So I limped to my car, grabbed my keys and locked the doors, then followed my partners outside. My leg still ached terribly, but I didn't want to be weak in front of Blaire, so I bit my lip hard and fought through it. I looked up towards the house and thought about my mom. She was home alone, my dad had left that morning to attend to business at the Quimby Suites in Sarasota.

We climbed into the Mazda and Blaire pulled down my driveway. "Now, listen," she said, looking at me like a parent does to their child when they're trying to help them understand something. "We're not going to Charlottesville or Gordonsville. He never would've just given up his partners like that, either out of loyalty or fear of consequences. He just said the first town he could think of along 64. I think he's full of it. There's no way to get real information out of him, but we can utilize him. If he thinks that he just broke himself out, he won't know we're on his tail. He'll meet back up with his crew, and we'll be right there behind him."

"We're just supposed to follow his every move?"

"How dumb do you think I am? No, when I was doing his zip-ties, I slipped something in his back pocket, a tracking device. It's small enough that he won't notice, and even if he did, it holds the resemblance of a quarter, unless you look closely at it, but he wouldn't."

"Well what are we tracking this tracking device with?" I asked.

"That's where we're going," she answered. "I went to see someone before I met up with you guys."

"Who?"

"The very person that divulged my real identity to everyone last year."

I smirked. "Gabe McDowell."

"Hello, Blaire," Gabe took up the whole doorway of his second-story apartment. "Hey, guys. Come in. Didn't expect you this late."

I hadn't realized the time. It was nearing midnight. My mother had texted me as I was in the car and I'd simply told her I was spending the night with Nolan. She was used to the two of us being out late together. I was guessing I wouldn't get any sleep any time soon since we had to stay on the tail of Rosen, but I would be far too stressed to get any sleep. I could sleep when I'm dead, right? That wasn't a very distant possibility.

"You guys already met?" I asked as Gabe led us to his tech room.

"It didn't take long for me to discover who gave me away last time, and it took even less time for me to find him."

"I thought she was here on a revenge trip," Gabe laughed nervously. I chuckled too, and I noticed the funniest thing. Now, I was exhausted and had a gunshot wound in my leg, so I may have been seeing things, but I thought for a moment I saw the slightest tickle of a smirk on Blaire's cold face. I suppose the only thing that made her smile was the idea of a "revenge trip".

"Anyway, this is, uh, what I put together." Gabe sat at his gaming chair and picked up a small screen from his messy desk. His hand was shaking. "Gutted my old phone and put the tracker inside it, so it projects on the screen. Not sure if the battery will run out or not, but take this charger just in case." Blaire took the phone and pressed the power button. A blurry map lit up the screen, with a red dot slowly moving along a field near my house.

"Looks like he already took our bait," Nolan said.

"Guess we should get going then," Blaire decided. "He'll contact his partners soon and meet up with them before long. So can I get–"

"Don't move," I said, my pistol pointed at Blaire's head. My hand was shaking, but I held it steady. "If anyone moves I'll pull the trigger."

I could see the fury on Blaire's face. "What are you doing, Chris?"

"I have a question," I said, sweat beading on my forehead. "You said you contacted Gabe before you met with us. How come you already had the tracking device plan in place before we even had a prisoner to use it on? I may not be a professional killer like you, but I'm not an idiot. You keep talking about 'last time' like you haven't forgiven or forgotten anything. Wouldn't surprise me if you *were* on a revenge trip."

"Chris," Nolan piped up. "Whenever we went to pick up your car, Blaire stopped here and picked something up. I didn't know what it was, I didn't even know Gabe lived here, but I guess it was the tracker."

"Why didn't you say something?" I asked, beginning to feel like the idiot I claimed I wasn't.

"You never asked."

I still held the gun on Blaire. I looked at her now. "Well then why did you meet up with him the first time?"

"That's what we were about to address," Blaire said angrily. "Gabe, can you please go get it now? Careful, though. Chris might blow your face off." Gabe looked at me before moving. I nodded, and he left the room. I kept the gun steady, but my grip grew weak as I realized my idiotic mistake. "No, I wasn't going to kill you," Blaire said. "But right now, I'm definitely considering changing my mind."

Gabe came back into the room, and I actually almost did blow his face off. Nolan also jumped at the sight of the long-barreled black sniper rifle. "Don't shoot me, please, don't shoot me," Gabe yelled, raising his hands and nearly dropping the gun.

Once again, the pistol was out of my hand before I realized Blaire had made a move toward me. She snatched it from my grasp and shoved it under my jaw so hard it drove me against the wall and I struggled to catch my breath.

"If I wanted to kill you, Chris, I would've done it the first second I saw you, and you'd be in the bottom of Lake Chesdin right now." Her face was inches from mine, and I decided I had been less afraid when I was in my kidnappers' car with a bullet in my leg. "Pointing a gun at me is a death wish, and I promise you this: if I ever see the barrel of that pistol again, I'll make it come true."

She lowered the gun and I sucked air, trying not to hyperventilate. Turning away from me, she tossed it back into my hands and I quickly put it away. Gabe handed her the rifle, and she looked through the bulky scope out the window. "Looks good."

"What'd you do to it?" Nolan asked.

"I programmed an angle of trajectory and slope measurement so that she'd know exactly how her bullet would hit depending on the distance. Based on her skill set, she could probably hit from eight or nine hundred meters with this. That's military numbers. I don't know where you got a hold of that scope, but it's the most advanced piece of firearm equipment I've seen."

"You're planning on taking that shot?" I asked her.

"You don't know me, Chris. You don't know my life, you don't know what happened before you met me. I met Bruce Smith long before this afternoon. Hate to break it to you guys, but I didn't get into this mess just to save your asses."

"Then why did you?" I asked quietly.

She lowered the gun and exhaled.

"I'm going to kill him."

"Blaire, you know we can't just let you kill him," Nolan said as we pulled out of the parking lot of Gabe's apartment complex. "This might be kind of your thing, but murder is murder."

"I agree," I said quietly. I hadn't spoken up till now after the dramatic incident inside, and I'd somewhat lost my right to give an opinion, but I figured a united front would help change her mind.

She didn't speak, though. She just drove. She seemed less confident now, her sharp wits seemed to be somewhat dulled. I wasn't completely sure what had upset her so much, whether it was my accusations or the thought of her apparent history with Bruce Smith, the man who was heading up our assassinations. Whatever the case, I could read her side profile. It seemed as though she regretted being here.

Nolan was in the backseat, so he wasn't able to read her as well, so he didn't tread quite as lightly as I. "Why are you suddenly out to get him? You said you met him a long time ago, what does that have to do with it?"

She still ignored him. I could tell she was frustrated, but not the same annoyed frustration that she'd had with me all day. She seemed stressed by Nolan's prying, like the feeling you have as a kid when your parents ask you why you're upset but you don't want to embarrass yourself. I glanced back at him, that blank half-glance that told him not to speak so much. It's odd the way we could so easily communicate with each other, just the slightest hint of an expression could tell us how to act.

I was unsure where we were headed. Blaire had the tracker in her left hand as she drove with her right. She slowed and pulled into the parking lot of the mall near the interstate exit. She parked far from any lamp posts, put the car in park, and killed the engine. "He still seems to be walking," she said. "We'll give him a head start so there's no chance of us accidentally catching up to him before he's with the others. Get some sleep if you want. I don't know how long it'll be."

Nolan was already horizontal in the backseat. I didn't personally know any rocks, but if I'd have to guess, Nolan slept similar to one. You had to give Nolan at least ten minutes to get his brain calibrated after waking up, if you actually managed to wake him. That was a difficult task as well, dangerous even, because if he found someone bending over him or grabbing him when he woke up, there was a good chance he'd send a strong hand into the face of whoever it was.

The silence was deafening as we sat in the dark car. Blaire rested her head on her hand as she studied the tracker. My anxiety and adrenaline were out of control due to the fact that I wasn't able to let them loose, I just had to sit still and quiet. I couldn't run, I couldn't yell, I couldn't drive, and I sure couldn't cry, which was what I wanted to do the most. I couldn't even hear her breathe. I was beginning to think I'd gone deaf, it was so quiet.

I ventured a glance at her, and I saw her eyes were closed. I couldn't blame her for being exhausted, but I was surprised to see her showing any human characteristic. But the emotion she was showing wasn't exhaustion, not physically, anyway. She wasn't falling asleep, she was trying desperately to hold something in. But she failed to hold it in, and I saw the single shimmering tear escape from her right eye, and leave a wet mark along the edge of her nose.

My lips parted in utter disbelief at the sight of Blaire Devereaux shedding a tear. She quickly put a hand across her cheek and wiped it away, and she looked at me, hoping I didn't notice, but instead she looked dead into the center of my eyes, and her lips parted as well.

"Blaire. . ."

She looked away quickly, completely ignoring me.

My sweaty, shaking hand crossed over the console and onto Blaire's forearm. The look in her eyes was pure bewilderment, like the look of a wild animal the first time it lets you touch it. She didn't move, and her wide eyes grew narrow, then soft. I saw her nostrils flare, and the moonlight glared off her glistening gray eyes. I realized there was one advantage I had over this black-haired captivating woman: I knew how to handle emotions. I'd been described as a feeler, not a thinker. If anything, people found me a bit odd in the way that I wore my heart on my sleeve. I knew people, I knew emotion, I knew hearts, and I could currently see Blaire's beating out of her chest. I stared into her eyes as they fell shut, and this time, she made no attempt at stopping the tears.

She set her head against the steering wheel and sobbed silently for two minutes or so. I didn't look at her, or offer any physical comfort, no matter how badly I wanted to embrace her and hold her head against my chest. Finally, as she stopped taking fast breaths, I heard her mumble, "I haven't cried in two years."

I said nothing. I knew she wanted to speak, I knew with all the emotion she'd just let flow from her eyes, she would open up. But she sat silently for a few more minutes. Finally, as I thought the moment was lost, she spoke again.

"I had a mother once."

"I think we all did," I answered, realizing it sounded sarcastic.

But she chuckled in despair. "I suppose, but having a mother was a big deal for me, because that's about all I had. Not that we were poor or anything, we lived decent, just the two of us. Believe it or not, I had a life. A real, normal, boring life. I went to high school, I had friends, well, *a* friend, and sometimes I was almost happy."

"I knew deep down there was a human in there," I joked compassionately.

"There was," she said, solemn once more. "The only normal thing about me was that I had one of those childish passions. I loved martial arts, as you can probably tell. I had always been in gymnastics through my childhood and high school. Martial arts was like gymnastics without the glitter. I was good, really good.

"Being a fighter the way I was led me to a different sort of friend group. I had always kind of known that karate kids were all potheads and hippies, it was sort of obvious. I started hanging out with them, just to hang out, not to smoke weed or anything like that, just to have friends. Turns out that pot played a big role in the things they did, and it wasn't just pot. It started out like that, but it grew into other things. We went to prescription meds, painkillers, and as we got older, cocaine. Not just doing it, but selling it, too.

"When you get into the drug world, people notice you, and they noticed me. I didn't know who Neil Trace was besides the fact that he had the same hussle as us, just a whole lot bigger. I knew he was interested in me for my skill set. I didn't realize how interested, though. He pursued me, tried over and over to recruit me, get me on his team, but I had enough common sense to say no. Turns out, 'no' wasn't an option. He got upset with me, threatened me, but I thought it was just some druggy bluff."

I was sweating immensely. I almost vomited from the anxiety I had over the story she was telling. I watched her rub her temples and sigh before she finished.

"I'd met Smith when I met Trace, he seemed like his right-hand man. I liked him even less than I liked Trace. He was outright insulting to me, and I could feel his eyes covering my body when he sat there next to Trace. It made me sick. Trace made his final threat to me, saying I wouldn't be the only one in trouble if I refused again. But like the stupid, stubborn idiot I am, I still refused.

"Smith killed my mother a day later, on my eighteenth birthday. That was the last time I cried. I didn't refuse after that."

I didn't speak, I couldn't. I couldn't cry, couldn't move, couldn't breathe. For the first time, I'd officially met Blaire Devereaux.

After thirty more seconds, my mind cleared. Her head was still on the steering wheel. I reached over, put a finger under her chin and picked up her head.

"Okay," I said.

"Okay?" she repeated, staring at me.

"Okay. We'll kill him."

The man who'd called himself Rosen had been at the same warehouse for twenty minutes now. We sat in the Mazda a block away, staring at the busted front door. I didn't even know what town this was, but it wasn't an attractive one. The warehouse we'd followed him to looked like no one had set foot in it in decades. Blaire decided she was going to go check the place out, so she stuck a pistol in her waistband and left us. I watched her cross the street and slip through the chain-link gate, then disappear around the corner of the building.

"What were y'all talking about last night?" Nolan asked me from the backseat.

". . .Nothing."

"Seriously?" he said, leaning forward. "After all this, you're not even gonna tell me what you two were talking about?"

"She opened up. She–I mean–well. . ." I sighed. "Bruce Smith, uh, shot her mother. That's why she wants to kill him. She cried, Nolan. Stone-cold Blaire Devereaux actually cried, like a human being."

I heard him let out a soft chuckle as he sat back in the seat.

"What?" I asked, turning around.

He smiled at me. "You crack me up, Quimby."

"What are you talking about?"

"I have known you for ten years, Chris. I can read you like a book, and you know it. And there is one thing so obvious right now that I don't even think you know about."

"Which is?"

"You love her."

I jumped when the driver side door opened and Blaire hopped back in. I gave Nolan one final glance as our conversation was abruptly ended. "They're in there," she said. She pounded a fist on the steering wheel. "He's in there."

"Let's go finish this," Nolan said sharply.

Blaire grabbed the duffle bag containing her rifle from the backseat. "Couldn't have said it better myself."

"Mr. Quimby, Mr. Bragg, join us, won't you?" Bruce Smith sat at a circular table, next to Rosen and two other men who I recognized from my kidnapping. Guns were aimed at our heads, so we dropped our own and let them clatter to the floor. As terrified and naked as I felt unarmed, it was part of the plan, and I stuck to it. Don't speak, Blaire had said. Just let him boast.

"It's funny that we meet this way," Smith said as we stood in front of the table. "I'll have to admit, I expected this mess to be finished long before I ever had to see your ignorant face in person, so congratulations on getting this far. I'm sure Trace will be overjoyed to hear that our little game has ended. I'm sure right about now you're still feeling very confident, I can see it in your eyes. You've got your plan down pat, right up to the moment that that backstabbing menace sends a bullet from her spot on the water tower across the street."

My stomach quivered. He was a step ahead of us.

He continued. "But I'm sure by now you realize that I'm not in line with her barrel. For her to fire through that top window, I'd have to be standing right over there, so your plan was most likely to get me to move over there, right? That's why you walked in here like you owned the place?" His hand slammed on the table and I did my best not to shrink back. "You think I'm an *idiot?*"

To think, it was going to end like this. All we went through, the bullet hole in my leg, the tears on Blaire's steering wheel. Oh, Blaire. It broke my heart the most to think about her, the years she spent as Neil Trace's assassin, only to fail in her ultimate goal.

I began mumbling The Lord's Prayer.

"It's been fun playing with you," Smith said. "But you couldn't have possibly thought you'd come out of this on top."

Rosen raised a gun to my head. Smith raised his own to Nolan's.

With one final breath, I heard Nolan whisper, "I'm sorry."

The ensuing *crack* was not the firing pin of a pistol striking the bullet, but rather Nolan's right foot slamming into the bottom of the plastic table in front of us. I was taken by surprise, not exactly sure what happened. Guns did soon begin to fire rapidly. My reflexes took control of me, and I took advantage of the split second that Rosen was caught off guard. I sent my shoulder into the table, which was now on-end. It knocked over Rosen, Smith, and one other thug, but it missed one man. Nolan was on the ground, but I saw him moving, now ramming into the table once more.

Months spent in my weight room paid off in the following seconds as I overpowered Rosen, my left arm around his neck and my right fighting for his pistol. Looking for a weak spot and finding one, I stomped my left foot onto his vulnerable knee and felt a crack. He screamed and the grip on his gun loosened. I ripped it from his hand, raised it, and shot the first man I saw, who turned out to be one of the unnamed thugs, who I recognized as having put the original bullet in my thigh. He fell to the ground, gripping his shoulder. In the back of my mind, I hoped he would survive the shot. I never wanted to be the deciding factor in taking someone's life, it wasn't my place.

Either way, I kept firing wildly now. Rosen was struggling from my grip, so I shut him up with the butt of the pistol. He grabbed his nose and I let him roll away, then I slid across the empty room to the walkway against the wall, to assess the situation. From what I could tell, Nolan was on the other side of the room, taking cover behind one of the steel framing columns along the wall, in a gun battle with the other hit man. I scanned the place, trying to find Smith, but saw no sign of him, until I heard the door slam in the corner from which Nolan and I had entered.

Blaire.

"Go, Chris!" Nolan yelled. "He's going after Blaire."

I wasted no time. I worked my way along the wall, running from column to column, covering myself from the remaining enemy fire. Nolan covered me as best as he could. I kept an eye on the two men I'd put out of commission by the table. They were in obvious pain, now only worried about surviving instead of coming out victorious. Finally, I made a last dash toward the steel door that Smith had gone through a minute ago. On the way, I snatched up the gun I'd surrendered when we'd first entered, and stashed it behind my waistband. Now I had Rosen's pistol and my own. Whipping the door open, I stepped inside and put my back against the wall, expecting to be ambushed by Bruce Smith. But he wasn't in the entrance room, he was already making his way to the water tower across the street.

I sprinted in pain out the door after him, crossed the road with hopes that no car would come at that moment, and none did. I couldn't see Blaire, and at the height and angle she was at, she couldn't see us. She was on the top, eye in her scope aimed through the warehouse window, waiting for the moment to fire. Meanwhile, the person she was aiming for was bearing down on her from behind.

He was almost up the ladder by the time I grabbed a rung. I had no clear shot at him, even as I watched him shimmy along the railing. He had yet to fire at me, and it seemed as if he hadn't noticed me coming close behind him. He took his time tiptoeing along the railing, gun held ready.

I reached the top a few seconds after I lost sight of him. I was in a hurry to catch up with him before he reached Blaire's position. I didn't want to make noise, that would only cause him to get a jump on me. So I hurriedly slunk along the railing behind him.

I'd never seen hands as large as the ones that hit my chest and sent me falling backwards, over the flimsy rail. Screaming, I grasped as whatever my hands hit, which turned out to be the steel edge of the track I'd been walking on. My gun fell a hundred and fifty feet to the asphalt below and broke into a hundred pieces. I caught sight of Blaire around the corner now. She lay along the track, rifle set up, finger on the trigger. She whirled as she heard my scream from behind her. Smith aimed his gun at her helpless head as she struggled for her handgun.

He cocked the hammer.

Her eyes grew wide.

And I shot him.

Good thing I grabbed that extra gun on my way out.

His scream mixed with mine as he fell onto the metal track, my bullet having struck him in the middle of his back. Blaire rushed over and yanked his gun from his hand, not that he was going to use it. I handed her mine, then took ahold of her forearm and let her pull me up.

We fell against the water tank, I with sobs and her with sighs. In the moment that I looked over to the warehouse, I saw Nolan Bragg emerge from the door, gun in-hand. He stared up at us. We stared back. He nodded. We nodded.

There are things in life that make you question every notion that you've ever thought, and the next thing Blaire did was one of them. I heard her head slide against the tank and land hard on my shoulder. She sniffled once, and softly mumbled, "Thank you."

I hadn't smiled in a month, since that day. Every thought I had was trumped by the memory of the man I killed. The life I took. The tears shed on my pillow and forgiveness begged for, the overwhelming weight on my shoulders as I stood along the church pews. But I also thought of Blaire, and knew I'd do it again every day if it meant it was his life taken instead of hers.

I sat in Nolan and I's booth at The Grind, only Nolan wasn't there. I wasn't the only one who'd ended a life that day, so had he. He was just as shaken up as I, and he'd been at his house ever since we made it home, Jennifer constantly by his side, kissing his forehead, holding his arm, nuzzling him. So I sat alone, staring at my reflection in my coffee.

The bell above the door rang, feet hit the floor all the way to my booth. I didn't pick my head up as she slid in across from me, I could picture her captivating face just fine, in fact it was the only thing I could picture besides Bruce Smith. Her slender hand slid across the table and touched mine. I looked up.

Blaire didn't smile, but her expression was soft, as were her eyes for the first time since I'd met her. She wore a loose-woven beanie over her black hair. Her cheeks had a tint of red, perhaps from the cold outside or from her human nature showing through again.

"Hi."

"Hi."

I smiled then, a little, and laughed softly. She looked at me, her lips pursed, holding back a smirk. "What is it?" she asked.

I sighed, shook my head, and looked her in the eye. "Nolan was right."

Part III

City of Love

Holding cells in real life are even more depressing than in movies. The entire room, which was much smaller than expected, smelled like urine, obviously from the metal toilet in the far corner, although I noticed several places where someone hadn't bothered to use the toilet. There were only two small benches, too narrow to sit on comfortably, and too disgusting to lay horizontal. So there I sat, cuffs cutting off circulation on my wrist, my seat cutting off circulation on my rear end, looking across the room at my best friend, Nolan Bragg. At least we were the only ones there, no intimidating biker with neck tattoos like you see in most movies. But in smalltown Dixon, Virginia, there weren't many tough hombres getting picked up every night.

We really couldn't catch a break with Justin Hobbes. The last time we'd messed with him, I'd made a daring escape off the balcony of a drug store, and that was six months ago. Now, all we were trying was a little friendly prank. When Nolan and I had seen his truck in the mall parking lot, there was no way we were going to pass up the opportunity to tamper with it. Of course, it took longer than expected, and when the patrolling officer questioned us, we weren't quick-witted enough to come up with a reasonable excuse as to why we were disassembling his tailgate.

Our rivalry with Justin and his little squad of thugs was lighthearted compared to what we'd been involved in recently. The roughest it ever got between us was a few punches, just to let off steam. Luckily, he didn't press charges, but he agreed with the officer that it might be "beneficial" to take us in for the night.

Keys jingled down the hall, along with two sets of footsteps. A horn buzzed and the door of the cell rolled open. In the doorway stood a female officer with a low center of gravity. Squinting at a paper, she read our names. "Christopher Quimby, Nolan Bragg, somebody saved you a rough night's sleep. Although, by the look of her, you might be in for somethin' worse."

She was right. Blaire Devereaux's expression was even more cross than usual. She stood, arms crossed, looking very unimpressed with the two of us. She didn't speak as the officer removed our handcuffs and led us down the hall, then bid us goodnight. In fact, she didn't speak until we made it the whole way out to the car in the back corner of the parking lot. At least she'd been nice enough to pick up my car from the mall. The sight of my '67 Mustang brought a little light air to the situation.

The first acknowledgement she gave me was a cold slap over the face. Then she turned to the backseat, pulled Nolan's chin forward, and gave him the same. She started the car and finally spoke.

"You two impress me every day. Just when I think you've reached the highest level of stupidity, you shatter the ceiling and find a whole new one. No, don't speak. I mean, for one thing, you couldn't talk your way out of that simple of a situation? I thought you guys were supposed to be slick or something. You've never watched Trailer Park Boys? The 'Joe' technique? Every cop knows a guy named Joe, act like you know him, they'll let you off right away. And doing something that stupid to Justin's truck, in public, for no reason. Don't you understand that getting arrested is sort of a big deal for people like us? Who knows what they could've uncovered. Just because the whole Bruce Smith case is closed doesn't mean there's not something else they could find out about me. That is the first and last time I will walk into a jail on purpose. Me walking into a jail is like a cow walking into Texas Roadhouse. If they'd ever connect my real name to any of my aliases, I'd catch quite a case."

We sat in a shameful silence for a few moments, feeling guilty for putting her in this position, until Nolan voiced the question we both had on our minds: "You've watched Trailer Park Boys?"

She shrugged. "I had an aunt in Canada."

"Well, sorry," I said genuinely. "Thanks for picking us up before our parents found out."

"Just don't forget I can spill your secret any time you give me reason to." She smirked and put an affectionate fingernail on my chin, but quickly scrunched her nose. "You need a shave."

We pulled into the driveway of my family's mansion a little past eleven o'clock. I noticed my father's Cutlass was back in the garage, which meant he was back from his trip to Outer Banks, where the fiftieth Quimby Suites hotel was finishing up construction. It was a big landmark for my mother and father, who'd started the company at the age of twenty with their first bed and breakfast. Once the business had grown, they'd bought many smaller properties to add to the Quimby chain, and were currently maintaining a steady modest growth every year. The Quimby Suites Headquarters were here in Dixon, where my father now worked with several of his executives. The business was growing, as was the family name, and the family wealth. And here I was, a rich eighteen year old with no goals and no concerns.

The three of us relaxed in the small basement lounge, the TV at a low volume. We didn't say much, just sat in each other's presence, enjoying our boredom. I watched Blaire as she sat on the opposite end of the couch, head resting on her hand. She probably knew I was staring, but I didn't care, it was a common thing.

It had been almost three months since she'd officially left the outlaw life, after avenging her mother's death and putting Neil Trace's last remaining hitmen behind bars. It had been a rough transition for her, and she was still struggling to lead a normal life. She'd hated the illegal life that she'd been forced to live for two years, but it was who she was. She was trained to be distant and cold, to not love or care about anyone or anything. You can't domesticate a wild animal in a few months, it takes time.

She'd done herself a favor during her time as a criminal in making sure to never divulge her real identity. After the showdown between the three of us and Bruce Smith's men, Blaire had been able to answer all questions by the police using real facts, since the name Blaire Devereaux had never committed a crime, except for one DUI which she'd committed only to appear like a normal citizen. Even whenever Smith had claimed that Blaire had once been a partner–which was true–nothing was made of it. Neil Trace's organization shot themselves in the foot with erasing all evidence of their involvement in their crimes. The only real danger Blaire faced was if she'd be identified by an eyewitness from her past.

She had no living immediate family, so Nolan and I had somewhat taken her in. She spent most of her time with us, since she had nothing else to do. She lived in a room at the original Quimby Suites in our hometown of Dixon, free of rent, of course. When she'd objected to this, my father had told her that he would never be able to repay her for saving my life–twice–and believe me, the loss of one room didn't make a dent in my father's business.

I loved her, she knew that, there was no hiding things from Blaire, but I had no idea how she felt about me. She probably didn't know either, her heart was so trained not to love, but I was patient. I knew if I made any advances too fast, I'd scare her off. She was new to this, so I let her take her time. I knew she cared about me, whether intimately or not.

Her eyes were closed, and I thought maybe she was asleep. She got more sleep here than she did at the hotel, mostly because she felt safer here. Years of looking over her shoulder didn't do well for a sleep schedule. But her left eye came open now, and she smirked. "Chris," she mumbled. "Am I that interesting?"

My face turned red and I turned away with an embarrassed smile. I looked at Nolan on the recliner, and I was surprised to see he wasn't asleep either. It wasn't hard to get that kid to sleep.

"Whatcha thinkin' about?" I asked him.

He bit the tip of his water bottle in thought. "Spring break is in two weeks. Why don't we have plans?"

"Hm," I grunted back. "That's true. Why don't we have plans?"

"Chris, your father literally owns fifty different locations for us to take a trip to," he pointed out. "There's quite a few in some of the bigger cities, right?"

"That's also true," I agreed. We had never spent much time being tourists in our own hotels. And there were several Quimby Suites destinations in the more attractive cities along the east coast.

We both looked at Blaire.

"It's not like I have plans. Ever," she said. "I'd love to leave my current Quimby Suites hotel to go stay in another."

"Settled, then," Nolan said. "Spring break trip."

"And where to?" I asked.

"We'll just have to figure that out, won't we?"

So we spent the next hour narrowing down the best destinations for our vacation. I brewed coffee, we did research, Blaire stared into space, as usual.

Nolan was frustrated. It seemed that just about every place he wanted to go on vacation, Blaire had had some illegal business there before and didn't find it safe to go back any time soon. The original plan had been Hilton Head Island, but apparently she'd had some dealings off the southern coast of South Carolina, so we decided against it. The next place Nolan wanted to go was Miami, but Blaire said that had been quite a hotspot for trade with South American arms dealers, so that was also out of the question.

"Well, where on earth are you not a wanted criminal?" Nolan said.

Blaire looked at me, then at Nolan. "Europe," she jokingly said.

He rolled his eyes. "Good one."

The thought came to all three of our minds at once. Eyes widened, faces brightened, and mouths gaped. "Europe!"

"All the free hotels you could ask for," said my father, Henry. "And you want to go to Europe."

He sat on the patio, swirling his wine glass, feet propped up in front of the fireplace. It seemed a bit early to be in the wine, but it was Saturday, he said, Saturday is just one long five o'clock.

"France, to be specific," I said.

"Paris, to be more specific," Nolan added.

"You two looking for a romantic getaway?" my father joked.

"Well, we were actually going to invite the girls," Nolan said. I'd brought him along for this because my father loved him as much as he did me. Nolan was studying law, as both his parents were attorneys, so he was an all-around business nerd as well, and as a result, he and my father bonded on the more dull aspects of life.

"Not that one you went out with a couple months ago?"

"*Psh,*" I scoffed. "Jennifer's friend? Absolutely not." *"Kind of a ditz, if you ask me"* I remembered Blaire saying about Heidi. I smiled to myself, then thought about the still-healing gunshot wound in my thigh that came not long after. That always did make memories seem less pleasant. I looked back at my father, "No, we wanna take Blaire. Blaire and Jennifer."

"Thought y'all weren't a thing yet," he drawled.

I took a deep breath and tried not to be frustrated. He had a way of drawing things out unnecessarily long. "Never said we were. But I don't know if she's ever even been on a vacation, and it's kind of the only place she's not in danger of being arrested, and at least it would mean more protection for us."

"Jared and Olivia are going to be home from college, but I guess you'll see 'em on Easter," he said as he thought. "Well, I don't see nothin' wrong with it, whole country might surrender when you land, anyhow." He sipped his wine and turned back to the fireplace.

"Great," Nolan said as we walked away. "Now to go convince *my* parents, the one whose child, namely me, was kidnapped six months ago and then shot someone soon after."

"Not that I didn't go through basically the same trauma," I pointed out. "Plus, I got a nice healthy bullet hole in my leg." I said it jokingly, but I'd never forget the man whose life I'd taken. It was in defense of myself and of Blaire, but it was hard to justify it to myself. I suppose it wasn't mine to justify, it was God's to forgive, and that I believed wholeheartedly.

"Paris sounds great!"

We were both taken aback by the reactions of Stewart and Estelle Bragg upon the proposal of our trip. The two were very business-like, professional people, as most attorneys are. But unlike most attorneys, they had good hearts, which had been passed down to their son. They had become more protective of their son since his kidnapping and the events that followed, but they'd grown to trust and like Blaire Devereaux. They'd even invited her to come with me to one of their fancy social gatherings with their fancy law associates. Mine wasn't the only family in Dixon with money, the Braggs had done quite well for themselves.

"Really?" Nolan asked. "You're okay with it?"

"We love Paris," Estelle said. "That's where we went on our honeymoon." She winked at her husband.

"That's cute," I said.

"That's disgusting," Nolan blurted.

I thanked and bid farewell to the Braggs, including Nolan, and drove home alone. I decided to throw on a pair of shorts and head up to the weight room on the second floor of the garage, where Nolan and I spent a lot of time. I was surprised to find Blaire's blue Mazda sedan outside, and sure enough, she was already in the weight room, doing what looked like a torturous core workout.

She sat up as I entered and cleared sweaty hairs off her forehead. "Hey," she said.

"You don't have to sneak around like this," I said with a smile. "You're a part of the family, you can let me know."

Her eyes seemed to flicker when I'd called her part of the family. She was, in a way, since she had no other family to speak of. My family cared for her, Nolan enjoyed her, and let's be honest, I was utterly enamored by her.

"I know," she said quietly. "Didn't think I had to tell you about every single move I make."

"You know I didn't mean it like that. What's the matter? You've been on edge for the past while."

She shrugged. It was becoming my least favorite thing that she did. The poor girl had never understood what it was like to talk about her feelings. Since she was a child, she'd been a tough, rugged girl, and the years of being a hired assailant had just about frozen her over completely. It was almost impossible to get through to her, but usually, if anyone could do it, it was me. So I crossed the room and sat next to her, leaning against the wall. "Talk to me," I said softly.

She rubbed her temples. "I'm sorry, okay? I'm just nervous about this whole Paris thing."

"Nervous, why?" This seemed like a new emotion for Blaire. She was usually always confident and prepared. "You know, we don't have to go to Paris if you're not comfortable with it."

"No, no," she said. "I want to. It was my idea, anyway. I'm just worried that someone will recognize me or figure out who I really am."

"But you *really are* Blaire Devereaux," I said. "The person who worked for Neil Trace wasn't you." I knew this wasn't really applicable and it was more figurative, but I thought maybe it would make her feel better.

"Whoever it was," she said. "They can still arrest *me*." She sighed and was quiet for a moment. I wasn't quite sure what to say. It was true, this was risky, but we had most, if not all of our bases covered. I wanted Blaire to live a normal life, and I would do whatever it took to give her that, even if it meant mine would no longer be normal.

Her head slid down the wall and landed on my shoulder, just like it had the day I'd saved her life. I'd felt joy before, but the amount of dopamine released in my body by one simple touch from this angel was far beyond anything I'd ever felt. I heard her mumble softly, "I just don't wanna lose this, Chris."

I felt a lump in my throat and my eyes started to burn. *Don't cry, you baby.* I choked it back and leaned down and kissed her forehead, then set my head against her own. "Me either."

The March morning air had a bite to it as we walked into Richmond International. Moods were abstract between the four of us. Nolan's girlfriend, Jennifer Poole, was all smiles, chipper and excited. Nolan was just trying to keep her under control, but I could tell he was excited to have a romantic trip with her. Blaire had her usual cool composure about her, not showing many emotions, but she gave me an occasional glance, and I returned a reassuring nod.

Richmond International Airport was a maze. Spring break had spiked the number of passengers coming and going. Those coming were most likely headed to Virginia Beach, hopefully to stay in a Quimby Suites hotel, and those going were like us, ready to leave the dull state.

This was no one's first time at an airport, so we made good time sending our luggage away, working our way through the metal detectors and such, and eventually boarding with ease. I was surprised at how smoothly everything went, but when you're planning for the worst, anything less seems superb. I could see color filling back into Blaire's face as we boarded. I offered her the window seat, but she said she couldn't react fast enough from the window seat if something were to happen.

"Nothing's going to happen," I assured her. "No one knows you, no one's out to get you. You're perfectly safe."

She smiled gently and gestured toward the window seat.

The Boeing 777, or Triple 7, was very spacious and the skies were smooth the whole way to Boston Logan, where we made our first stop, and boarded another Triple 7. Blaire spoke very little, but I caught her dozing a few times along the way, which gave me a bit of relief.

I occasionally heard Nolan and Jennifer talking and giggling in the row ahead of us, and I was somewhat jealous of the good time they were having. Not that I wasn't, but it was much more fun on a trip such as this when there was a bit of romance in the air. It was difficult for me not to make more obvious moves on her, but I was just afraid of scaring her off or hurting her. A heart as cold as hers was delicate. But if things were going to progress, where else but the City of Love?

Our second stop was in Lisbon, Portugal. This was also a massive structure, with thousands of people speaking a language that I was quite unfamiliar with. Blaire came in handy then, seeing as how she was almost fluent in seven languages.

It was odd the way she'd changed over these months. She'd become quieter, for she'd never really had the social life that had been suddenly forced upon her in the past season. Usually, she was apt and competent in the combat situations that we'd been in with Neil Trace and his hired men, but now that we were past them, she was in a new world. Sometimes I felt as though I was holding her back from who she really was, but the way she talked about it, she had no interest in being who she "really was".

Our total flight time, including our stops, had been close to thirteen hours, but due to France being six time zones ahead of Virginia, it was only five in the afternoon when we touched down in Charles de Gaulle Airport in Paris.

We stood at baggage claim for a good twenty minutes, watching it go around, everyone taking their bags, and ours nowhere to be found. I was frustrated, Jennifer was worried that she'd lost her entire wardrobe, Nolan was consoling her, and Blaire suggested foul play, as per usual. I assured her this was a common mishap by airlines.

"You'd think if it was a common mishap they'd learn how to fix it." She rolled her eyes. "This sucks." It sounded funny coming from her mouth, such a casual slang term.

"You four are a Quimby party?" came a French accent behind us. We turned to find a polite-looking female customer service agent. Her English was a bit lousy, which was understandable.

"Yes, we are," I replied.

"Your bags are moved here. Follow."

So we did. I was a bit confused as to why our bags had been moved. As far as I knew, none of us carried anything that would've set off a red flag. I felt a bit uneasy, a sixth sense I'd grown from my past two deadly experiences. I could see it in Blaire's eyes, the expression that used to be her only one, a look of danger, awareness, an acute sense of everything going on around her. The girl was a bloodhound, and it was obvious when she smelled danger.

The woman led us behind the service desk and into a small office, where a short man with slick hair sat behind a desk, our four suitcases lined up next to him. As soon as the door was shut behind us, two other men were revealed, both with pistols aimed at our heads.

You've got to be kidding.

Blaire's left foot went into one of the men's gut and as he faltered, she snatched his gun from his hand as a viper would strike a rat. Out of reflex, I leapt toward the man at the desk as Nolan made an advance on the second gunman. The short man stood with astounding speed and smashed the barrel of a pistol against my nose. I coughed and grabbed my nose, right as a wet rag was placed on it. I wondered who'd come to my aid so quickly, but I was soon unable to think, my sight was blurry, the room grew quiet...

The first thing I heard was the voice of a man. He spoke in English, with an American accent. I wondered if I was in Virginia, if the past day had been a dream. But as I opened my eyes and saw my three friends laying next to me on the cold floor of a dank room, I realized this had all been reality.

"Well, it is apparent that you are definitely the group we believed you to be," said the American voice. "I'm in the presence of heroes, I see. The very ones who took out the last of Neil Trace's organization. Mr. Quimby, Mr. Bragg, we're very indebted to you."

"Is this the way you thank heroes?" Blaire mumbled next to me.

"Oh, Miss Devereaux, thanks is the last thing you deserve," the man said. "You are the very pot who called the kettle black. You are no better than the people you killed three months ago, no better at all. You ma'am, are much more than Blaire Devereaux, you are also Janice Downey, Kate Sanders, and Veronica Teague."

Blaire's lips parted and her face sagged, hearing the names of her aliases. That was the moment I knew we were in trouble.

The man went on. "Well, how can you be surprised? When the eyewitness descriptions of three east coast criminals matched perfectly, it was apparent that they were the very same person. Those three were wanted for armed robbery, kidnapping, and auto theft. There was also an identification made by a witness on a security camera photo in Charleston, South Carolina, after a ship was looted in the bay. Whenever the three of you made your heroic effort, I did some reading up on you. Whenever Trace's men claimed you to be a former accomplice, it was shoved off as unprovable, but all the publicity turned out to be your undoing, Miss Devereaux. There was a seventy-two percent match from that blurry security camera photo to your new photo in the police database. We were waiting to make a move on it, but when you four hopped on a flight here, we decided to meet up with you now."

"Who are you?" she asked. "Where'd you get all this information?"

The man reached into his suit and removed a polished gold badge, the words *Federal Bureau of Investigation Department of Justice* in thick letters. I heard Blaire and Nolan cuss. Jennifer was still struggling to regain consciousness.

"Special Agent Phineas Wexler, FBI. That's right, Miss Devereaux, we found you. Good luck kicking your way out of this one."

She stared at the agent, her face so pale she could have been dead. "Arrest me then."

Wexler smirked. "No."

"Where are we?" came Jennifer's groggy voice, unaware of the conversation she'd interrupted. "Are we in France?"

"Yes, you are."

"Then how can you hold us like this?" I protested. "This is out of your jurisdiction."

"Well, for one thing, Mr. Quimby," he said. "Officially, we're 'assisting' the local police force, which is very much legal. Also, you're technically not on French soil right now."

"The embassy building," Nolan said.

"Correct. 2 Avenue Gabriel on the northwest corner of *Place de la Concorde*. So we are very much in our jurisdiction, and if we weren't, I simply don't care."

My head pounded. It must've been chloroform that had been shoved in my face back at the airport. My senses were slowly becoming sharper. The room seemed to be a random basement crevice, maybe a janitor's closet at one time. Pipes lined the ceiling, along with one dangling bulb. Wexler sat cross-legged on a wooden chair, his FBI-issued Glock Model 22 in his right hand.

"Why won't you arrest me?" Blaire broke the silence. "You've got substantial evidence backed up by however many eyewitness accounts, plus I'm sure Neil Trace and his guys in prison are more than ready to testify against me."

"I would love to arrest you, Miss Devereaux, but our meeting is much more complicated than that. As much as you do not deserve it, the Bureau is prepared to make a proposition."

"A proposition?"

"A proposition?"

"Indeed, a proposition. Believe it or not, there are folks out there who are much worse than you, in this very city, even. So, the

Bureau deemed it justifiable to trade one retired criminal, yourself, for three active, much more dangerous ones."

"How do you expect to make that trade?" Blaire asked, but the look on her face told me she was catching on.

"We're not going to make it," Wexler said. "You are. You're obviously a very capable group, and you're the perfect channel with which we will capture our three targets and get them extradited back to the States."

"And in return?" Blaire asked, her nostrils flaring.

"Freedom."

Blaire didn't speak, so he went on. "For the rest of your life, you'll never have to watch over your shoulder, dodge cameras, avoid publicity, unless of course you commit another crime. Every charge will be dropped, you'll be free to live a normal life, have friends, fall in love, if that's your thing." His eyes flashed to me for a millisecond. "It really isn't that complicated, seeing as how you haven't been convicted, so we don't have to go through the exoneration process. The charges can simply be dropped and forgotten, if you follow through."

"Freedom?" Blaire asked, still hung up on that word.

"Like Blaire Devereaux never even jaywalked."

She sat back against the wall. She looked at me with hopeful eyes, I nodded. The two of us turned to Nolan, who nodded. The three of us looked at Jennifer, who looked like a five year old caught in 'adult problems'. She simply shrugged and hid in Nolan's shoulder.

Blaire gripped Nolan's arm and mine in a show of thanks, then looked back at Special Agent Wexler. "Got yourself a deal."

"Gabriel Matthieu is a mastermind of heists. Whether they're jewelry stores, banks, he even made a stab at the Louvre once, but no one's that good. The man plans them out, has them executed, and has the loot sold or stashed away before anyone can turn the lights on. There's plenty of evidence against him, it's just the fact that he's impossible to get hands on. The reason we needed you to handle this is because the police in this city are absolutely incompetent, not to mention half of them are dirty."

Phineas Wexler flipped the page and continued. "Marius Chevrolet is a bit more dangerous. He runs a powerful street gang in the 10th arrondissement, and he carries plenty of weight in other parts of the city as well. He's an absolute thug. Anyone he doesn't like disappears, and anyone he does like lives in constant fear of rubbing him the wrong way. Other gangs hire him and his misfits to do the dirty work they can't do themselves. He's wanted for kidnapping, attempted murder, and murder."

"Did you say his name was Chevrolet?" Nolan sat with a tilted head near the other side of the conference table. He chuckled. "Imagine your last name was Lamborghini, or Tesla."

Blaire looked at him with considerable disappointment. "Like the founder of Lamborghini, Ferruccio Lamborghini? The famous inventor Nikola Tesla? Where do you think brand names come from?"

He slouched in his chair. "Definitely didn't miss your constant scolding."

Wexler looked like a high school teacher waiting for his students to stop talking. When they finished, he spoke. "*Anyway*, the thing that connects Matthieu and Chevrolet is one man: Elio Baptiste, the king of illegal exports and smuggling in Paris. He smuggled and distributed Gabriel Matthieu's stolen merchandise out of Le Havre in the English Channel. As for Chevrolet, like I said, he does all his dirty work, and the two organizations work well together. So we think the connection between these men can be a way to kill three birds with one stone, or, three stones and a girlfriend, I suppose. Either way, you get it. All of these men have worked in the States, doing just as much damage there as they do here, which is why we want them to be extradited. Like I said, the law here is weak, and we're here for the crimes they committed in America, so they're going to stand trial there. We've been getting intel on all of them over the past months and we've learned of something big in the making, involving all three men, so the timing is perfect here. We do appreciate you all planning your trip here this week," he added sarcastically.

The conference room was in the basement of the Embassy of the United States in Paris, down the hall from where my friends and I had been held. This was apparently secretive business, hence the discrete conference room. My three partners and I sat along the table, along with Special Agent Wexler's two partners, who didn't speak.

After ten more minutes of Wexler explaining the situation, he passed us photographs of all three men, and closed with, "Look, you're the lucky ones in this situation. If Blaire would've been captured anywhere else, there's a good chance they would've booked her and convicted her, but sometimes it's worth it to give up one criminal for three. I've noticed that you've been trying to live a normal life over the past months, and I want that for you, but you absolutely cannot stray from the mission whatsoever or else they'll shut it down. We gave you this chance because we believe you can get it done, so don't let us down." He sighed, as if exhausted from showing sincerity. "You've got the information, get out of here. If we want to talk, we'll contact you. If it's really me, you'll see my initials, followed by a crossed-out triangle. Until then, just follow the plan. Stephens will show you the way out. Don't forget your luggage. Goodbye." He gestured to our four suitcases along the wall, along with a duffle bag that we hadn't brought along. As I picked it up, I immediately recognized the weight and sound of metal packed inside.

The tall, skinny partner beckoned us and led us down the hall, up the stairs, and out the back of the foyer, into a courtyard that merged into a park. Without a word, he turned and left us. The four of us silently walked into the grassy park and found an unoccupied bench.

We didn't speak for a while, just sat, processing everything that had just happened. There was a light mist in the air, making everything damp and giving me a bit of a chill. It was warmer in Virginia than here. I wore only a pair of jeans and a T-shirt. The cool air, not to mention the adrenaline and anxiety of what had just transpired, left me shaking as I tried to calm myself on the bench.

"So much for spring break," Nolan said with his usual light sarcasm.

Jennifer had a bored expression. "I wanted to eat bread on the Eiffel Tower like every other French person."

I smiled. "Don't worry, Jenn, we'll–"

"We should go get hotel rooms," Blaire interrupted and stood abruptly. Without waiting, she walked down the sidewalk toward the street. Nolan and I made eye contact. I was afraid something like this would happen. She'd been trying for months to become a normal person, live a normal life, and now it was like she was relapsing, going back to what she was before.

I hurried up next to her, trying to keep up with her fast pace and talk at the same time. "Hey, look, don't worry about this. It's just one time, one *more* time. Then no more, for the rest of your life. This is it, you'll be free again, from everything. Just one more time."

She didn't look at me as she said, "Three months ago was supposed to be 'one more time'."

The *Hôtel Château Frontenac* was in the 8th arrondissement of Paris, just down the *Avenue des Champs-Élysées* from the embassy, better known as the Chancery. The street was often known as "the world's most beautiful avenue" and it was hard to disagree with that. If circumstances were different, I would've been enjoying myself in the chilly, stereotypically European weather.

The meeting between Gabriel Matthieu, Marius Chevrolet, and Elio Baptiste was to be the day after tomorrow, per Special Agent Wexler. That meant we had a day and a half of reconnaissance and planning, so Blaire obviously wanted to get started right away. My rear end had barely touched my mattress before she barged in the door, telling me we were leaving in five minutes, then stood in the doorway to make sure I didn't dilly-dally.

"How'd you get a key to my room?" I asked as I hurried to put my shoes back on.

"I didn't," she answered blankly.

"Okay. . .then," I mumbled. I couldn't help but smile. This was vintage Blaire, in her natural habitat, bossing me around, mysteriously knowing everything about everything. This was the Blaire I'd fallen in love with. S*hut up, Chris,* I told myself. *This is a serious situation.* Still, I couldn't help but enjoy it.

It was just the two of us as we walked down the hallway. "Aren't we waiting for the other two?"

"I told Nolan not to worry about it tonight," she replied. "He's with Jennifer, I feel bad. Let him have at least one romantic night before this goes down." I was surprised that she'd jeopardize something this important so Nolan could have a romantic evening. Perhaps I'd rubbed off on her a bit after all.

We went into the center of the city to the *Petite Ceinture*, translated as "little belt", an abandoned railway station that had turned into a hotspot for homeless migrant camps. It was definitely not the Paris that you see in tourist guidebooks, it was dangerous, depressing, and foul-smelling. But this was the place that the men were supposed to meet, according to Wexler's informant.

In some places, the tracks went under an old brick bridge, and brick walls rose up on either side to meet it, so the tracks were in somewhat of a hidden ditch. There weren't as many people here, and it was well-hidden in the shadows, so we decided this would be one likely spot for the three of them to meet up. Of course, it would also make sense for them to stay amongst the derelicts as to blend in and not arouse suspicion.

We also found several spots for the three of us to hide in waiting–we'd made the obvious decision that Jennifer need not come along. The arching support of the stone bridge provided several small crevices, a well-hidden spot. We could also take a different approach, random pedestrians strolling along through the scenery across the bridge. This was, of course, if they did decide to meet here. If they met in the homeless camps themselves, then we could also disguise ourselves and blend in. After an hour of scouting it out, as the sun fell behind the cityscape, we headed back toward the hotel.

The evening was cool, the mist still floating along the streets, making my hair damp, but only making Blaire's complexion glow. The moisture clung to her pale cheeks and shimmered under the streetlamps. I knew she was sworn against makeup, but it was hard to believe someone's face could be so perfect naturally. I was only experienced in high school girls that wore pounds of face paint to cover up blemishes caused by the very products they insisted on covering themselves in.

"Different circumstances," I said as we walked. "And I'd be having a good time with you."

Her face looked tired. "Yeah, but they're not different. This is how they are, this is how they'll always be. Won't change."

"Don't be so negative. It is different this time. We actually have a chance to end it."

She shook her head. "You don't understand, Chris. You can exonerate me, put every criminal in jail, try to give me a normal life, but I'm still me. My problems follow me everywhere. Followed me four thousand miles across the ocean. I was born into these circumstances, and there's no way to change them."

I knew what the next day was. When I woke up at five in the morning, it was the first thought to come into my mind. I battled with it throughout the next two hours, as I made myself a cup of coffee using the single-cup maker in the room. At home, Nolan and I would spend thirty minutes at a time trying to toss the cup of coffee grounds into the maker, betting on who'd make it first. I couldn't even make myself relive that memory, though, because of the dread on my mind considering this day. Nolan and Jennifer came to drink coffee, and the three of us bounced our concern off of each other. Blaire didn't come.

The twenty-fifth of March fell on a Thursday this year, also in the midst of a life-or-death situation. I struggled to decide how to act with Blaire. Nolan told me to be the optimist that I normally was, but I only worried that it would make too much of a day that Blaire wasn't interested in speaking about.

It was odd to think that someone as cold and robotic as Blaire could have a birthday, something that seemed so domestic. But today was that day. Today was also the day *before* the meeting between Gabriel Matthieu, Marius Chevrolet, and Elio Baptiste, when we'd be putting our lives on the line in order to get the charges against Blaire dropped. But the reason that I was anxious about today, the reason I was dreading seeing Blaire's face this morning, was that of a specific anniversary. The third anniversary of the death of her mother, killed by Bruce Smith, Neil Trace's gunman.

When the digital clock on the nightstand blinked 7:00, I decided I had to see if she was still in her room. "Be careful what you say," Jennifer cautioned. "She might not be a normal girl, but she's still a girl."

"Also," Nolan raised a finger. "I would be a little wary of whatever booby-traps she left for an intruder." I grabbed a small package from the counter and left the room.

I knocked once, held it, then tapped again, and repeated, signaling my first initial in morse code, the way Blaire had instructed us to. There was no reply. I did it again, still no reply. I tried the door, but it was locked, as expected. Growing concerned, I knocked loudly, calling her name. "Blaire? Devereaux?"

"What?" came her soft voice a foot behind me. I leapt and fell against the door, scrambling to pull the pistol from the back of my pants. She stood casually in the hall, her usual adequate composure about her. She held a croissant in her left hand and was gripping my forearm with the right. "Are you really about to pull out a gun in a monitored hotel hallway?" she asked, giving me her usual disappointed glare. I glanced to the middle of the corridor, seeing the black 360°

camera staring me down. I let the tail of my jacket cover the butt of the gun and brought my hands back to my front pockets.

"Sorry," I said awkwardly. "You didn't come get me this morning, I didn't know you'd been out."

"I went for a jog," she said, brushing past me to unlock her door. "I do just about every morning."

"You don't seem very worn out," I noticed. Not a shimmer of perspiration was visible on her face.

"That was three hours ago," she explained.

"At four a.m.?" She didn't speak, as if confused as to why I found this odd. "What have you done since then?"

"If you want me to live a normal life," she said, finally making eye contact with me. "Stop making me give you a step-by-step of everything I ever do. I went for a cup of tea at a café, got a croissant in the lobby. Still interested?"

She was on edge, as expected, but she was usually on edge to begin with. She unlocked the door and I followed her into an immaculately clean room. It seemed as though she'd just arrived, everything neatly in order, within arms reach to quickly grab and leave. Things like this were beginning to make sense to me. She wanted to be able to pull up stakes and leave the area as fast as possible, without any trace that she'd ever been here.

I still held the small cardboard package in my hand, and I reached it out to her now. She looked at me, then at the box, then at me, then back at the box. "What?" she asked bluntly.

"Well. . .Happy birthday."

Her sharp eyebrows scrunched as she looked at me suspiciously. Slowly, she reached out her hand and took it from me, then cautiously unfolded it. She held up the 9mm brass bullet, and her suspicious expression now became confused. "It's spent," she said, noting that this was just the slug with no casing.

"You fired it," I explained. "It's the bullet you saved my life with. Back in October, when you shot Miranda Blaine in the leg the second before she was going to shoot me. I know you want me to forget that, but I won't."

She smirked. "How'd you get your hands on this?"

"Don't you think I'm capable of pulling some strings and making some moves? You're not the only one with secrets here."

"Don't forget you saved my life not long after," she mentioned. I remembered, although I wished I could forget, shooting Bruce Smith in the back while hanging off a water tower as he'd aimed his own gun at Blaire's head. I'd never seen a person die until that day, and I'd been the one to do it. "Sorry," she said quickly, regretting bringing it up. "But really, I am grateful. Don't forget that."

She sat on the edge of her bed, a blank expression across her pale face. "You know what today is, don't you?"

"Uh, your birthday," I said flatly, although I knew what she meant. She looked up at me with an expression that told me to drop the act. I nodded solemnly, looking at my shoes.

"I had always been lucky, my birthday usually falling on spring break. It's weird, senior year feels like so long ago, but that day feels like yesterday. She woke me up with waffles on my nightstand, and took me to the mall to buy a new phone. Later I went to hang out with my friend, my only friend I still had since I'd started working with the dealers from my martial arts club. Allison Mixon, my friend since third grade. She bought me new Vans, pink ones. I don't know what she had in mind, she had to have known I'd never wear that color. . ."

Her dark eyes were wide, like endless black holes. "Got home at ten o'clock. She was dead on the kitchen floor." She pushed the last sentence out in a painful whisper. She breathed heavily, dropped the bullet on the floor, and fell back onto the bed.

I frantically stood over her, asking if she was alright. Her eyes were still wide and unblinking, she stared at the ceiling, as if blinded by the memory flooding into the room. She reached out and grasped my arm. "I'm fine." Her lips began to form another word, then froze. Finally, she pushed it out. "Chris. . .come here."

I didn't know what she meant, but I sat on the bed next to her and mumbled, "I'm right here." Glancing over, she blinked once, then continued staring.

"Lay down."

I had grown confused and uncomfortable, not understanding what she wanted from me. Still, I obeyed, laying next to her. I was a bit frightened by the way she continued to stare at the ceiling, and by the awkward command she'd given me. But gently, she rolled over, set her head on my chest, and I watched her sober eyes slowly fall closed. I felt cool tears on my neck as she sobbed quietly.

I'd seen Blaire show more emotion than most people had, even felt her simple gestures of affection, but I'd never seen her so vulnerable, so broken, so in need of compassion. Holding back my own tears, I gently wrapped my arms around her and repeated, "I'm right here."

For the second time since I'd known her, I heard her whisper, "Thank you."

The entirety of Blaire's birthday involved a whole lot of nothing. We decided against going back to the *Petite Ceinture*, since middle-class

Americans taking multiple trips to a French homeless camp would raise red flags among most of the community. So the four of us went to eat at a small bistro on the *Avenue des Champs-Élysées*. We sat on the small patio of the restaurant, fighting a light chill, sipping red wine.

"The only thing I like about France so far," Nolan commented. "Is that the legal drinking age is eighteen. Makes me feel like an adult."

"Fighting for your life against drug lords and hitmen doesn't make you feel like an adult?" I asked flatly.

He shrugged. "Sometimes the opposite. Lying on the floor with a gun pointed at my head and taking constant orders from guys in suits sure makes me feel pretty low on the totem pole."

Blaire spoke up, more to herself than to us. "Welcome to my world."

Rain. Wind. Cold. As I looked out onto the balcony of my room, I was seriously wondering what on earth led us to believe Paris in March would be a pleasant trip. Not that the city wasn't still intriguing and beautiful, but it wasn't exactly the stereotypical spring break. Then again, there were several more reasons this wasn't a stereotypical spring break.

An unmarked envelope had been delivered to Blaire's door that morning. We skipped to the bottom of the note to begin with, making sure it was legitimate. Just as Special Agent Wexler had described, in the bottom right corner were the initials "PHW" followed by a small triangle, with a diagonal line crossing through it. We decided it was valid, then looked over two lines.

⊐⊏⊡>∨⊏<⊏⊓∨ ⊔⊏⊓⊐⊓⊐
>∨⊡⊡><⊏⊡⊡

"What is this?" Nolan asked, annoyed. "*National Treasure?*"

"Oh! Oh!" Jennifer yelled. "I know this. I actually know it."

The three of us looked at her. She hadn't said much this entire week, and I was surprised to see her speaking up now.

"It's a pigpen code," she explained. "Freemason's code. I read about it in a book, *The Lost Symbol*. It was about Freemasons and Washington D.C. Letters are set out on four separate grids, and their position on the grid is used as the letter."

Everyone looked at Blaire, who was staring widely at the note, stumped. She looked at Jennifer, then realized she was being stared at. She opened her mouth, couldn't find words, closed it again. I could see her turning red, angered and embarrassed that she wasn't familiar with the code. I was also surprised that Jennifer had come up with the answer that even Blaire couldn't. By this time, I had pulled the code up on my phone, and I set it down next to the note.

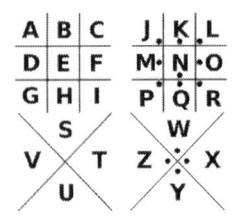

```
A | B | C     J .K. L
D | E | F     M·N·O
G | H | I     P | Q | R
  \ S /         \ W /
 V  X  T       Z ·X· X
  / U \         / Y \
```

After a few minutes of reading and copying, we discovered the note to read, "Montsouris bridge twentyone". It was simple and vague, but we quickly made sense of it: The meeting was at the bridge at *Parc Montsouris*, where Blaire and I had been the night before. It most likely meant twenty-one hundred hours, or nine p.m.

The time was set, the place was set. Now all we could do was prepare, and pray.

I could smell it, I knew it was coming. French rain smelled the same as American rain, and that was the smell lifting off the city as I stood on our balcony. We were leaving the hotel separately, at different times, from different exits. We could've been being monitored by anyone at any time. If anyone in this city knew Neil Trace and Bruce Smith, which someone probably did, they would know who we were.

Nolan had walked out the hotel's back entrance ten minutes ago. Jennifer had had a panic attack earlier in the day, passing out in the bathroom. I pitied the poor girl, getting into the whole mess that Nolan and I had just fallen into six months ago, and having to wait here all night while he went to capture three gangsters. I also missed Nolan, missed the close friendship that we had before this had all started. He and I hadn't spent much time talking on this trip the way we usually did, having been so focused on the operation at hand.

Before he'd left, I grabbed his shoulder and pulled him into an aggressive hug. He patted my back and grasped my neck in his little-brother sort of way. "Be careful, Chris," he mumbled to me.

"You too, you too." I gave him a healthy slap on the back and he kissed Jennifer goodbye, then left.

He was headed to the bridge, to the small ledge underneath it amongst the cross beams. It would serve as a good vantage point, while Blaire and I took the hiding-in-plain-sight approach.

"Ready, *mon amour?*" Blaire asked me.

I was taken off guard at the affectionate name, but understood the act. We were to be the empty-headed couple taking a stroll along the bridge and admiring the scenery, too entranced by each other to notice the gang meeting below us, or so it would seem.

We strolled out the front door of the hotel holding hands, smiling at each other, swinging our arms and talking in hushed voices.

We'd decided it would make sense for us to be speaking English, seeing as half of this city were tourists from other countries. Rather to be heard speaking a different language fluently than speaking in French badly. We made sure to act as if we had no specific route, taking the long way along the most populated and scenic sidewalks. Blaire giggled a couple of times, which sounded nothing like her, and startled me the first time I heard it. Every so often, she would stand on her tiptoes–although she was only two inches shorter than me–and pretend to whisper sweet nothings in my ear, while in reality she said, "Laugh and put your arm around me." I did so, putting a hand around her waist and pulling her toward me. She giggled, loudly accusing me of tickling her, and I dramatically denied.

To anyone watching, it was an adorable picture, as long as they didn't notice the bulging Ruger pistols tucked away in our jackets.

We were right on schedule, the bridge coming into view two minutes before nine, as we entered the *Parc Montsouris*. We wanted to be there right on time because there was no way of knowing how long this discussion would take. We wanted to be there while they were off-guard, talking to each other.

The bridge was more of a tunnel for those underneath it. It was fairly wide and cast a long shadow, especially at his hour of the night, so much so that as we came onto the bridge, we could scarcely see the tracks beneath us. We hadn't thought that through very well. There were several trees overhead, though, so it was also difficult for them to spot us, as there was no visible moon on this misty night.

Three people, two women and a man, strolled onto the bridge from the other side. Trying not to meet their eye line, I jokingly acted as if I was going to push Blaire off the bridge. She let out a shriek, then giggled, falling against the railing, and pulling me against her. We held still, face to face, our cloudy breath evaporating around our faces. Her pupils dilated as they stared into mine, and for a second I forgot where I was.

She could see the people behind us walking past, and as I followed her eyes, I saw them grow wide, and looking back to me, she mumbled something, grabbed my face, and kissed me, then again. I knew this was a diversion to get the passers-by to look away, but I suddenly felt as if I had no care in the world whether we lived or died tonight, this was all I wanted.

But it ended before I could finish the thought. She pulled away, catching her breath. I tried to act as if what had happened hadn't phased me at all. She quietly apologized, and I told her I understood. The two of us turned then and casually gazed down onto the bridge, straining our eyes in the dark to see the figures of our targets. But we saw nothing.

We also didn't see the man behind us, the one who'd just passed by. "Chris!" Blaire yelled a second too late, and I felt a powerful set of hands throw me over the railing, and watched the ground below come up to meet me.

My eyes opened, but I saw nothing, at least for the first few seconds. Blue splotches flashed across my eyes, and as I became aware of my surroundings, I also became aware of the suppressed gunshots coming from above me. Afraid, I scrambled to my hands and knees, then quickly changed my mind. The pain shooting through my back flattened me onto the cold ground again. Gasping for breath through the pain, I felt the cold raindrops landing on the back of my neck and running down into my mouth. But I soon realized the water coming from my mouth wasn't water, but blood.

Now I began to panic, remembering all I'd heard about people spitting blood before they die. I pushed frantic words out, begging for help. Rolling onto my back, I gazed around myself. I'd luckily fallen to the side of the train tracks when I'd been pushed over the railing, hitting the stone wall that ran up twenty feet high as it met the landscape that the bridge was built off of. It had slowed my fall as I bounced off it, or I would've been dead on impact. But I was afraid the end wasn't far off.

The tunnel formed by the bridge was in front of me, a pit of darkness, where I had no way of telling if Nolan was there or not. As raindrops splashed into my eyes, I saw Blaire's silhouette on the bridge, on the outside of the railing, standing on the ledge and holding onto the cold iron. With her other hand, she was firing to the left at someone I couldn't see. From the sound of it, they were firing back. Both guns had silencers, but the sharp hissing of air still pierced the night.

But there were more than two guns, for I heard more shots, most of these not silenced. I knew Nolan's pistol also wore a suppressor, but I didn't hear it now. Painfully reaching into my jacket, I removed my Ruger and started firing wild shots toward the bridge. I made out Blaire's pale face as she turned to look down at me, and her mouth fell open. It was hard to make out what she mouthed, but I was fairly sure I saw her say, "Thank God."

My eyes had adjusted to the darkness, and I was sure there was no one else in the tunnel, no gangsters having a secret meeting. I did see another figure, leaning over the wall, but I didn't fire, hoping it was Nolan. I soon learned it wasn't, as I saw a muzzle flash as the person fired down at me. Panicking, I wildly fired five shots, hearing them ricocheting off the wall, until one pierced muscle, and the figure disappeared.

The gravel crackled behind me, and I tried to aim around my head, but I heard frantic whispers. "Chris, no! It's me, it's me." I craned my neck to see a bloody face appear, standing over me. I gasped as I recognized Nolan's wavy brown hair sticking to his forehead. "Come on. I got you." He grabbed me under the armpits, and ignored my painful screams, except to tell me to hush.

I still felt blood dripping from my mouth, I tasted its sourness on my tongue. Nolan pulled my limp body along the tracks for what felt like two hundred feet, but was more like fifty. We came to a narrow stairway built into the side of the wall. He pulled me to my feet and threw my arm over his shoulder, despite my desperate cries. I tried my best to put my feet on the small steps, but Nolan did most of the work.

Although I was dizzy and nauseous, I maintained consciousness. My back was stabbed with pain from my neck to my tailbone. He pulled me into the park, toward a secluded bench. "Stay here," he said.

"Nolan," I managed to say. "What happened?"

"We got set up. Now stay here and don't make noise."

"Wait, Nolan," I cried. "I'm spitting blood. I'm scared. I'm dying."

Fear covered his face as he leaned over me. He wiped the blood from my lips and opened my mouth, squinting. Sighing, he said, "No, Chris. You're not dying. You bit your tongue."

"Well it sure feels like I'm dying."

"I know, buddy. Your spine's probably fractured, but you gotta stay here. I'll be back soon, I gotta go help Blaire. Chevrolet's men are everywhere." With that, he ran off, back to the bridge.

I couldn't tell whether the shooting faded because I was losing consciousness or because they'd stopped firing, but I was sure I heard police sirens and a familiar voice before the darkness closed in around me.

"Miss Devereaux, Miss Poole, Mr. Bragg, Mr. Quimby."

We were led into the basement conference room of the Chancery. Special Agent Phineas Wexler sat at the head of the table, fiddling with a pen, a packet of papers in front of him. Nolan pulled a chair out for me, on which I sat stiffly, the brace around my back holding my torso tightly, making it difficult to sit. I managed. Nolan sat next to me, bandages around his forehead from the bullet that had grazed him. Jennifer was on his other side, and Blaire sat silently on the other side of me, and she grasped my hand tightly, nervously.

Wexler wasted no time. "Well, you've obviously not completed the total task which was assigned to you." I was sure of it now, he'd been the voice I'd heard before losing consciousness. "Gabriel Matthieu and Elio Baptiste are still running the streets of Paris, free as birds. I understand that the information which was given to you by me was false. The informant who'd described the supposed meeting between these men has since confessed to working for the very men we were trying to capture. In the process, you were able to take down and capture Marius Chevrolet and two of his hitmen. They are all currently awaiting trial. In spite of this, our deal had been for all three of the gang leaders. Correct?"

"Yes, sir," I heard Blaire push out in despair.

Wexler didn't speak for twenty seconds. He stared down at the paper in front of him, still twiddling the pen in his fingers. "Yes, the goal was three crime lords, in exchange for one mediocre criminal. But you gave us one crime lord, and two of his own mediocre criminals. When I look at this case, and I look at the three of you, there is no shadow of a doubt in my mind that you've done all in your power to complete this assignment. You did your country a service, and you did the city of Paris a service. You put your lives on the line, sustained serious injuries, trying to complete the task assigned to you."

Our tired heads looked up from the table, into the narrow eyes of Phineas Wexler. He kept speaking. "I believe the appropriate reward for your effort, and your achievement, is the same deal that we'd originally agreed upon." Blaire's lips parted, none of dared take a breath. Wexler clicked his silver pen, bent over the paper, and scribbled a signature. He then slid it across the table to us.

"Blaire Devereaux, you are hereby released of all charges against you. You are free to go home. All four of you."

The only sound in the room was Blaire's exhale.

A week after Marius Chevrolet, the hitman of all hitmen, had been captured, Nolan, Jennifer, Blaire, and I were dropped off at Charles de Gaulle Airport, for a ten a.m. flight home. I walked side by side with Nolan, forever indebted to him for dragging me out of certain death. I used a cane, and was still constricted by the velcro brace around my torso, but overall intact.

That night was still foggy to me, since I hadn't been a part of much of it. Nolan and Blaire had fought off Chevrolet and his men for ten minutes, until Chevrolet suffered a gunshot wound to the shoulder. Most of the men dispersed, aside from his right-hand man, and another thug who'd been shot in the arm, supposedly by me, although the memory was vague.

Walking across the airport parking lot, as I was trying to refresh my memory of the battle, it resumed in front of my eyes. A black SUV screeched to a halt thirty feet in front of us, and suicide doors swung open, two men emerging.

"There they are," Blaire hissed.

A short man with curly hair emerged from the driver's seat, French pistols in either hand. He was athletically built, and slim. I immediately recognized him from the pictures Wexler had shown us: Gabriel Matthieu.

From the backseat stepped a mountain of a man, a buzzed haircut, wet trench coat, and HK416 rifle in hand. Elio Baptiste.

No one dared to breathe. The morning was quiet, aside from the distant sound of jet engines. But the silence among us was deafening. My fingers twitched, Jennifer breathed heavily, Nolan exhaled calmly, and Blaire had no expression. Making nary a sound, we let them begin the endgame.

"*Mademoiselle Devereaux*," Baptiste shouted in rich French, then in broken English, "The time has come, for to revenge."

Still, we didn't speak. I studied the man as he confidently gloated. This was the man who ran the streets of Paris, along with the most elusive thief in the better part of France. Baptiste had a scar across his forehead, similar to the one Nolan would have once he healed. His thick neck seemed like a continuation of his round face, and he wore a confident smirk, looking at these four American children who'd captured one of his most powerful allies.

A nineteen year old high school graduate, now a barista at a small town coffee shop; the eighteen year old son of two attorneys, whose future was full of battles of law, much different than the one currently at hand; a rich man's kid, who, until six months ago, had only to worry about where the next party was; and a twenty-one year old girl, whose chance at a normal life had been stolen out from under her time and time again.

"You taken someone special to me," Baptiste continued. "Arrested him. But you do not get away with it. Now, Americans, you will, how you say–"

No one will ever know what mocking declaration Baptiste was trying to get across here, because in the second he spent trying to find demeaning enough words, Blaire pulled her pistol from the back of her waistband with speed unknown to our assassins, and shot him in the chest. And in the same second, I pulled my own handgun from where I'd hidden it in my inner jacket pocket, and fired two shots into Gabriel Matthieu. The two men fell to the ground in two separate thuds, their blood flowing together in one pool on the cold asphalt.

The writhing groans were drowned out by the ringing in my ear. The foggy morning was still as two men lay in front of us. Neither were dead, that hadn't been the goal. My shots had been wild and might've killed Matheu had he not been wearing a protective vest, but the bullet in his shoulder held him to the ground. Blaire's accuracy had landed her bullet far enough to the left to miss Baptiste's heart. She could've killed him had she wanted to, I knew that much. But she hadn't, which I thanked God for. Now we stood frozen, guns still raised as Nolan advanced on the two, removing all weapons and training his pistol on them as they lay on the ground. This had all been expected, we'd planned for it since we'd left the Embassy. Agent Wexler and his men were waiting a half mile away for our call. By the time they did arrive, airport police had closed off the scene, and it took all of twelve minutes for seven different witnesses to give matching accounts of what had happened.

Wexler approached us, removing his sunglasses and crossing his arms. "I'd like to rescind my previous statement. You *have* completed, nay exceeded, your assignment, for which this city, this country and your own homeland, are forever indebted to you for. Once I return to the States, we will be in touch. I'd like to have a chance to formally thank you, in a much more suitable environment. Until then, I beg you, please try to live that normal life you've so desperately fought for. *Bonne continuation.*" With that, he left us.

"Are you alright?" I asked Blaire as I noticed her staring blankly at the ground. "What's going on?"

She shook her head and gestured to the men writhing in pools of blood as paramedics struggled to clean their wounds. "You can exonerate me, drop the charges, send me home, give me a normal life, but look at that. I told you Chris, there's no such thing as different circumstances. I am who I am, and it can't change."

"Yes, you are who you are. You're Blaire Kickass Devereaux. The one who saved my life when you owed me nothing, the one who fought to protect us and the people we care about. The one who destroyed the very men who took your life away from you. The one who took down three of the most powerful criminals in France. And the one who I care about more than I do myself. You talk about the evil in this world and in your life and how you can never escape it. No, you can't, none of us can. This world is evil. But it can't control us. Do you know how I know that? Because right then, when you had the drop on Baptiste, you could've aimed five inches up and ended his life, but you didn't, because that's not you. You can talk all your life about all that's wrong with this world, but you're what's right with this world. The circumstances don't determine the outcome, the response does."

A single tear fell down her soft, perfect cheek, and I wiped it away with my thumb. I saw Nolan in the corner of my eye, crying on Jennifer's shoulder as they had their own emotional conversation. Blaire bit her lip and put her forehead against mine. I watched the corner of her mouth curl slightly, revealing matching dimples, and I felt her take both my hands in hers.

In a broken whisper, she said, "Let's go home."

Part IV

Signet Ring

". . .and to everyone who has made this possible over the years, all who have helped my family and I in the hardest of times, and those who never doubted that Quimby Suites Limited would keep climbing to the top. My sincerest gratitude and thanks to everyone here tonight, for all that you've done. Let us raise our glasses, to all of us!"

"To all of us!"

I watched my father sip his champagne and finally step down from the stage, the small jazz band resumed playing in the corner, and conversation grew loud once more. I glanced around at the roughly two hundred guests in the ballroom of the Quimby Suites Hotel in Outer Banks, who'd come to celebrate the completion of it, it being the fiftieth destination of the company. Many of those fifty had been hotels that my father had bought out from other companies, so this was one of the few he'd actually constructed. Either way, the name Henry Quimby was rapidly growing in popularity. Most of his executives, managers, their spouses, and everyone in between were here now, sipping champagne or chardonnay or any of the other wines my father had imported from Spain. Everyone dressed equally as exemplary as the next, from ankle-length ball gowns to three-piece suits.

Here I sat, in my own blue pinstripe suit, Quimby Suites "Q" lapel pin, and gold cufflinks. I felt proud to be my father's son, as I always did. Even if I was the youngest of three, recently graduated from high school with no career path, I was still treated like a Quimby.

As for my best friend sitting next to me, Nolan Bragg did have a career lined up for him since the day he was born. His mother and father had met while opposing each other in criminal court, so practicing law was in Nolan's blood, that was obvious. He'd led Dixon High School's mock trial team to state runner-up this past winter. He was distinguished, mature, and smart, while I was sometimes the opposite. I was happy for him, though, after all we'd been through in the past nine months, being kidnapped, getting into shootouts, and most recently, taking down three of Paris' most powerful criminals. But here we still sat, alive and well, although the scars of our conflicts would never fade. There was a still-red scar across the side of Nolan's forehead, where a bullet had grazed him two months ago. I had a scar and a numb spot on my thigh where I'd been shot this past January, and I was still going to physical therapy after fracturing my spine in Paris.

Next to Nolan sat his girlfriend, Jennifer Poole. We'd met Jennifer last October, serving us coffee at The Grind, a coffee shop in downtown Dixon. The two had hit it off, leaving me somewhat in the dust. Not that I wasn't involved in my own fruitless romances.

"There she comes, Chris," Nolan said, nodding toward the entrance of the ballroom. Just as I'd been thinking of her, the source of all our recent woes showed up in a black dress that complemented every feature. Straight black hair falling to her shoulders, and cool pale skin that never showed a single blemish. Eyes so blue they appeared an icey gray, like cold stars dancing in her iris. I watched the eyes of the younger men at the banquet follow Blaire Devereaux to our table and sit at the chair which I had pulled out for her. I couldn't blame them, I was equally as captivated by her beauty. She thanked me formally and took a glass of champagne that my father had come over to offer her, although I knew she wouldn't drink it.

"Glad to see you here, Blaire," he said, formally kissing her cheek.

Smiling, she replied, "Of course. So sorry to be late." Once he'd left, she turned to me and much less sensitively said, "Sorry."

I checked my watch. Late? It was eight o'clock. We'd been here two hours, eaten an hour ago. We were all staying at the hotel, she was only three rooms away from me, and I'd spoken to her before I'd left. I'd texted her and called to make sure she was alright, and had hardly gotten a response. She wasn't any regular girl, but she definitely communicated like one. Still, not wanting to upset her, I held my tongue and simply said, "That's okay. Everything alright?"

She exhaled. "Yes, just running behind."

My eyes narrowed, and I couldn't keep myself quiet. "Blaire, it's eight o'clock. You're two hours late. Plus, I'm not sure if you've ever 'run behind' in your life."

"You're right," she hissed through gritted teeth. "I've been in my room for the past hour vomiting and taking tylenol, because I'm just a little hesitant to see Wexler again."

I sat back, sorry that I'd flustered her. Special Agent Phineas Wexler of the FBI had made a call a week ago saying he'd like to meet with us, and I'd invited him to the banquet this evening. Wexler was the very man who'd granted Blaire her freedom this past March after we'd taken down three of Paris' largest criminals over the course of a few conflicts. I understood that she was a bit ambivalent towards him, even though he'd given her her life back, he still brought back memories of her life before.

"Well, you're in luck," I said, gesturing around the room. "He's not here, either."

"I feel like an FBI agent would be a little more prompt," Nolan whispered, leaning over to join the conversation. "He said he was coming, didn't he?"

I nodded. "Said he'd be here sometime tonight. I guess maybe he didn't want to be greeted at the door, but he's on the guest list, we know he's coming."

"He'll be here," Blaire said coolly, scanning the room.

I followed her gaze to the far corner of the room, where sat the manager of the Charleston, West Virginia Quimby Suites, along with what seemed like a girlfriend, although by the look at the two of them together, she must've been more focused on his pocket book than his attractivity. It wasn't the couple Blaire was interested in, I knew, but the table. This wasn't the same place that I'd met Blaire, but essentially the same layout, and the table in the exact spot. It was the first place I'd ever laid eyes on her, sitting with legs crossed in a long black dress, a glass of chardonnay in her hand, throwing glances at Nolan. At the time I'd been jealous, but I soon learned the reason for her interest wasn't romantic, but rather that she'd been ordered to kidnap him.

"Crazy, isn't it?" I said aloud for only her to hear amongst the chatter at the table.

"What?" she asked, although she most definitely knew what I meant.

"Less than a year ago you were at that table, back in Virginia, on a mission for Neil Trace, and now you're here, amongst the very people you were working against."

She nodded soberly, looking at her lap, seemingly ashamed. I apologized with a hand on hers and she nodded back, setting a finger on the gold signet ring on my left pinky finger. "What's this?"

"Was my father's," I answered. "And his father's, and his, and his."

"How'd your great-great-grandfather get it?"

I chuckled at the question, a commonly asked one. "Well," I began, trying to piece together a sentence. "Abner Quimby made his fortunes a little bit differently than my father. He wasn't exactly a hard worker, but he was a genius."

"He was a thief," Blaire reached the conclusion.

"Well, yes. He'd fought in the First World War as a boy, and you know how times were going into the twenties. He was a father of four trying to provide for his family, so yes, he did live somewhat of a life of crime. He grew quite good at it, actually. But popularity was his eventual downfall. He spent the nine years leading up to the Second World War in prison, but was paroled in order to look after his family and his oldest son's family while he was fighting. That was the beginning of the hardest times for our family. The next two generations had a rough go of it, but my own father was the one to get the Quimby family back on track, and you know that story."

"I appreciate the history lesson," she said in her usual sarcastic way. "You still haven't told me where the ring comes from."

"Oh, well, like I said, Abner became pretty popular among criminals in the twenties, and that ring was *supposedly* snatched right off the hand of 'Scarface' himself."

"Sure it was," she said without a hint of belief. She smirked at my wild story.

"Look for yourself," I said, slipping the ring from my finger and showing her the underside of its head. Carved out of the gold was the inscription "*No. 1*", a popular nickname used for Al Capone, him being known as Public Enemy Number One.

She showed the slightest interest after seeing my proof, but still shrugged. "Anyone could've written that to match the story."

Smiling, I had to agree. Sliding it back onto my finger, I said, "Either way, it's a family heirloom. My older brother gets the company, I get a ring. Even-Steven."

"Steven!" came my father's booming voice from behind me. He took an empty seat next to me. "You're forgetting, your brother's on his way to a college degree. Look at him over there, talking business with all those old fellas. Don't act like the company just fell in his lap."

"You didn't go to college," I mumbled. "And you don't know that I wouldn't have wanted to get a degree, too, but Jared's four years older. He had first dibs."

He smirked and gave me a raised eyebrow. We both knew I was full of it, I had absolutely no desire to go to college, due to the evidence of his success without the aforementioned extra schooling. Not to mention my overall neither-here-nor-there personality. I, the black sheep, whose natural hatred for books whose covers didn't read Lewis or Hemingway or Christie or Doyle or the like caused a hatred for school entirely, who only cared for these classy events for the fact that it allowed me to showcase my astounding fashion sense, who, even if given the entire company with a bow and a box of chocolates would've still been unsatisfied. It was plain and simple, I was a ne'er-do-well derelict.

Okay, perhaps that was a bit exaggerative, but I did feel a pinch of jealousy upon seeing my brother's success. Even my sister

Olivia, two years my elder, was working on getting a complete cosmetology license. My mother liked to reassure me I would find a calling that would get me somewhere in life, unlike playing baseball and drag racing my Mustang, which was basically all my life currently consisted of.

Oh, well. Far be it for me to let silly things like the future ruin the moment herein. I absorbed my father's healthy slap on the back as he wandered off to shake hands and kiss babies. Turning back to my three companions, I noticed the anxiety level among them was rising. Knees bounced rapidly, fingernail polish was picked at. I'd been trying to keep my mind off of Wexler, but his absence was bothering me. I had no idea the nature of his visit, whether just to formally thank us for all we'd done or to lead us into more trouble.

But the large clock on the far wall kept ticking, and at nine-thirty, there was still no sign of him. The crowd began thinning out then, and an hour later, my father was thanking the last of the guests and writing a check to the jazz band. The four of us–Nolan, Jennifer, Blaire, and myself–headed sluggishly toward our rooms on the fifth and top floor. The elevator was deafeningly silent as everyone drowsily leaned against vibrating walls, both exhausted from the evening and depressed at Wexler's absence. As we reached the top floor, the jerking stop nearly sent me to the ground, but I shook myself awake and stumbled out the door.

Do you know that feeling as you near someplace and the intuition of trouble seems almost tangible? As Nolan and I reached our room, I looked down the hall to where Blaire stood, staring at her doorknob. Jennifer, across the hall from her door, asked what the problem was. Blaire slipped her keycard into the slot and we heard the door unlock, and she gently pushed the door open. The look of bewilderment on her face told us all we needed to know. Quickly, I unlocked our door and shoved it open, to find the disaster it had become.

The room had been turned inside out, suitcases emptied, clothes strewn about, the room safe busted open, mattresses on the floor, every drawer or cabinet in the place hanging open. From Jennifer's exclamation down the hall, we guessed hers looked the same. We slowly entered the room, back to back, having learned to go about these situations warily and calmly. We made a thorough search of the place and found no one still there.

Judging by the look of the safe, it appeared the intruder had used some kind of powder and fuse to burn through the deadbolt, but we'd left nothing in there for them to find. Frankly, we had nothing to hide, here in our room, at least. It had originally looked like a robbery, but we took a quick inventory and found nothing missing. The pure silver watch I'd received on my eighteenth birthday six months ago was still in place in the chesnut box along with three other watches, a gold crucifix necklace, and a set of silver cufflinks. Nolan had left his wallet on his nightstand, and although it's contents littered the floor, they were all accounted for.

Trying not to soil the crime scene, we left everything the way it was and went to check on the girls. We found Jennifer cross-legged on the floor, crying amongst the mess that looked similar to our room. I left Nolan there to console her and went to Blaire. She was standing still at the foot of the bed, her eyes scanning the place. Again, it seemed to be the result of the same type of unorganized raid as ours. But in this case, the intruder had given a very definitive clue to their reason for this assault. A sheet from the notepad upon the nightstand had been ripped out and taped against the front wall, and scribbled upon it was the name "*WEXLER*".

Blaire stood, looking exhausted at the sight of the mess and the feeling once again of being up against someone. For the past three months since Paris we'd had absolutely no conflicts with anyone, not even amateur rivalries with my old classmate, Justin Hobbes. But this felt like more than just a grudge. In my mind, I was crossing off possibilities. It obviously wasn't a robbery, because the crook had taken their time about the place but stole nothing. It wasn't an attempt on our well-being, because we'd found no booby-traps or ambushers waiting for us. The way in which things were emptied and thrown on piles told us that this wasn't some kind of rude ransacking, but rather an exhaustive search of our possessions.

We stared at the note left on the wall with Agent Wexler's name written on it. There could be several reasons for this: One could be that this was a warning against Wexler's safety, that they were showing their ability to infiltrate and cause damage; an unlikely one would be that this had something to do with revenge *for* Wexler or for something that Wexler *did*; but the most likely reason that we deducted, having taken the state of our belongings into consideration, was that the intruder was out to find Wexler, or some sort of information on him. That would've explained the rigorous search through our things. They were after something, but we were even more in the dark than them, so their search was probably fruitless.

The four of us joined in Blaire's room, and my father showed up soon after, along with two men from hotel security. "Nolan called me. What on earth happened?"

"Someone was after something," I explained. Attention was on me as I spoke, and out of the corner of my eye I saw Blaire silently pull the note off of the wall and slide it into the bosom of her dress. Taking this as a sign to not give up our reasoning, I played dumb. "Could've been an attempted robbery, maybe a prank, I don't know."

"Well this is ridiculous," yelled my father, turning to the two guards. "We're not even open to the public yet and we've already had the rug swept out from under us and our most important guests burglarized. How difficult can it possibly be to protect this place?"

"We apologize, Mr. Quimby," one man stammered. "We must've been too focused on the gala. What would you have us do, now?"

"Well, for goodness sakes, it's a bit too late for that now, isn't it? Go back to your posts, I'll be having a word with your supervisor." The two defeated officers tucked their tails and walked sullenly down the hallway. Turning back to us, my father asked, "You're all okay, right? Did anything get stolen? Should I call the police?"

"No, nothing stolen, no harm done," Nolan assured him. "I think the police would only make more trouble."

"And, let's be honest, Dad," I said, nudging his shoulder. "I don't think that's the kind of publicity we want for the grand opening of the hotel. It would probably be best if no one hears about this, don't you think?"

His attitude changed after I'd pointed this out. "You're probably right. As long as you're all okay, and you don't think you're in any serious danger, we'll just keep this amongst ourselves. Especially don't make a big deal of it to your mother, or she might have a heart attack. Now if you'll excuse me, I need to have a word with Sergeant Dennehy." He stomped down the hallway to give an earful to the security supervisor.

Blaire shut the door and turned to us. "Alright, Nolan, put on some coffee, let's go over this."

"They, whoever it was," Blaire began. "Must've learned about our situation with Wexler, they might've even been waiting in the ballroom for him to show up. That means it's not a coincidence that he happened to not show up tonight. If he broke his word and didn't show up, there had to be a good reason. He's probably aware that someone is after him. He's an FBI man, I don't think he would go back on a plan without it being an emergency."

We'd gathered around the room, coffee calming our rattled minds. Jennifer had quickly recovered from her episode. She'd grown harder over the last few months after going through all that we had alongside Nolan. She was maturing, although I'd learned that getting used to a life like this wasn't very beneficial for a girl as sweet and attractive as herself. Blaire was evidence of that.

"So basically," Nolan said. "Wexler's the one on the run this time."

Jennifer, cross-legged on the bed in Nolan's oversized hoodie, meekly spoke up. "Seems like we need to find them before they find Wexler."

Eyes turned to her. This was a bold statement, especially coming from her, but she was right. It was somewhat our responsibility to protect him, one reason being we owed him for granting us freedom from the law, and another being that we'd been somewhat pulled into the situation as a result of our relation to him. Slowly, Blaire nodded and said, "You're right. Can we all agree that this is our responsibility?"

Heads nodded, and we moved on.

"Okay, so Blaire," Nolan began. "You were the last one out of the room. Did you see anything suspicious, anyone checking out our rooms?"

"No. . .I did pass the laundry guy on my way out. He had a cart full of towels and things."

"We don't have a laundry guy. . ."

Eyes flashed to me. "We have two laundry *women*, Annamarie and Melinda Wilson, sisters, both like fifty plus. They were sitting two tables away from us tonight, not on duty. The only laundry they'd have would be from the other banquet guests that are staying here. But I'm sure we don't have any man doing laundry for us. The only male employee besides the manager and security would be Arthur, the maintenance guy, and I saw him at the same table as the Wilson sisters."

"Well, whoever this was was definitely pushing a laundry cart," Blaire said.

Rising from my seat, I hustled to the hallway and looked to either end to see the blinking security cameras. Waving my partners behind me, I headed double-time toward the elevator.

"Where are we going?"

"The security office, where the camera footage is," I explained. "I want to see this so-called 'laundry man'."

We brushed past my father pounding his hand on the desk of Sergeant Dennehy and went back to the surveillance room, where screens lined the wall and live feeds of the entire premises were displayed. Scanning the wall, Jennifer pointed out the fifth floor hallway, and a split-screen view of both directions were clearly shown. Currently the corridor was empty, but we had to figure out how to rewind them to the past few hours. My brain was fried from the gala and now the present goings-on, so I let Nolan work his way around the control panel.

"The screens are all labeled," he narrated. "If I can find the fifth floor hallway. . .here it is. I'm not sure how to rewind. This looks like it–"

The screen shook as if to rewind, then went back to the live feed. "What happened?" I asked, standing up. Nolan pressed another button, and the rewind symbol showed on the screen, but it only went back five seconds.

"Oh, no. Oh, no." Nolan rubbed his forehead. "The first button must've been to clear the footage. Now there's nothing leading up to ten seconds ago."

"Are you serious?" Blaire exclaimed. "How hard is it to find the rewind button? There's literally like five to choose from, and you pick the one that deletes everything."

"Why didn't you do it then?" he fired back. "You're sure quick to accuse after the fact. You didn't know which button it was, either."

"I know I wouldn't have pressed any random button before I knew what it did. That's what happens when you're not careful."

"Don't talk to me about being careful, you're the criminal that got us into this."

Jennifer slapped Nolan coldly across the face. "Shut up," she said. Nolan stood, flabbergasted at having been put in his place. She turned and said the same thing to Blaire, who wasn't accustomed to being yelled at by another girl, someone who she knew she wasn't allowed to knock unconscious. "You guys are like children. Yelling at each other isn't going to help anything. And for another thing, Blaire isn't a criminal and you know it, and no one knows how to use the buttons and *you* know it. So everyone just apologize and shut up."

"You tell us not to act like children and then you make us apologize," Nolan objected.

"Nolan Edgar!" she said through gritted teeth,

He rolled his eyes and said a feeble "sorry".

Blaire sat back down and said, "I know." Jennifer shrugged her off, satisfied.

"What are you doing?" Blaire asked as I sat at the control panel.

"Well he didn't fly onto the fifth floor, so he had to have gotten in the elevator on the ground floor. I'll go through the feed from both of those elevators." I did so, finding nothing from the main elevator in the lobby, so I found the second one, amongst the ground-floor hallway. Rewinding to a few minutes before Blaire would've seen him, we waited to see the mysterious laundry man. After five minutes, I was growing frustrated, until I saw a male figure coming from the far end of the hallway. I was hopeful that this was our man, but as he grew closer, I realized he was wearing a black suit and tie, and I recognized him as the manager of the hotel. Discouraged, we waited ten more minutes, but no one passed by the elevator, and by that time, Blaire had already made her way down to the ballroom.

"Doesn't make sense," I said, leaning back in my chair, upset.

We sat in silence for a minute, until Blaire let out a groan. "No, Chris, I think you were wrong to begin with. He did fly to the fifth floor, so to speak."

"The roof," Nolan deducted.

I hit the table, knowing there was no camera footage left of the man. I tried to hold back my frustration with Nolan for deleting the footage, but he was obviously overwhelmed with guilt over it, so I let it go.

We were silent in thought. "Was he wearing any gloves when you saw him?" Jennifer offered.

"No, I thought about that, but I checked the doorknob, they were clean. He must've put gloves on before he went in, and kept them on."

"How did he even break in?" I asked.

"Electronic card locks aren't hard to manipulate. If he had the right device with the right amount of electrical friction, he could've easily broken through it."

"So the only place his fingerprints would be would be the laundry cart," I said. "Which he probably took with him."

"Wait," Nolan said. "If he didn't have the gloves on when you saw him, there's a chance he didn't have them on when he was coming onto the roof. He might've not had them on at all until he got to our door."

The four of us looked at each other, knowing this was the only lead we had, and decided it had enough potential to follow, so without another word, we headed out the doorway toward the elevator.

Blaire cut into her room to grab whatever she thought she'd need in the case that we came across a print. Then using the password my father had given to me, we made our way to the maintenance room of the fifth floor. From there we took the ladder that ended in a trap door onto the roof. The trapdoor fell right open, the latch having been broken by the intruder as he'd forced his way in. I'd nearly forgotten how late it was until the cool moonlight glowed on our skin. I decided it must've been past midnight by now.

Once on the roof, the first thing we tested was the trapdoor itself. Having just been constructed, every part of the roof was new, so any print on the metal latch would've been easily discernable. Blaire shook what looked like baby powder onto the entirety of the latch, gently covering every inch of it. Then holding her flashlight directly on it, she gently blew into the powder.

Meanwhile, I was in a childish daze at how attractive I found this.

Best case scenario, all of the powder would've floated away except for that which was on the fingerprint. The oils from the finger would cause the powder to stick, leaving only the fingerprint, which could then be lifted using clear tape. That was similar to the way it's done in the forensic science field, except in those scenarios, where the participants come prepared, a magnetic powder is used, and then a small magnetic pen clears away all of the powder that hasn't bonded to the print. This is much more accurate than random generic powder and a breath of air. Still, this was all we had to work with, and I was glad Blaire was there to lead the way.

But, in this case, no powder remained. Every speck of it disappeared in a white cloud, leaving no print. Blaire tried again, and then one more time, growing more frustrated at each failed attempt. Finally, she stood, telling us to stop being lazy and find somewhere else that he might've left a print.

Shining a flashlight along the rooftop, I found the ladder that led from the roof to the ground. It was in the alley on the northern side of the hotel. The suite balconies were on the east side, facing the water, while the front entrance was on the west, facing the inner streets of Nags Head, Outer Banks. Shivering at the height, I stepped back and gazed over the rim from a crouch position.

"Move," came a voice behind me that nearly sent me sprawling over the edge of the building.

"Don't sneak up on someone when they're looking over the edge of a seventy-foot drop," I scolded Blaire.

"Grow a pair," she shot back, and proceeded to dust the handles and rungs of the ladder. Her general testy attitude was understandable, but it didn't help the circumstances, and I was growing tired of it.

Shining my light down to the alley, I strained my eyes and made out what looked like a large dumpster, with one of the lids open. Studying it, a thought came to mind and I made my way to the ladder.

"What are you doing?" Blaire asked me as I side-stepped her.

"I want to look at something," I vaguely explained, then eased my way down the ladder, pretending to not be terrified of the altitude. I made sure to only touch the rungs with the edge of my sleeves so as not to soil any fingerprints that were already there with my own. Once I'd made my way to the bottom, I approached the blue industrial dumpster, shining my light into the heap of garbage.

Just as I'd thought, two black latex gloves laid on the top of the pile.

I called to Blaire, and she made her way down with tremendous swiftness. I showed her my discovery. She shrugged, saying, "Those could be anybody's."

I sighed, frustrated at her negativity. "Actually, they couldn't. This dumpster belongs to Quimby Suites and no one else, and, as a matter of fact, no Quimby Suites employees wear black latex gloves. The standard issue are white, with the gold Quimby "Q" specially printed on the wrist. Not to mention any gloves thrown away inside would've been thrown into a trash bag. You'll notice the only other loose garbage in here is cardboard and that broken chair." Satisfied with myself, I crossed my arms and waited for her argument.

But none came. Instead, she looked at me incredulously and simply said, "Who are you?"

"I'm what you taught me to be," I answered, trying to raise her spirits with credit.

She gave me an affectionate light slap on the cheek, saying, "Nice job, Quimby." She had no idea, but my heart was overflowing with joy at having been praised by her. She gloved her own hands, reached into the dumpster, and carefully collected both gloves, placing them in a plastic bag she'd brought along. Sighing and glancing up at me, she meekly said, "I'm sorry for being so tense. I'm just so stressed over all this."

I squeezed her hand and smiled. "I know."

She smirked at me with the slightest hint of warmth and headed back up the ladder with our evidence.

As Nolan and I were packing up our belongings and preparing to leave the hotel, my father passed by the open door and asked what was going on.

"We've got a lead on what happened here and who did it," I explained. "We've got to head home early."

"The rest of us are staying for the weekend," he said. "I thought that's what you all were planning to do."

"We were planning on that," I said. "But we weren't planning on getting burglarized. Things come up, we need to deal with them before the trail is cold."

"What trail?" he asked, irritated. "You're eighteen, you shouldn't be following trails, there's police for that. After all the trouble you've gone through with drug dealers and murderers already, you want to hunt down the strange person that broke into your hotel room? You're asking for trouble."

"No, they're asking for trouble," I said, my voice slightly raised. "You're right, we have been through a lot of stuff in the past year, so I understand enough to know that I can handle this. For goodness sake, you want me to do something with my life, but you won't let me."

"This isn't doing something with your life," he thundered. "This is throwing it away."

I picked up a suitcase in each hand and brushed past him, saying, "It would be throwing it away if I didn't do something about this. Tell mom I'm sorry." Without waiting for his answer, Nolan and I met the others in the hallway and made our way to the parking lot. Nolan and Jennifer rode in his Audi, and Blaire and I climbed in my Mustang. Tires squealing in the silence of the dark morning, we made tracks for Dixon.

"Gabe McDowell, man of the hour." I gave the tall twenty-one year old a pat on the back as he invited us into his messy second-story apartment.

"As happy as I am to see you all," Gabe said. "I'm sure there's some kind of trouble bringing you here."

"What, can't your pals pay a friendly visit once in a while?" Nolan asked.

"At seven in the morning on a Saturday?" he asked. "Looking like you just crashed a wedding?"

I'd somewhat forgotten that the four of us were still dressed for the banquet. I had tossed my waistcoat into the backseat of my car, a button was missing on my vest, and my bow tie was hanging on for dear life. Nolan looked equally as ragged, Jennifer still wore his sweatshirt, and Blaire had changed into casual clothes at some point that I hadn't noticed. She looked calm and refreshed as always, despite having not slept. I'd tried to convince her to catch a few hours' sleep as I drove, but she insisted on keeping her guard up, for whatever reason I wasn't sure.

"You're right," Blaire said, holding up the plastic bag containing the black latex gloves. "We need your help. What do you know about fingerprints?"

"I've got a minor in forensic science," he said. "Believe me, I've done my fair share of fingerprint analysis."

"You can analyze it, but can you identify it?" Blaire asked.

He smirked with a hint of pride. "Doing as much work as I did with this in college, I soon figured out a back door to the IAFIS identification tool."

"IAFIS?" Jennifer asked.

"Integrated Automated Fingerprint Identification System," I blurted out before anyone else could. I'd also taken a forensic science class my senior year, so forensic protocol was actually one of my strong suits.

"Well, it looks like first things first, we need to get a clear copy of the print," Gabe said. "Come on back here." He led us through the apartment, kicking pizza boxes and empty orange juice jugs aside, into the second bedroom, which had become his computer/tech room. This was what led us here. Ever since Nolan's kidnapping, Gabe had proven that he was capable of helping me out in situations such as these.

From a bottom drawer he pulled a small glass jar of what I recognized as magnetic powder. He put on his own pair of latex gloves, then carefully laid our evidence on an empty space on the table. The gloves turned inside out, he flattened them out and began brushing dust onto the fingertips. "It'll be harder to see," he explained. "Seeing as how this is black powder on a black glove, but if it's there, we'll find it." He shone a bright lamp directly on the glove as he made his way across its entirety. "Am I allowed to ask whose print this is supposed to be?"

"Whoever broke into our hotel rooms last night and ransacked them," I explained.

He stopped brushing and looked up at me. "Everyone okay? Did he take anything?" I assured him we were all well and that no damage had been done, but I still held back the most confidential information, wanting to leave as many people out of harm's way as possible.

Once the glove was completely dusted, Gabe pulled the sheath of the brush back, opening the magnet on the tip. The loose dust now stuck to the brush, leaving only the dust that had bonded to something. Magnetic powder sticks to the oils on human fingertips better than baby powder. He went over the glove several times, until no excess dust remained. Finally, raising the glove up to the light, he gave a satisfied chuckle. On the thumb of the glove was a broken but clear fingerprint.

"Will that do?" Jennifer asked hopefully.

"Oh, it'll do."

He quickly took a picture of the print on his cell phone, which he then plugged into his computer. On his desktop screen, he clicked an icon named "IAFIS Shortcut". He then uploaded the image onto the site, zoomed in on the fingerprint, and clicked on a button labeled "Scan".

"This seems very illegal," Jennifer commented from under Nolan's arm.

"'Everything they do in the S.H.I.E.L.D. is illegal'," I quoted.

"Very much so," he said, swiveling in his chair. "That's why I have my own wifi router, and why I'm doing this on my smaller computer, the one that's IP address isn't traceable and that I don't care if it gets overrun with viruses. So let's all please agree that this never happened. Yes?"

"Yes."

In that same moment the loading screen on Gabe's computer disappeared and appearing on the screen was a spreadsheet-style list of names. "Three hundred fifty-two possible matches," Gabe explained. "It's not the most clear print, so not bad, considering there's 56 million criminal prints and 250 million civil prints in the database. We can cancel out some of the obvious people who we know aren't the suspect."

"We know it was a man," I said.

"At least thirty years old, no more than fifty or sixty." Blaire said. "Caucasian."

Gabe proceeded to select filters only containing white males between the ages of thirty and sixty. The results narrowed down to thirty-seven possibilities. "Fourteen of these are criminal fingerprints, so there's mugshots to go along with them." He began clicking through every image, giving Blaire time to make sure it wasn't the man she'd seen. After she'd seen every man, she defeatedly sat back in a chair.

"None of them," she said.

"Are you sure?" Nolan asked, but quickly rescinded the question after the piercing look she gave him.

"Hold on," he said. "There's four more pictures, 'government officials', it says."

He began flipping through the images, but only made it to the second when Blaire popped from her seat, yelling, "Stop!" nearly making me jump out of my skin. "That's him. That's him, that's him, that's him."

"Is it him?" Nolan asked sarcastically. He didn't even receive Blaire's glance this time, rather a backhand over the head as she still stared excitedly at the screen.

"And the winner is: Howard Statham. Obviously of English descent but it says here he is a former Special Projects Investigator for Central Intelligence, from 2000 to 2015. Doesn't say what happened or why he left the position, but he's only forty-five years old, I highly doubt he retired in 2015."

"Not like the CIA is going to say if or why they fired him," Nolan said. We nodded in agreement.

"The CIA doesn't say much at all," Blaire said. "Not even to their employees. Why do you think the secrets of the government have never been told? If no one knows the secret, then there's none to keep at all. We'll get nothing out of the CIA, so we'll have to skip a step and go directly after Statham."

"That won't be hard," Gabe said. "His last known address is listed here. He lives in Culpeper, north of here. About halfway between us and Washington D.C."

"Can you pull up the address on a map?" I asked.

"Currently doing so." Gabe entered the address and clicked the search icon, and was soon brought to a map view of the supposed address of Howard Statham.

"Seems kind of in the middle of nowhere," Nolan voiced.

Gabe switched onto a satellite view, so we had an aerial picture of the landscape itself.

"Looks. . ." Blaire had a rare moment of confusion. "Looks like a farm, of some kind."

The room shared equally confused expressions. "So," I began. "Respected CIA agent gets fired. . .moves a hundred miles away. . .lives on a–is that a pig? Lives on a pig farm, at the age of forty-five."

"Sounds like the opening scene of a Hallmark movie," Nolan commented.

"Fingerprint doesn't say whether he's married or not," Gabe announced. "So maybe that's why he's attempting to restart his life, maybe he found love."

The only response was a "hmph" from Blaire. She copied the address onto her cell phone and said, "Thanks for the help, Gabe. It doesn't go unnoticed." She left the room.

"What?" I asked as the rest of us scrambled to follow her. "What are we doing?"

"What do you think? We're going there. We're going to talk to this guy, we're going to find out what's going on. Normally I wouldn't take such a hasty approach, but for some reason, I find myself concerned for the wellbeing of another person. Wexler is a government agent. There's a reason he didn't show up last night. This Statham guy is trouble, and it seems to me like we need to find him before he finds Wexler, like Jennifer said."

"Why couldn't we try to find Wexler before he does?" Nolan asked.

"What good will that do?" Blaire asked, wearing her disappointed-in-you expression. "That would only make it easier for Statham. We'd lead him right to Wexler. Do you not think before you speak?"

Nolan sighed and waved a hand. "See, why'd you have to add the last part? What's the point of insulting me?"

"It wasn't an insult," Blaire shot back. "It was a legitimate question."

I rubbed my forehead. The tension between these two was becoming a problem. Two people who are used to being the smartest in the room, used to being the decision maker. Nolan hated being hounded like this more than most people, due to his natural courtroom argument ability. Blaire wasn't used to working with a team, especially a team of amateurs like us. She had very little patience for shortcomings.

Jennifer turned Nolan around with a shove and headed out the door with him, saying goodbye to Gabe. Blaire rubbed her face, still angry. I took hold of her forearm to get her attention, which soon proved to be a mistake. She glared at me, then my hand, then back at me. Quickly I loosened my grip and put my hand at my side. "Sorry," I said quietly. "Let's go."

While Nolan and Jennifer went to get a change of clothes for those of us still dressed for the banquet, I drove Blaire and myself to the Quimby Suites in downtown Dixon, where she had been living for the past five months. It was the original hotel, the first my father had constructed. Blaire lived in a deluxe suite, alone, although she spent very little time there. My father had insisted she stay here, until she wished for someplace else, due to his feeling of gratitude to her for all she'd done for his child. I could tell she was somewhat embarrassed to be living under my family's charity, but she didn't complain. She could've lived in the backseat of her car, for all she cared. Like I said, she was only at the hotel when she had to be, mostly just to sleep, if she wasn't crashed on the couch in my basement lounge. Her usual absence led the place to look barely lived in. The only evidence of occupation one could see without opening closets or cabinets was a laptop lying on the couch, a charging cord nearby. This was the first of two rooms in the deluxe suite, the second being a bedroom with an attached bathroom, which I was sure was equally as neat.

  She went into the bedroom to retrieve something while I waited awkwardly on the couch. I'd been to this room a total of two times in the five months that she lived here: once to move her in, although she had very little belongings to move in, and once to pick her up for a company dinner in Richmond. No matter how close we'd grown, I was still somewhat intimidated to be in her hotel room, especially due to the fact that I'd developed a painful adoration for her. I loved her, it was all but obvious. I made no effort toward her, though. For one thing, she was a beguiling twenty-one year old woman, while I was hardly out of high school, only eighteen years old. The odds were stacked against me, for once, which was utterly depressing. For another thing, I was too afraid that my outward feelings of intimacy toward her would scare her off, ruin the friendship that we'd built. Blaire wasn't accustomed to trust and affection toward people. She'd come around a bit since she'd settled down in Dixon, but her general personality was standoffish.

  I was shaken from my thoughts upon her reentrance. She carried a black plastic case in one hand and a small weekender bag in the other. She didn't explain what they were, only headed for the door, saying, "I'm ready, let's go."

"What is all that?" I asked, trying to catch up to her as she stepped out the door.

"Two extra pistols and ammunition, plus silencers for both," she said in a low tone, holding up the black case.

"And the duffle bag?"

She shrugged. "Anything else we might need." It wasn't surprising for her to be vague, but I trusted her. I took my own pistol from the glovebox of my Mustang and we switched vehicles to her blue Mazda. It was more trustworthy in this situation than my fifty-some year old relic.

As she merged onto the interstate and headed north toward Culpeper, I took inventory. Including my own handgun, and the one Nolan had stashed in his vehicle, there were four pistols, one for each of us if need be, although I was fairly sure Jennifer had never fired a gun in her life, and would be rather hesitant if the occasion arose that she had to. Either way, we would be prepared. Like Blaire said, the case also held two barrel silencers and two loaded magazine replacements. They would only be able to refill the guns in the case, as the brand wasn't the same as my own.

I closed the case and stowed it in the backseat. As I unzipped the weekender bag, Blaire made a noise in her throat like a frustrated mother whose child couldn't get their hands off her things. "Be careful with that stuff, please."

She was capable of using the word "please".

The bag was full of intriguing tools I'd never used or even seen before. A pair of what looked like military-grade night vision goggles, which only reminded me the the movie Step Brothers; a set of ear pieces, which I guessed were meant for two-way communication; and an unmarked plastic bottle that looked like it was meant for contact solution, although I had a very strong suspicion that that was not the case. I held it up to her with a questioning expression.

"Don't sniff it," was all she said.

"Chloroform?" I asked. When she didn't answer, I said again to myself, "Chloroform." I closed the bag and set it in the backseat, hoping to myself that there'd be no need for any of the contents of the bag.

Although the ear pieces would be cool.

The town of Culpeper, Virginia was an attractive place, not a large town, although bigger than Dixon. We'd caught up with Nolan's car on the interstate and were now driving a length ahead of them as we cruised down main street. We seemed to stick out somewhat, a shiny Mazda and a black Audi obviously driving as a pair. We kept a lookout for anything that might've given us any information about the Statham farm before we made our way out there. The address was roughly five miles out of town, and the nearer we came, the more the landscape looked like Dixon's surrounding scenery. There were many farms and wooded areas outside of Dixon, the town having only been reintroduced as a corporation a few decades ago.

My stomach twisted every mile that we drove. I wanted to throw up, I knew it would've made me feel much better, but I knew there was no possibility of that when Blaire was nearby. I had had very little time to think since this had all begun. I hadn't slept a wink, I wasn't sure any of us had. But Blaire spoke very little while driving, so I'd trailed off in thought a few times. Normally, I would've broken down in tears at some point, but I'd had no chance to. Everything was progressing so fast, Blaire never wanted to stop to catch her breath.

My heart skipped a beat and my stomach convulsed as the recognizable white house came into view. The matching barn sat to the front left along the driveway, with the small pen of three pigs at its side. A long garden ran along the other side of the driveway, freshly planted vegetables showing green leaves, and a row of flowers sprouting along the front. Blaire drove past slowly the first time while we scanned the area.

"Looks so. . .normal," I commented.

"That's the idea, I'd say," she replied.

Once out of sight we found a wide shoulder on the side of the road, visible only to passers-by. Nolan parked next to us and the four of us stepped out of the vehicles to discuss our next move.

"Okay, Jennifer," Blaire said. "Ready?"

Nolan and I exchanged glances, and he ventured a "Huh?"

"Yep," Jennifer said with a brave smirk.

This time I tried. "Huh?"

Blaire sighed at having to explain herself. As she reached into her car, she said, "Jennifer and I are going to walk to the house to ask for help with our flat tire."

"What flat tire?" I asked before thinking. ". . .*Oh.*"

Blaire winked sarcastically, the first time I'd ever seen her do so, even if it wasn't genuine. The weather was dreary and a light rain had begun to fall, so she slipped on a blue rain jacket that didn't seem her style, but I supposed that was the goal. There was a good chance Statham had done his research and would know what we looked like. I watched her tuck a pistol into her back waistband, covering it with the rain jacket. She also produced the set of earpieces from the weekender bag and placed one in her ear.

"Dibs," I called out, sensing that the other receiver would go to one of us.

"I don't think dibs applies in this situation," Nolan said confidently.

Blaire shrugged and handed me the earpiece. "Have to respect dibs."

As the girls prepared to leave, Nolan ventured a protest. "I don't know how safe this is," he said, looking at Jennifer.

"Don't you believe in me?" Jennifer asked him.

"Well, sure..."

"Then don't worry about it. I'm safer with her than anyone else, no offense." She gestured to Blaire, who didn't disagree. Without any further discussion, we tested the function of the earpieces, made sure they worked properly, and the girls set out down the road toward the Statham residence.

Nolan and I sat nervously against the car, not speaking. The girls were out of sight now, but in my ear I listened intently. All I heard at the moment were footsteps on asphalt, and soon, the pattern changed to a louder, crunchier step. They'd reached Statham's gravel driveway and were approaching the house. My stomach did flips and my palms were moist. A chill had fallen over me in the weak drizzle of rain.

As I heard a knock on a glass door, I made a knocking motion with my fist to show Nolan what was happening. There was silence for ten seconds, then another knock. "Someone's coming," Blaire whispered.

A door opened, and the voice I heard saying, "Hello," was clearly that of a woman. "Can I help you?" she asked.

"Hi there! Yes–" The chipper and friendly voice startled me at first. I was amazed to realize it was Blaire speaking. She'd disguised her tone as that of an average college girl, so much so that I almost thought I was listening to Jennifer. "We're so stupid. Our poor car got a flat tire down the road and I'm so dumb with car things, you know, we were just wondering if there was someone around here who knew anything about cars and changing tires and that kind of stuff."

The rambling was such an accurate disguise it almost annoyed me to listen to. It reminded me so much of my female former classmates that I could hardly pay attention to the conversation. But I strained my ears to hear what the woman at the door was saying. The first part of her reply was indistinct, but I picked up when she said, "I'm the only one home now, my husband left earlier today, and I just don't know anything about fixing a tire either, um. . ." She mumbled, evidently searching for a way to help, or to get these girls off of her front porch. "I could call someone, maybe. . ."

"No, no, that's okay," Blaire said, cutting her off. "We can ask someone else down the road. Maybe I'll call my boyfriend, he knows about all that car stuff." She giggled at her silliness, a laugh so empty-headed and feminine that I wanted to tell her to stop, but I didn't risk it. The woman apologized once more and they bid each other farewell. I heard Blaire and Jennifer's footsteps off of the porch and back down the gravel driveway.

For the first time, Blaire spoke to me. "Did you get all that?" she whispered.

"I think so," I replied. "So Statham was home earlier, but he left?"

"That's what she said, but she's lying."

"I think so, too," I heard Jennifer whisper, evidently leaning toward Blaire's ear.

"It was obvious," Blaire went on. "She came outside to talk to us, closing the door behind her, as if keeping us from looking inside. But I saw a pair of men's shoes inside the door when she opened it, and they looked wet and grimy, as if someone had recently worn them. Plus, the way the driveway looks, no one has left since before the rain. The gravel is evenly wet, no rocks have been turned over. It's a one-car garage but there's another one parked outside of it, and the gravel underneath it is dry."

"So you think he's there?" I asked, seeing her and Jennifer come into view down the road.

"I think he's there. And even if he isn't, his wife is obviously aware of the situation. We're going to keep an eye on the place until dark, and if he doesn't come out, we'll go in after him."

A treeline bordered the edge of the Statham property to the east, two hundred yards from the house and barn. We lined the edge of it, Nolan nearest the road, Jennifer fifty feet inward, I another fifty feet, and Blaire the farthest back off of the road. From her vantage point, she could see parts of the back of the house, where she'd relayed her discovery of a back door leading onto a patio, with a connecting sidewalk that circled to the front porch. I was even with the house itself, a two-story white-siding home in desperate need of a power-washing and weeded flower bed. I could see Jennifer, arms wrapped around herself, staring into the darkening landscape. I pitied her, deeply. She didn't belong here, she belonged at The Grind, where Nolan and I had first met her. She lived alone in Dixon, in an apartment on Main Street above the music shop. Nolan was all she had, aside from a few girlfriends. It pained me to see her being pulled into the seemingly endless troubles we'd fallen into.

My soul nearly left my body upon hearing the crunch of footsteps behind me. I was growing better at repressing my fright, but my hand was still on the handle of my pistol as I whirled toward Blaire, approaching me.

"One of these days you're going to shoot me because you're so jumpy," she said.

"One of these days you'll learn not to sneak up on me like that," I shot back.

"She doesn't belong here," she said, gesturing to Jennifer. I told her I'd been having the same thoughts. "Next time we'll leave her at home."

"Next time?" I repeated. "There's going to be a next time?"

"There's always a next time, Chris. I know you don't think there will be, it always seems like this will be it, this will put it all to bed, but it won't. It's who we are. It's who I always was, and now it's who you are. You don't have to look for trouble, it'll find you. Always will. I know you think I'm inhuman and heartless but I know how much you care about me, and the closer I become with you and the more I come to like you, the more guilt I feel for pulling you into this terrible life. You think you owe me something but I'll always be the one paying back the misery I caused all of you."

"Blaire, I've told you before that you're what's right with the world. Like I said in Paris, the circumstances don't determine the outcome, the response does. And you're right, I do care about you, just as much as I care about my own family, just as much as I care about Nolan. There is not a single ounce of regret in my body for all that we've been through, because it gave me you, and you are the one thing I can't afford to lose."

Back in January, when Nolan had been attempting to remove a bullet from my leg, in an attempt to shut me up, Blaire had grabbed me by the face and kissed me. Not a day went by when I didn't think of that time, and every time I became upset over it, knowing she'd only done it out of instinct to distract me from my pain.

It happened again in March, as she and I had been acting as a couple in Paris on our mission to bring down the most powerful criminals in the city. On that occasion, for a split second, I thought perhaps a small part of it was real, but again, as I looked back, I knew it meant nothing more to her than it does an actress in a movie.

But this time, on the edge of the darkening trees, the sound of raindrops echoing from the canopy, I watched her jaw twitch, her face flush with pink, her mouth come open in hesitation, and she rushed forward, caching me by surprise as she kissed me.

What felt like a minute was no more than six seconds, and at the end of those six seconds, she stepped back, staring into my soul, her mouth open. I stood equally still, too afraid that any move I'd make would ruin the perfect moment. Anything I'd say would scare her off, make her feel foolish, so I didn't speak. I waited for her to, but she didn't. Instead, she rotated her gaze from me onto the house, then up into the sky, which had concluded its darkening and now was as black and endless as her dilated pupils. My watch said it was just after nine p.m. She turned to me, trying to find words, finally closing her lips. After an even exhale, she said, "It's time to go."

I gathered myself, regained my composure, and followed her towards our companions. Jennifer joined up with us as we made it toward the road, where Nolan awaited us. Blaire repeated the order she'd given me.

"Does everyone know what's going on?" she asked. "Everyone remember your job?"

The three of us nodded.

"Okay, Nolan and Chris, make your way to the front door. I'll creep up to the back patio. Jennifer, are you alright with being on your own?"

"Yes, I can handle it."

"Good luck, everybody." Without another word, Blaire slunk back down the treeline. Nolan kissed Jennifer's forehead as she donned her night-vision goggles, then set out to keep watch. We'd assigned her this job in hopes that it would keep her out of harm's way as much as possible. As she crept through the grass, the pistol in her hand looked entirely out of place.

Before we headed out into the open, Nolan pulled me into a powerful hug, the same way I had to him in Paris. "What have we become?" he hissed.

"Who we have to be," I said. "This is something we have to do. This is our fight, and I wouldn't want to fight it with anyone else. Let's finish this."

"I love you," he said.

"I love you too."

He took a deep breath and stepped away, nodding. "Let's go."

Our steps were as silent as our breaths as we approached the front door, avoiding the loud gravel. The rain had picked up even more, and I shivered under my soaked t-shirt. The garage was unattached and was catty-corner in front of the house. Nolan's path directed him along the front of it, while I was crouched at the end of the barn, thirty feet of open space in front of me. As I prepared to make my way to the front porch, a blinding motion-sensored flood light lit up a twenty-foot circumference around the garage door where Nolan was standing. He took off at the same moment I did, the two of us racing through no-man's-land to the flower bed that lined the front of the porch. I crashed into a hydrangea bush and, pressing my back against the wall, made eye contact with Nolan on the opposite side of the porch steps. I struggled to keep my breathing under control. We listened as the curtains were pulled back, then released after ten seconds. We waited another minute and a half, until we were sure whoever had looked through the window was no longer there.

Nodding to Nolan, the two of us turned and peered up through the railing of the porch, getting a view of the front door, a window on either side. When we looked back toward each other, I could see him mouth the word *"Window"* along with a lifting motion. I nodded in agreement, and prayed the windows wouldn't be locked. By the look of the house and it's features, they were installed in a time before locking windows.

In one fluid motion we were over the railing and against the front wall, next to our respective windows. One hand holding a suppressed pistol, the other pressed upon the window rail, we opened both windows at the same time. Leaning down, I slowly stuck my head through the hole.

I was familiar with the barrel of the Smith & Wesson SD9 that was pointed at my forehead, because Blaire had once held the same model on me at my own home. But this time, the barrel wavered and trembled in the thin, pale hand which held it. My eyes traveled from the gun, to the hand, to the body, to the face of Mrs. Statham as she held her pistol five inches from my eye.

"Forgive me, ma'am," I said. "It appears this is not the front door."

"Shut the—"

"Ma'am," came Nolan's interrupting voice behind her. "You're much too pretty to use such foul language, especially in your own home, which is quite lovely, might I add. On that subject, we must be careful as to not cause any bloodshed that might stain this gorgeous rug, or these soft linen curtains."

She didn't move, for she felt the press of steel against the back of her head. I also didn't move, so as not to startle her into any sudden movements, her finger was shaking on the trigger enough as it was. I couldn't help but smirk at Nolan's theatrics. He winked at me from behind her.

"I want to know where your husband is, Mrs. Statham," he said.

"Not here," she whispered.

"I don't believe you."

I could tell from the sharp exhale that she'd prepared to scream. By the time Nolan could cover her mouth, she'd already shrieked the first syllable of *"Howard"*. His hand muffled the rest of her cry, and she fell to the ground as she struggled. Frantically crawling through the window, I yanked the gun from her grasp and slid it away.

"Chloroform's in my pocket," Nolan hissed, still struggling to silence her screams.

As I dabbed the liquid onto the curtain and pressed it against her nostrils, I said, "I'm sorry you made us do this, but you should've obeyed. Don't worry, you'll just have one heck of a hangover when you wake up in a few hours."

I thanked Nolan and we set off through the first level of the house. But we hadn't made it through the kitchen when we heard the second cry. "Is that Jennifer?" I asked.

Nolan shook his head.

Bursting out the back door, I found Howard Statham himself, standing in the middle of the patio, his gun pressed hard against Blaire's temple. "Welcome to the party," he shouted at Nolan and I. "Look at what you've gotten yourselves into now. All I wanted was Wexler. You could've given me him, but instead you go to all this trouble, for what?"

"We don't know any better than you where he is," I stated as Nolan and I stood in the doorway, both guns aimed at Statham. He was twenty feet away, and he held Blaire in front of him. I knew neither of us could hit the shot.

"Well she better think it up fast," he said, jabbing his gun harder into Blaire's head. "Because I'm taking her, and she's going to take me to him."

In every dangerous instance that we'd found ourselves in thus far, there'd been confidence in my mind knowing Blaire Devereaux was nearby if things went wrong. But as I saw the desperation in her eyes as they bore into mine, I knew we were in trouble. Even in the darkness I could see the red blood coming from a deep cut near her right eyebrow, where he'd hit her with his pistol, provoking her scream.

He took her around the house to the car that was parked next to the garage and threw her into the passenger seat, then climbed in himself. His tires threw gravel as he sped out, knowing Nolan and I would be firing a barrage of shots at his tires and windows. Our bullets struck the doors and bumper of the silver SUV, but it didn't stop. I screamed in desperation, cussing, crying, firing until my gun clicked empty. Nolan had already set off for our car parked down the road.

There was a gunshot and a shatter of glass inside Howard Statham's car, and before it reached the road, it veered off of the driveway directly into the brick mailbox. As I sprinted down the lane, rain piercing my face, my shoes had become so wet that one slipped off, and I left it lying in the grass.

I reached the car at the same moment that the driver side door opened and Statham fell out of it, struggling to his feet. With a warcry, I grabbed him by the collar of his shirt, pulled him upright, and sent my right fist into his jaw, a mixture of rain and blood spattering off of his face. As he fell away, I grabbed him by the shirt and slammed him against the hood of his car. He whirled towards me, but I blocked a punch with my left forearm and struck him across the cheek with my right fist. His body grew stiff and he fell to an unconscious heap on the ground.

Nolan grabbed me by the shoulder and pulled me away, his gun trained on the criminal. My tears of desperation became that of joy upon seeing Blaire climb out of the car. We fell into each other, an embrace nearly powerful enough to knock me to the ground.

I'd seen Jennifer come out of the backseat, but in my mindless stumbling, hadn't processed it. As she crashed into Nolan's arms, I tried to form a question. Blaire answered first.

"She was already in the car," she explained. "Jumped out from the backseat and knocked him off course. He got one wild shot off before we took the gun from him and we crashed into the mailbox."

"Heck of a mailbox," Nolan commented, kicking the unaffected bricks.

"How did you know. . ."

Jennifer pulled her earpiece from her left ear. "I heard everything he said. Got to the car first." She gestured to Blaire, who displayed the one she'd been wearing when Statham had a hold of her.

As I pulled Howard Statham to his feet, Blaire pointed at a circular cut on his cheekbone. "Guess the family heirloom came in handy after all." I looked at the gold signet ring on my pinky finger, red with blood.

"Guess it did."

Special Agent Phineas Wexler sat at his desk in the study of his country home in Northern Virginia, twenty miles from Washington D.C. Blaire Devereaux, Jennifer Poole, Nolan Bragg, and myself sat across from him. He'd offered us all a drink, although the only one of us that was of-age was Blaire, who hadn't touched a drop of alcohol in the near-year that I'd known her. I'd accepted a cup of coffee that Wexler's wife had offered me.

It had been twenty-two hours since the FBI had arrested Howard Statham at his Virginia home. As to why he'd been hunting Wexler was yet to be divulged to us. Statham being a former CIA agent, and Wexler being FBI, we weren't on the edge of our seats waiting to be let in on the secret. It was likely we would never fully understand, although Wexler promised to explain the situation on a later date. He'd been flown home that morning from an undisclosed FBI location after having been in hiding from Statham.

Blaire sat with three stitches and a bandage over her eyebrow after having been worked on by the on-scene paramedic at Statham's farmhouse. Otherwise we were unscathed, physically, anyhow. Nolan and I had contacted our parents in the early evening, and gave PG descriptions of what had unfolded. Jennifer's parents lived a fair distance away and knew nothing of her goings-on. Blaire had no family to speak of.

We had been driven to Wexler's home in the early evening, shortly after he'd arrived home. After customary greetings, he'd invited us to his study, where we currently awaited his word.

"I apologize for breaking our arrangement to meet at your father's banquet in the Outer Banks," he said. "Give him my regards, I'm sure it was a lovely event. But I know you didn't believe my intentions were pleasure rather than business. I did have a proposition to make that evening. Of course, after what has developed since that evening, my proposition has changed."

Nolan leaned forward beside me. Jennifer's foot bounced. Blaire was still.

"My original proposition for that evening was directed at Miss Devereaux, but over the last twelve hours, I've arranged to make a greater proposition, to the three of you." He pointed three fingers at Blaire, Nolan, and myself. "As I understand, you two are unemployed, and as it is, have no direct career path. As for you, Mr. Bragg, I know you are a promising student of law. My offer for the three of you is as private investigating consultants. I decided since it appears you can't keep yourselves out of trouble, you might as well use your skills to prevent it from happening in the first place. Officially, you'd be freelance, but unless anyone comes to you personally, you'll be working under me, paid by the case. Your licenses will be provided and notarized by the Bureau, all you'll have to do is sign. Should you take the deal, Mr. Bragg, your studies at the law school of your choice will be completely funded by the Bureau."

Coffee sloshed out of my cup as I set it down hard on the desk in front of me, trying not to let it slip from my suddenly sweaty palm. None of us spoke.

"I understand, you'll need time to consider," Wexler said with a friendly smile. "Take your time, talk with your families. Miss Poole, I hope you won't feel, er, left out."

Jennifer raised her hands and shook her head as if relieved to be left out of the offer.

"Very well, then. Here is a draft of the private investigating licenses for you to read over. If you could contact me within a week with your answer, here is my card. I really appreciate you coming here tonight, and I will forever be indebted to you for all that you did in my defense."

I rubbed my forehead, Jennifer stared at Nolan, Nolan stared at the floor. Blaire hadn't blinked.

I strolled into the lobby of Dixon's Quimby Suites the Tuesday after returning home. Blaire hadn't answered my texts or calls since the previous evening. Stepping to the manager's desk, I greeted Mr. Teller. "Hey, Bob. Do you know if Miss Devereaux is around today?"

Bob Teller looked up from his desk and raised an eyebrow at me. "No, Chris. What makes you ask that?"

"What do you mean?" I asked. "This is her hotel."

"I thought you knew. . .she left early this morning with a packed suitcase. I watched her drive away."

I stole Bob's master key from his desk and made it to the fourth floor in fifteen seconds, tearing down the hallway to the room that had been Blaire's. Unlocking the door, I threw it open. I had to check the door again to make sure I'd come to the right room. It looked nothing like it had the last time I'd been in it. Trash littered the floor, made up mostly of empty glass bottles of liquor that had been cleared out of the mini bar. The bed was unmade, the bathroom was a mess, but nothing remained of Blaire Devereaux, aside from a few drawers and hangers of abandoned clothing.

As I whirled, trying not to hyperventilate, I fell onto the bed, feeling something solid underneath me. Reaching for it, I found her cell phone, with every one of my missed calls still on her lock screen. She'd left it behind. She'd packed her bag, checked out of her room, and drove away.

As mysteriously as she'd come, Blaire Devereaux had disappeared.

Part V

Rendezvous

I felt the bead of sweat form and trickle from my brow into my eye, causing a severe burning sensation. I pursed my lips, trying to prevent my diaphragm from retracting and pushing every ounce of breath out of my body. Blood rushed to my face, causing a tingling, and I feared I would pass out. My feet pressed hard against the ground, I utilized every muscle in my upper body to fight back.

"Help," I hissed, feeling the pressure release as Nolan grabbed the bar and pulled it the rest of the way to the rack. Taking a moment to breathe, I finally sat up on the bench and wiped the sweat from my forehead.

"You're alright," Nolan said with a slap on my back. "Four out of five reps is good."

"I used to lift that weight easily every day in May," I said, standing up from the bench press.

"Sure, during baseball season," Nolan said. "That was almost three months ago. We were both in much better shape then. I can't put up that much now, either. Don't worry, you'll get back there."

The pre-workout energy drink I'd consumed was beginning to wear off and give me a headache, and causing my head to tingle and itch. I stared at the floor, allowing my brain to recover from the intense workout. I often grew light-headed during lifts like these, the strain on my muscles causing increased pressure on the blood vessels in my brain. I knew my body would be sore the next day, especially since Nolan and I hadn't had a strenuous workout like this in weeks.

He was right, I was out of shape. All of our recent affairs had caused me to lose interest in discretionary things like cardio, lifting weights, and other pursuits of self-care. My hair was longer than usual, and I only shaved Sunday mornings so as not to embarrass my parents when walking into church. At least I hadn't gained weight, due only to the fact that I found little interest in eating more than I had to. My mother worried over me at times, telling me it seemed that I'd let myself go. "I'm eighteen years old," I would tell her. "I can take care of myself."

Since graduating high school two and a half months ago, I'd lost contact with most of the friends I'd made in class, excluding Nolan and a few baseball teammates. Most of the friends I had had moved to college or to a bigger town by now. Most graduates found it pointless to remain in Dixon, Virginia, any longer, because the small town held very little career opportunities. Nolan and I still received invites to old friends' college parties on occasion, but rarely made an appearance. That was another reason for my lack of effort in well-being. In the past, my romantic endeavors had led me to greater commitment to my appearance and popularity. But this was another area in which I'd lost interest, since the only person I ever found myself thinking about romantically now had disappeared from my life completely two and a half months ago.

I often became frustrated with myself for the depression I felt. I was lucky to be a part of the Quimby family, my father an exceedingly successful hotel proprietor, the neoclassical style mansion we lived in, the 1967 Mustang that I called my own. I felt a certain amount of shame for feeling unfulfilled after all I'd been blessed with, which was what kept me quiet about my feelings of melancholy.

Nolan's lifestyle hadn't necessarily taken a turn for the worse the way mine had. He'd left his high school friends and interests in the past as well, but now had a greater path ahead of him. He was in classes at the Virginia School of Law twice a week this summer, his tuition being funded mostly by scholarship. Meanwhile, he and Jennifer Poole were nearing a year's anniversary in their relationship. Needless to say, my best friend had plenty of promising circumstances to keep his head above water.

Sighing myself out of my depressing thoughts, I rubbed the cramp out of my tricep and splashed the contents of my water bottle in my face. Upon checking my heartbeat on my watch, I realized it was past nine o'clock.

"It's later than I thought," I said.

"You're right. You want to go get something to eat in town?"

I shrugged. "Kind of tired."

I heard him sigh, not like an agreement that he was also exhausted from our workout, but like he was exhausted by my negative attitude. "You say the same thing every night, man. How can you always be so 'tired' from all the sitting around you do, all the coffee you drink, all the sleeping you do."

"I don't sleep that much," I said defensively.

"You fall asleep on your couch almost daily, which doesn't make sense seeing as how you go to bed at nine thirty and get up at eight."

Ashamed, I mumbled, "Doesn't mean I sleep." I didn't sleep well, I hadn't for weeks upon weeks. The loneliness that caved in upon me as I stared at my ceiling was like a thunderstorm in my mind night after night. It was impossible trying to sleep knowing there was still something out there, a door left open in my mind, driving me crazy more and more every night as I struggled and cried and tried to understand what had happened, why it happened, how it happened.

Every night the memory of Blaire Devereaux weighed heavier on my mind.

Nolan rubbed his forehead. "You just need healthier habits, Chris. You need to eat more, work out more, make more out of your day. Just go into town with me tonight. It's Friday. It should be illegal for an eighteen year old to sit around at home at nine oclock on a weekend."

His chipper attitude raised my spirits enough to make me agree to go out with him. He clapped in excitement, saying, "The boys are back in town." We made our way down the ladder from the weight room above my garage, then strolled up the walkway to the house.

As we walked past the front porch to use the side door, I heard a vividly recognizable voice. "How hard is it to get your attention?"

We stopped in our tracks and turned back toward the front porch. The evening was dark but from the light of the single bulb above the front door I could make out the figure sitting on a rocking chair. My stomach turned, my face flushed. It was a feeling I hadn't felt in far too long a time. I was afraid, and it felt good.

Nolan and I walked side by side up the front steps and faced Special Agent Phineas Wexler. He sat cross-legged on my father's chair, casually fidgeting with the end of his gray tie. He held a manilla file folder on his lap. Going on with his original statement, he said "You're quite oblivious to your surroundings. My car is parked in plain sight in your driveway, and I chose a well-lit area to sit and still I have to call out for your attention."

"After not having to deal with your kind of people for a few months, I stopped worrying about being ambushed in my own home," I said sharply.

"This is no ambush, Mr. Quimby," he said. "And I'm not sure what you mean when you say my 'kind of people'."

"The kind that brings trouble," Nolan said for me, just as on edge as I was.

"Is this how you greet an old friend?" he asked.

"We've got nothing against you," I said. "But with all due respect, when we turned down your job offer, we did it in hopes that we wouldn't be dealing with you or anyone similar to you anymore."

"I understand that," he said apologetically. "Which is why I was hesitant to come here this evening. But, believe it or not, I've always favored you boys, ever since our original dealings in Paris, and especially since all you did for me when I was in hiding from Howard Statham. That's why I thought I would come by with a small, one-time offer for a mostly danger-free job that wouldn't take up twenty-four hours of your time."

"What makes you think we'd be interested?" Nolan asked.

"Simply the type of person that I know the two of you are."

"Elaborate," I said.

"Look at you." He gestured to our sweat-soaked clothes and tense muscles. "You crave action, you crave stimulation, so much so that you go to the trouble of pumping creatine and other compounds into your bloodstream just to use it to strain your muscle to the very last fiber and wear out every inch of your body just to feel the satisfaction that the pain brings. I've seen the potential in the two of you since we met, and I knew back in June the reason you turned down my offer wasn't because you didn't want it, but because it didn't feel right considering the circumstances. I didn't come here planning to bribe you or to try to convince you to do this because I knew I wouldn't have to."

I felt violated at the psychiatrist-like evaluation he'd made of the two of us, but I felt more frustrated at the fact that everything he'd said was true and there was no denying it. I wanted it, and as well as I knew Nolan, the look on his face told me he wanted it too. Looking him in the eye, I half-questioningly nodded. He nodded back. We both nodded at Wexler.

A smile brightened Wexler's face and he slapped the file folder against his knee. "Excellent. Now, if you have somewhere more private and comfortable for us to speak, we can go over this. I'd also appreciate a cup of coffee."

The three of us sat at the back patio five minutes later, dimly illuminated by the string lights that my mother claimed added an aesthetic to the area. The coffee I sipped only made my insides tremble more intensely. The summer evening was warm and humid and my body was still trying to cool down from our workout. Wexler drug out a minute of silence as he sipped his coffee and looked around the backyard. The house sat at the front of a twenty-acre lot surrounded by white pines, common in our area. My father valued his privacy, which was why he'd bought the surrounding land when he'd purchased the home eighteen years ago. The majority of the property was forest, which we occasionally hunted, along with a natural pond not visible from the house.

"I would've liked my property to be as private as this," Wexler said. I'd been to his country home in Northern Virginia before, and I remembered his neighbors to indeed be a bit too close for comfort. I tapped my foot anxiously now, annoyed by his small talk. He noticed this and changed direction.

"Alright, then, I suppose we'll get down to business," he stated, laying the file folder on the coffee table we sat around. We sat forward as he opened it up. "It's a simple endeavor, really, and, like I said, should put you at no risk for harm, assuming you don't screw up. The Bureau has been in contact with a trusted informant from a technology organization somewhere in Central America that claims to have information regarding national security. A deal has been made between the Bureau and the informant for compensation of the risks they've taken in providing us with the information, along with full immunity regarding this situation. The informant still refuses to come directly to the Bureau, out of fear of being discovered by the members of the organization that they are compromising, so they've requested a public rendezvous to trade off their information for our compensation."

He paused, letting us absorb all that he'd told us.

"I'm guessing that's where we come in?" Nolan deducted.

"Precisely," Wexler said with satisfaction. "My supervisor suggested the two of you when we were deciding who to send to the rendezvous, and there was no question that you would be the right fit. You are of a generally inconspicuous age to anyone watching, and you will fit in perfectly with the surrounding population."

"Surrounding population of where, exactly?" I asked.

He laid a finger on a line on the casefile. "Virginia Beach. The informant said they'd come no closer than one hundred miles to Washington D.C. and since they were traveling from the south, we proposed Virginia Beach, a densely populated area in August. You two seem like the beach-going type, so I trust you'll be a good fit for this venture. There is a suite reserved for the two of you at the *Paradise Hotel* near the beach."

"My father owns a hotel in Virginia Beach," I pointed out. "If that would be more convenient—"

"No, no," Wexler cut me off. "You must follow the instructions to a T, do not deviate whatsoever. My SSA is very particular about that."

"What's an *SSA*?" I questioned.

"'Supervisory Special Agent'," Wexler said. "My boss, Lance McGuire."

"So, when is this happening?" Nolan asked.

"The meeting is set for one week from today at one o'clock in the afternoon. The suite is already reserved, so you can arrive at any time, just present the clerk with the invoice included in the file there. There are more specific instructions in the file, which I will leave with the two of you in hopes that yours will be the only eyes to see it. Can we agree on that?"

"Yes."

"Good. A second rendezvous point is listed, a diner off the highway between Virginia Beach and Washington D.C. I will meet you there next Saturday where you'll provide me with whatever you receive in the trade. If you have any questions, which you shouldn't, my phone number is on the file."

He stood and shook both of our hands. "It was a pleasure to see you boys again, and I believe implicitly that you'll be successful. I can show myself to the car, thank you. Good evening."

He left us and walked around the house, and shortly we heard him drive away. Only then did Nolan and I look at each other. A smirk crept to his face as I felt one creep to mine. Leaning in, I said to him, "You were right."

He raised an eyebrow. "About what."

"The boys are back in town."

That night I slept no more than two hours, but for different reasons this time. I was anxious, excited, scared, all emotions I hadn't felt in months. Wexler was right about my crave for action. I often read Sherlock Holmes novels and short stories, and I drew comparisons between myself and Holmes. I was nowhere near his chemical genius, but I often remembered a quote from *The Sign of Four* where Sir Arthur Conan Doyle spoke through Holmes about the use of cocaine. *"I suppose that its influence is physically a bad one. I find it, however, so transcendently stimulating and clarifying to the mind that its secondary action is a matter of small moment."*

While I had never experienced the effects of cocaine, nor did I plan to, I felt I had the same need for this tonic invigoration that our lifestyle had been full of in the past year. Now that it had disappeared along with Blaire, I had found myself in the same situation as Holmes, trying to fight off the ordinariness of my life. Finally Wexler had come to feed my addiction.

I woke before the sun, which hadn't happened naturally in weeks, but I felt dizzy and unfamiliar as I slid into a pair of shorts and a t-shirt. My brain wasn't accustomed to early rising anymore, I decided, so I brewed a cup of coffee to try to warm up my mind. I shuffled onto the front porch and sat on my father's rocking chair, awaiting the near sunrise.

The car was parked in the driveway before I noticed it, which caught me off guard, but not more than the appearance of the car itself did. I'd seen it a hundred times in the last year, but not recently. The few streaks of sunlight leaking out of the distant mountains glimmered off the passenger door, showing the slick blue color of the body. In the dim light I could make out the unique silhouette of the Mazda sedan. Leaning forward, I studied the vehicle until its driver stepped out.

I felt myself shudder in the cool morning as I recognized the figure approaching the front porch. I tried to speak, but could only hear myself distantly. Every time I blinked, she was ten feet closer. My eyes tried to focus, but couldn't.

She reached the porch. I tried to stand up.

Blaire reached out and grabbed my face, but I couldn't feel her hands.

She kissed me.

I woke up.

Sitting up in my bed, I scanned my dark bedroom, mind whirling, trying to determine what had just happened. My breaths grew heavy, my eyes burned, tears began to flow before I could stop them. I heard myself mumble words, my hands went to my head, my face became hot. Falling back down, I shoved my face into my pillow and screamed, cried, cussed.

That dream was as close as I'd come to Blaire in two months. The excitement I'd felt the night before was a distant thought, completely drowned out by my newest vivid encounter with the memory of her.

Once I'd slapped myself three times and blinked for ten seconds to make sure I was really awake, I glanced at the clock. It wasn't quite five, but I rolled out of bed anyway. I couldn't sleep anymore this morning, I didn't want to.

I made my way around the quiet, empty, dark house. My parents were on an anniversary trip to Fort Myers, where Quimby Suites had just added another coastal destination. My older brother, Jared, was beginning his fourth year of his business degree, while my older sister, Olivia, the middle child, was living in downtown Dixon, a street away from the hair and nail salon she co-established alongside a fellow cosmetology school graduate. So here I sat, like Kevin McCallister, living in my own world while the rest of the family was conquering the real one.

I sat staring at the coffee maker as it heated up with groaning and whirring noises from within. Finally it coughed and spurted and trickled the dark blend into my cup. I stepped warily onto the porch, examining the surroundings to be positive I was awake this time. This time I did see the headlights pull into the driveway, although it wasn't the blue Mazda of Blaire Devereaux. Instead, it was Nolan's black Audi crawling up the lane and parking in front of the garage. I now understood Wexler's surprise at having not been noticed on the porch, because despite my feeling of complete visibility, Nolan didn't notice me until he was nearly up the steps. He cussed and nearly fell back down them upon seeing me, saying, "That's twice in twelve hours that someone in that chair has nearly given me a heart attack."

"You're the heaviest sleeper I know," I said. "Surprised you couldn't sleep either."

"I probably would have fallen back to sleep," he explained. "But I knew you'd be up. Figured I'd keep you company and tell you my idea. But first, coffee." He disappeared into the house and in five minutes was back on the porch, watching the steam from his cup evaporate in the morning air. Sensing my anticipation, he said, "Oh, are you waiting to hear my idea?"

"Stop dragging it out," I said, annoyed.

"Well, it's just this: There's nothing keeping us here, right? The meeting in Virginia Beach is next Friday, and it's probably necessary to be there a day early at least to get a feel for the area, so. .

.why not be there five days early instead? Wexler said the place is already reserved for us. I'd only be missing a few classes this week, so no worries there, and you can't tell me you had plans. I figured we could leave tomorrow afternoon."

The smirk had leaked onto my face before I'd even had time to consider the idea, which Nolan took as confirmation. It was a good idea, I couldn't deny it. "Let's do it."

Olivia texted me Saturday evening asking me to drive with her to church the next morning since we were the only two members of the family in town at the moment, which I couldn't refuse. It was nice to have my sister back in Dixon. We'd been close in high school, her being only two years older than me, but she'd left for cosmetology school after graduation and had lived several hours away.

On the drive home from church, I told her about Nolan and I's upcoming trip to Virginia Beach. I left out the details of the exact purpose for our going, which was more difficult than I'd imagined. It was my nature to spill everything to her, and it pained me not to this time. I explained that we'd decided to have one last trip before Nolan's classes started full-time.

"Well at least you're doing something," she said. "I thought you'd never say yes to anything fun ever again since. . ." She trailed off.

"Since when?" I asked from the passenger seat.

She sighed and shrugged as if afraid to say. "Since, you know, Blaire left, and stuff."

I sat silently, trying to put together a sentence that wouldn't sound overly defensive but also wouldn't give away the fact that she was right. "She didn't control my happiness."

"She didn't personally," she admitted. "But you can't always tell when someone affects you the way that she did until they're gone."

"She didn't affect me," I lied.

"Chris, I've been in love before–"

"In what?" I cut her off. "Who's in love? Are you saying I'm in love? You think I was in love with her? That's so ridiculous. What do you know?"

"You're rambling," she said. "You're getting all defensive because you don't want to admit it."

"Who do you think you are?" I said, my voice raising. "You were barely even around when she was? How would you know who was in love? Why do you want to bring all this up now for no reason? Who cares if I was? What does it matter now? Maybe I was, I don't know. Okay, sure, I was. Who cares?" She didn't speak during my monologue of an argument. I realized now what I had admitted, and although I'd admitted it to myself before, I'd never said it aloud.

"You loved her," Olivia said. "And it's okay. You act like it's wrong to love someone. For someone that turned your life upside down the way she did, I'd love her too, for goodness sake. I was there that first night you met her, at dad's anniversary gala, remember? I saw you walk up to her table and try to work her over like you could all the other girls around here, but it didn't work. She didn't show a bit of interest in you, but you still wanted her. She kidnapped Nolan, tied him up and threw him in a corner and you still wanted her. You two went through more hate and love and hate and love than a married couple, and you still wanted her. That's love, and it's okay."

I sat silently, my throat aching as I tried to hold down a sobbing fit. I didn't understand her purpose for bringing this up, and I told her that.

"Because now that you understand that you loved her," she explained. "You'll understand that she loved you."

I let a tear fall from my eye, then another, as she went on.

"It's so obvious, Chris. How many times did she risk her own life to take care of you? When she shot that woman to help you and Nolan get away, when she came *back* just to help protect you from that Smith guy, when she took a bullet out of your leg, when she bailed you out of jail in the middle of the night, people don't just do that because they feel obligated. You were the only person she wanted to be around. How many nights did I come home to find her on our couch, or sitting with you on the patio? I know there's moments that have happened between you two that no one knows about, and I'm not asking you to tell me."

I missed her next sentence as I absorbed that one. I thought of every moment we'd had, every time she cried against me out of grief or fear or exhaustion, the three times she'd kissed me, although only one of them had been genuine. Every vivid memory that made my heart ache to think about, now seemed different. Olivia's evidence made sense, every piece of it. Was it because I *wanted* to believe she loved me, or because it was true?

"All I'm saying, Chris, is that this wasn't a wasted bond that you two had. You affected her as much as she affected you. You made a difference in her life."

My unavoidable pain came out verbally. "Then why did she leave?"

Olivia looked me dead in the eyes. "Because that's how *much* she loved you. She knew you wanted that job with that creepy FBI guy, and she knew what it was going to do to you and to your relationship.

She gave up her good life here so that you could keep yours. She left because she cared more about you than about herself."

I made no further attempt to hold back my tears.

Nolan hadn't been to Virginia Beach in almost a year, since he'd been kidnapped and held at Launa Payne's *Rêverie* club. I'd purposely avoided that street, that entire part of town for that matter, for his sake and my own. By six in the evening, we'd arrived at the Paradise Hotel, and by six-thirty, we were settled on our fifth-floor balcony, letting the saltwater-scented breeze soothe us.

Nolan held the casefile that Wexler had left with us, and was glancing from it out to the shore, then back. The hotel was in the perfect location, overlooking the beach, just down the shore from the pier at which we were supposed to meet.

"This is a good spot," Nolan said. "I wonder why it was so important to Wexler that we stay here, though."

"Seemed like his SSA or whatever he called it, that McGuire guy, is somewhat of a micromanager."

"I looked that guy up," he said. "He just got hired for the position a few months ago. He's an outside hire, but I have no idea where he came from or what he did before the Bureau."

"What happened to Wexler's old supervisor?" I questioned.

"Your guess is as good as mine. The article on the Bureau's website just said McGuire was 'replacing' Robert Something-or-Another as SSA over about ten special agents, Wexler being one of them, obviously. SSA is just a step up on the hierarchy from a special agent, the way I understand it. SSAs have bosses, and their bosses have bosses."

We sat silently for a minute, gazing over the beach and its surroundings. As the sun went down, the population migrated to the boardwalk and the shops that ran along it. Standing, I gestured down to the boardwalk and said, "I don't know about you, but I'm going to enjoy these couple days before we put our lives at risk for the hundredth time this year."

A hand gripped my shoulder and shook it. I reflexively struck at whatever force was trying to subdue me, and felt my hand make contact with my attacker's jaw. In the next instant my eyes opened, the grip was released, and Nolan's voice was cussing me out. I sat up in my bed, finding the only source of light to be the lamp on the night table. Barely a sliver of orange was visible from the sliding glass balcony doors.

"First of all," I started. "You should know better than to shake me awake like that. Second, why are you trying to wake me up in the first place? The sun's not even up yet."

"There is nothing healthier than a jog on the beach and then a morning workout," Nolan said. "I figured we could get a jog in before the sun is all the way up and then a little workout down in the hotel's weight room."

Not an ounce of my body wanted to listen to him, but my brain agreed. Reluctantly, I slid out of bed and dressed, then followed him out to the beach. The jog did feel good, more so for my mind than my body. Since Wexler's visit and my talk with Olivia, I was beginning to progress somewhat in my mental state, not to mention Nolan's constant optimism and support helped me along the way. I felt somewhat at peace with myself and excited for what was to come.

The feeling was brief.

We returned to the hotel a little before seven. The place being rather large, we didn't know our way around and decided to ask the front desk for directions to the weight room. As we approached, the receptionist was dialing the phone and held up a finger to us. "I'll be with you in a moment."

She was no older than twenty-two, I guessed, and had the stereotypical features of a beach-goer: tan skin and hair the color of the sand outside. I couldn't tell whether or not she was attractive, my perception of the idea had been completely rewired over the past year. But as we waited, Nolan gave me the recognizable eyebrow and side-eye that every wing-man gave his best friend. He was gesturing for me to flirt with the receptionist, but the idea of flirting was a lost art of mine, and I simply returned a scrunched nose.

We continued communicating with nods and facial expressions while she spoke on the phone with someone who I guessed was a hotel manager. "Mr. Thomas, there just seems to be some trouble with Miss Janice Downey's credit card. . .Well I'm not sure, it just says it's invalid. . .Okay, I'll talk to you then. Thank–" I heard a dull tone before she finished, and the expression on her face told me that this Mr. Thomas wasn't easy to work with. She quickly put on a pleasant face and turned to us. "How can I help you?"

Nolan explained that we were in search of the weight room and she directed us down the hall to the left. As we walked, Nolan whispered more persuasion to make a move on the receptionist, but my mind didn't process his words, it was still processing hers. Gradually my feet moved slower, my mind moved faster. The image of the receptionist in my mind turned to that of Phineas Wexler. The name the receptionist had just said was the same name I heard Wexler say five months ago.

Janice Downey, one of many aliases of Blaire Devereaux.

I whirled and scrambled back down the hallway toward the front desk, forcing myself to slow to a walk once within the receptionist's vision. My heart pounding and mind racing, I tried to act casual as I asked, "Did I hear you say the name 'Janice Downey'?"

She stared at me with side-eyes, taken off guard at the intrusion. Suspiciously, she answered, "Yes."

"What a coincidence," I pretended. "I can't believe me and Janice are in the same hotel."

She gave a fake smile, seeming confused and uninterested.

"Oh, sorry," I said with a chuckle. "She's just an old friend that I haven't seen in a while. I'd love to talk to her, do you happen to know what room she's staying in?"

Of course she knew what room she was in, she was the receptionist. But her hesitation and awkward expression told me her answer before she said it. "I'm sorry, we're not allowed to give out other guests' information."

I leaned into the tall desk and said in a friendly, between-us tone, "You sure?"

She seemed conflicted but genuinely apologetic as she said, "My boss is really strict and I just don't want to break any rules. I'm really sorry."

Discouraged, I assured her I understood and left. Nolan had caught up by then and followed me to the elevator, where I explained the development, or lack thereof.

"That's a crazy coincidence that she happens to be at this hotel," Nolan said.

"Coincidences don't exist with Blaire," I said. "She knows we're here, she followed us."

"You're sure the receptionist won't tell us what room she's in?"

I tapped my foot on the tile elevator floor. "Not just yet, but I'm not done trying. If Blaire's here, I'm going to find her, one way or another."

We plotted in our room for an hour, thinking of a way to find Janice Downey's room number. From the description of Mr. Thomas, it appeared that no receptionist would be willing to give up the information. Our only possible access to the hotel guest list would be on the computer at the front desk or the manager's office. The latter was ruled out immediately, because we had no urge to get into trouble with Mr. Thomas, especially when we were on an official assignment. We eventually decided some reconnaissance would be necessary before we could make any attempt at the computer, and we spent another ten minutes thinking of exactly what kind of reconnaissance would be worth our while.

Finally Nolan, who'd been lying on his back in thought, leapt to his feet with an excited clap. "I got it! Say we locked ourselves out of the room. They'll have to have replacement keys, and when she checks which room we're in, you can watch her screen and try to catch a glimpse of the guest list. Even if you don't see Blaire's fake name, at least you'll know how to find the guest list in case we get access to the computer."

He high-fived me with enough excitement to make my hand burn. I had to give it to him, this idea was better than anything I had in mind. But once he settled down, I ventured a protest. "Why do I have to be the one to ask for the key? She's already suspicious of me for bothering her the first time."

"Because you're the charmer," he said. "You need to get on good terms with her, loosen her up in case we have to make another attempt to get the room number. And the fact that you already bothered her will just make it seem like you came back because you're interested in her. Don't act like you can't do it, I've seen you work over dozens of girls with a lot less effort."

"Maybe a year ago," I said. "I've barely spoken to a girl our age since we graduated, let alone flirt."

"What about the girls from the party that the Virginia Tech guys invited us to?"

"All I did that night was throw ping pong balls into solo cups," I said. "I don't even remember talking to a girl there."

"Because you didn't *want* to. Every girl in the place was checking you out that night, but you didn't even notice because you didn't care."

"Exactly."

"This time, you do care, because if you screw it up you're not going to find Blaire. So suck it up and let Chris Quimby be Chris Quimby."

We spent the afternoon on the beach, trying for a moment to forget our current endeavors and relax, ease our minds and prepare for what was ahead. As the afternoon grew into evening, we decided the time had come to make the move on the receptionist, our newest patsy. We gathered our things and made our way up the path to the Paradise Hotel, making sure she noticed our entrance, then took the elevator to our floor.

It was impossible for anyone to know that this was all a plan, because we purposely *had* locked ourselves out, leaving both keycards inside. We made a show of attempting to open our door and realizing we had no key, just for any eyes or cameras that may have been on us. Then I hustled down the hallway, back to the elevator, leaving Nolan by the door.

The receptionist looked up as I approached, and I saw her take a deep breath, which could've been for any number of reasons. The first possibility, although very unlikely, was that she was nervous to speak to the handsome young man; or the second, which was more probable, was that she was wearily preparing to assist yet another annoying guest.

"I'm really loadin' you down with questions today, aren't I?" I joked to seem more friendly and affable.

"That's what I'm here for," she said with a polite smile.

"Well, I'm sure you noticed my friend and I aren't the sharpest tools in the shed, so it's probably no surprise that we locked ourselves out of our room." I chuckled, causing her to as well. As I spoke, I made sure to lean against the tall desk in a comfortable manner, and to remain inconspicuous as I attempted to catch a glimpse of her computer monitor which sat at an angle.

As she turned to the computer, she said, "No worries, it happens more than you think. Can I get your name so I can confirm your room number?"

"Quimby," I said. "Chris Quimby."

"*Quimby*'. That's fancy," she said as she clicked an icon labeled 'Guest List' on the home screen. Then she stopped and looked at me with a questioning face. "I recognize that name. Where have I heard that?"

"There's a 'Quimby Suites' hotel a block from here," I explained. "My father's."

"That's what it is," she said. I noticed as she searched the guest list that it was arranged by room number, not alphabetically like I'd hoped, so I didn't see the surname 'Downey' as she navigated. Eventually she pulled up my guest profile and confirmed that we were in room 513.

She turned around and unlocked a cabinet to find our replacement key. As she did so, I made a nonchalant scan of the lobby, finding the 360-degree camera in the center of the ceiling. As I measured its view in my mind, I roughly determined the blind spot to be anywhere to the left of the desk or behind it. The raised counter and L-shaped design hid anyone behind it from the camera's view unless they were standing. I decided if we were able to get behind the desk in a crouch position, we could access the computer without being seen. The only problem would be getting there in the first place, because the nearest hallway was ten feet from the desk, so whoever tried to get behind the desk would be on camera for more than a second unless something were hiding them.

As she turned back around and handed me the card, she asked, "If your dad owns a hotel down the street, what are you doing staying here?"

I had no immediate answer to this question, because *I* didn't even know why I was staying here, but I conjured something in my mind. With a shrug and a smirk, I said, "The view is much nicer."

I caught her off guard with the blatantly flirtatious statement, but she answered on the same level. "Well, you made the right choice," she said with a blushing smile.

As I turned to leave I open-endedly told her, "Thank you. . ."

"Alice."

"Thank you, Alice."

I fell down on my bed, groaning at how mentally exhausting my little stunt had been. I hadn't acted that way around a girl in so long it felt unnatural and embarrassing, and although I didn't admit it aloud, I hoped desperately that Blaire would never find out about it, for multiple reasons. One of these being that I had made a complete fool of myself, and another being that I didn't want her to think I'd come full circle and returned to my default personality. What was I thinking, anyway? This was Blaire. If she was anywhere near us right now, she knew everything that was happening at any given moment.

The act wasn't over, I had to carry it out until we left the hotel, or at least until we discovered Janice Downey's room number. Every time we passed through the lobby, I smiled or waved, once I winked, which felt disgusting. At times I saw other receptionists, an older woman, a tall, middle-aged man, and a short, angry-looking man who wore a name tag that read "Manager". I assumed this man was Mr. Thomas. Once, on Tuesday afternoon as I strolled through by myself, I saw Alice and approached the desk nonchalantly, as if deciding to pay her a visit. She smiled as I leaned my elbows on the desk.

"This job has to be boring," I said.

"Believe me, you have no idea." She rolled her eyes with a giggle.

"Are you here all day?" I asked.

"Not quite. Some days I have the morning shift, some days afternoon, some days both." She made a disgusted noise in her throat. "That just reminded me that I have the night shift tomorrow night."

The prospect of accessing her computer during the night appealed to me immediately, so I pried further. "Wednesday? You have to sit here all night?"

She nodded. "Until six a.m. Thursday morning. Not allowed to leave the desk, just in case some idiot decides to check in or call the hotel in the middle of the night."

"Maybe I'll pay you a visit, keep you company," I said.

Alice blushed and pursed her lips with a suppressed grin. "I'd appreciate that."

Throwing her my most charming smile, I left the desk and went to divulge my advancements. Nolan and I sat down and I explained the prospect of Alice's late shift the following night.

"So what's your plan, then?" Nolan asked. "Seduce her into telling you what room Blaire is in?"

"Please shut up," I said, disgusted at his suggestion. "No, this is where you come in."

"Me?" I saw his expression become nervous.

"Yes, you. Wednesday night I'll distract her and find some way to get her away from the desk. You'll sneak in and get to the computer, pull up the guest list, and find Blaire's room number."

"But how do I get to the desk?" he asked me. "You said there was a ten foot space where the camera could see me."

"That's true," I said, raising a finger. "But it won't be a problem if the camera isn't on when you get there."

By eleven o'clock Wednesday night, both of us had thrown up at least once. The simple fact that we had nothing to do but wait only made the anxiety increase. We planned to make the move after one a.m., when there'd be very little chance of anyone being in the lobby to witness our infiltration, so we'd spent hours upon hours waiting in our room for the clock to give us our queue. The more I thought about the upcoming events, the more nervous I became. What if Alice didn't cooperate?

What if she wouldn't leave the desk? What if she wouldn't turn the camera off? My biggest issue with this plan was that much of it hinged on the actions of the patsy. Blaire had taught me time and time again not to leave anything up to chance, or to the judgment of the pigeon.

An hour passed, then another. At one o'clock I got dressed in what I imagined would be an attractive outfit, although that was another of my skills that had long since been lost. Nolan said the t-shirt complimented my biceps, but I only wore it because the black fabric would hide my nervous sweating better than any other color. By the time I had physically and mentally prepared myself, the clock read 1:27. I told Nolan goodluck and headed down the hallway alone.

Alice sat leaned back in the swivel chair, scrolling on her phone when I entered the lobby. The smile on her face as she noticed me boosted my confidence. She was happy to see me, and would most likely comply with my suggestion.

"I was *this* close to dying of boredom," she said with her fingers pinched.

"I'm glad I could save you from it," I replied.

We lingered in small talk for a minute until she said, "Why don't you stay a while?"

"I will, but I don't really have a place to sit, and I don't feel very private. Why don't we head out the back exit, maybe walk out on the boardwalk?"

She gave a sorrowful look. "I told you I can't leave the desk. Mr. Thomas can be such an ass, I just know he'd throw a fit if I left."

"Is he around?" I asked.

"No, he went home a few hours ago. Me and the cleaning crew are the only ones here."

I lowered my voice and spoke intimately. "Well how about you shut off that camera view so no one will ever know you left?" I never broke eye contact with her, trying my hardest to make her risk her job for a random guy she'd met a few days ago.

She couldn't hide a smirk, and slowly, she turned to her computer. I watched her pull up a dozen live camera feeds, select the one that displayed the two of us, and click "Hide Feed". In the same instant, the view became black, and the two of us were figuratively invisible. I tried to hide my surprise at her cooperation. It was hard to believe I'd interested her to this extent.

Just before she rose to accompany me, she turned back to her computer. "Just to be safe," she said, as she did the one thing I hadn't anticipated. With three clicks she locked the computer, and now the only display on the screen was a password prompt.

Nolan was screwed.

I froze as my mind began to whirl, fighting panic. She noticed this and asked, "Everything okay?"

Everything was not okay, not even in the slightest, but that wasn't what I told her. "Of course," I said with no breath. "Let's go."

I spent a painfully dull half hour on the boardwalk with Alice, whose last name, I learned, was Trace. Through gradual prodding, I learned that she had no knowledge of any relation to Neil Trace, which was probably true, but the thought still lingered in my mind. Otherwise, I learned she was going into her junior year at the University of Virginia and was scheduled to move back onto the campus in the last week of August. She was talkative, which made it easier for me to think of the current problems at hand, as well as to not discuss my own recent affairs. I waited for Nolan's panic text, but it never came, and by the time I left Alice back at her locked computer and found my way back to our room, I found my best friend sitting on the edge of his bed, smiling at me.

"I got it."

"You got it?" I asked incredulously.

"Yep, it worked perfectly. No one was around. Janice Downey is in room 308."

I stared at him with no reaction, trying to read his face. "The computer wasn't locked?"

"Nope," he replied. "I was surprised too. It opened right up."

His face was unwavering, as if unaware of my confusion. I stood silently for several moments, until he asked me what was wrong. "Nothing," I said. "We'll go to her room first thing in the morning. Good job." I said nothing more, neither did he. Both of us went directly into bed, though neither of us slept. I felt strange around him now, like we weren't on the same team. From what I was aware, he'd never lied to me, especially in a situation as dire as this. And I had no clue as to what he had to gain by lying to me now. Had he been too scared to sneak down to the reception desk and made up a lie to save face? Had someone contacted him and forced him to lie against his will? Or was there something more serious developing–was he, for some reason, conspiring against me?

I'd known Nolan for a decade, and only once did I ever find myself at odds with him, and that was in ninth grade when we asked the same girl to homecoming. He was more of a brother to me than Jared ever was, not that that was Jared's fault, but our years of age separation had caused us to never become as close as other brothers I knew. Nolan had been the one, since third grade, to know everything about me, do everything with me, without a moment of hesitation. I'd made and lost a lot of friends during my time in school, but in the end they all drifted away and meant nothing to me, even more so since we'd graduated. All except for Nolan. The more I thought of this as I stared at the wall for the remainder of that night, I knew there was no way he could be working against me, at least not on his own accord.

Either way, the next morning as we set out for room 308, my pistol was tucked in the back of my waistband. I walked behind or beside Nolan, never in front. I'd watched his expressions and reactions all morning, and the only emotion I caught from him was severe nerves, although I was acting the same way, so I had no reason to believe he was nervous from anything aside from the possibility of meeting up with Blaire.

My heart was pounding out of my chest, my stomach turning in knots so powerfully it hurt to walk. By the time we reached the door, I was on the verge of throwing up and was beginning to hyperventilate when Nolan grabbed ahold of my shoulders. "Pull yourself together," he said with pleading eyes. "You know there's nothing to be worried about. If Blaire is in this place you know she wants to see you as bad as you want to see her. Please relax." His expression seemed more sorrowful than his words, as if he pitied me.

I breathed heavily still as I knocked on the white door. We tried to stay out of view of the peephole as we awaited an answer. To my surprise, I heard stirring within the room immediately, and footsteps neared the door. As I heard the privacy latch unlock, my right hand moved slowly to the handle of my Ruger, but as sweaty as my palm was, it would be impossible to get a worthy grip if necessary.

I watched the door handle turn and open slow enough to let my heart skip two beats, and all breath left my lungs as Janice Downey revealed herself.

"Can I help you?"

The woman staring at me was the farthest from Blaire Devereaux that I'd ever seen. She was nearly four times her age and had hair whiter than the door that she'd just opened. At first I hadn't seen her, she was no more than five feet tall, and the original pleasant smile on her face faded as she saw my despondent expression.

"Are you Miss Downey?" Nolan asked awkwardly.

"Yes," the woman squeaked. "Janice Downey. Is there something wrong?"

"Um, no." He glanced at me. I felt bad for my rudeness in ignoring the woman, but my face had been covered in an ice cold sweat the moment I'd seen her, and I didn't have the willpower to even meet her eyes. "We just had you confused with someone else," Nolan said politely. "Sorry to bother you. Have a nice day."

The sweet woman thanked him and shut the door just before I fell against the wall. Nolan caught me and led me to the elevator, apologizing a dozen times and telling me to keep it together until we made it to our room.

I cussed, punched the wall, and threw a healthy fit until Nolan brought me back to earth. He sat across from me and spoke in a fatherly tone. "I know this sucks, and it's not what you expected, but it's over now. It's one more thing we don't have to worry about. We can focus on the task at hand, which we have one day to prepare for now, by the way. Can we do that? Can we do what we came here to get done?"

I picked up my head and looked at my best friend. Whatever was going on in his mind, whether or not he knew more than he was telling, I didn't care at this moment. "Can you promise me something?" I asked.

"Anything."

"When this is over, and we get whatever we're supposed to get, and we go home, will you help me?"

"Help you what?"

"Find her."

His eyes narrowed as if pain had struck his heart. He sighed sorrowfully and looked me in the eyes. "Yes. I promise."

Shortly past eleven that forenoon, Nolan and I left the hotel with plans to walk through the planned events of the following day. From the back door of the lobby, the hotel pool was on our left, although the day was dreary and a weak mist floated off the ocean, leaving the pool meagerly populated. Only a bored mother supervising her two children as they splashed endlessly in the water, and two girls a few years younger than us in vogue lifeguard sweatshirts that could be purchased at any and every boardwalk shop. They sat criss-cross next to each other, unspeaking, faces buried deep in their cell phones. One glanced up as we walked by, elbowed the other, who raised her head. They were out of my peripheral vision by then, but I felt rather uncomfortable as we walked away, knowing we were the topic of discussion.

It only bummed me out as we walked, thinking of a year before when I would've humored them, shot them a wink or a smirk or a stupid comment. I myself had owned a lifeguard sweatshirt years ago when my fashion was up to date with every fad. I'd been voted best dressed in my high school class, although in a class of less than eighty, senior superlatives were almost like participation trophies. The one I was truly proud of was Nolan and I's title of "best bromance" which we had secretly nominated ourselves for.

We'd grown out of so much in such a short time. How thrilling it used to be to prank Justin Hobbes, drag race in the streets of

Dixon, throw parties at the house that my parents worked so hard to earn. I'd never worked a day in my life for any man besides Henry Quimby. How easy life had been when I felt no shame in living under the accomplishments of my father. The term "trust fund baby" had grown more derogatory as the years went on. The older I was, the more I felt the need to make something of myself. Both my older siblings were well on their way to successful lives, financially and socially. Jared had even brought up his plan to be engaged within the next year.

My thoughts piled rapidly as I watched my feet step on the wet planks of the boardwalk. I had to branch out on my own, stop blaming my melancholy on Blaire and the trouble she'd brought. Maybe I'd ask Wexler if the position he'd offered as private investigating consultant still stood. We'd originally planned to take the offer until our third party disappeared, at which point it no longer felt worthwhile. But since this week had begun, since the thrill of danger and secrecy had returned, I knew that if there was anything I could construct a meaningful life out of, it was this very lifestyle.

Nolan tugged on my shirt to pull me toward the pier as I'd been lost in my trance. We walked to the end of the six hundred foot fishing pier where the rendezvous was to take place. In the casefile was the code phrase that we were to initiate the conversation with, along with the response that the informant should give. That was all the communicating we were to do with them.

The more we read over the file, the more it puzzled me. It seemed so unnecessary, the lengths we were going to just to receive one item from a stranger. Either the informant was severely paranoid, or McGuire, who'd led the planning of the task, was just excessively cautious. It would be understandable for him to be a bit green and careful, being new to the job. Perhaps he was just covering every possible pothole. Still, I felt off about this new SSA.

My stomach fluttered as we reentered the hotel lobby and my name was called by a semi-familiar voice. "Chris–uh, Mr. Quimby and Mr. Bragg, a package was dropped off for you." Alice smiled personally behind the desk. "Were you expecting one?"

"We were," I said, and hastily went to receive what had been left for us, the so-called "compensation" that we were to trade off with the informant. I'd nearly forgotten that part of the plan since we'd read over it, but it was clearly written in the casefile that it was to be dropped off at the hotel for us on Thursday.

"I had fun last night," Alice whispered with a smirk.

"What–oh, yes, yeah, so did I." I'd forgotten about the goings-on of the night before, especially my boring stroll on the boardwalk with Alice. Now I had to keep up the act at least slightly so she wouldn't assume I'd been using her, which I most definitely had been. In my mind I wished desperately that she wouldn't ask to see me another evening, when her comments were interrupted by a voice from the office behind the desk.

"Mr. Quimby, you say?" The short man who I'd assumed to be the manager, Mr. Thomas, hustled out and around the desk, one hand outstretched to shake mine, another reaching for my shoulder, which I hated. He displayed every sign of a Napoleon complex: the way he controlled the conversation, taking ahold of my shoulder and leading me from the desk; his abuse of power over subordinates like Alice; his overblown appearance, framed in his suit like a mannequin, although his pant legs couldn't have been more than a twenty-eight inseam. Everything about him was a red flag to me, which led me to listen warily as he spoke a hundred miles an hour.

"So, young man, I understand you've got some relation to Quimby Suites down the road. Doing a little spying on the competition?" He raised an eyebrow but chuckled obnoxiously, letting me know it was a joke, but the way he held eye contact made it obvious he was trying to read me as hard as I was trying to read him. He didn't give me a chance to answer yet anyway. "No problem, no problem. We've got nothing to hide." Now he stopped and stared at me, at which point I realized it was my turn to speak.

I stuttered through a chuckle. "No sir," I said with a polite smile. "Just decided this place would be a nicer spot for us. Closer to the beach, a nice pool area, you know. Which it has been, by the way. Very nice." I wanted to loosen him up a little bit with a complement to boost his ego.

This side tracked him better than I'd hoped. He gave an exaggerated thank you and rambled on about how long he'd been managing the Paradise Hotel, how successful he'd been, and so on. His words were tuned out as I fell into thought. Again I questioned the FBI's insistence that Nolan and I stayed at the Paradise Hotel, and now I wondered if Thomas was any part of the reason. How he could've been, I wasn't sure, but he seemed like the type of man who knew what went on in his hotel. Very Terry Benedict-esque, or at least he tried to be.

By the time we'd circled back to Alice's desk, he gave me a healthy pat on the back and told me to enjoy my stay. He said something about saying hello to my father for him, but I had already turned back to Nolan. I was about to ask him what he wanted to do for lunch when Alice jutted in. "You guys just missed your friend."

"Who?" I asked.

"Janice Downey. She just came down off the elevator."

"Really old woman? Even shorter than your boss? I ran into her already, it wasn't who I thought it was."

She looked confused. "Uh, no. This Janice Downey is about my age. Blonde hair, almost your height, maybe."

I stared at her. Her face was naive and confused. "You're sure?" I asked.

"Yes, I'm sure. I talked to her earlier this week about her credit card."

"Where'd she go?"

"Just now? Out the back door towards the boardwalk."

I threw the back lobby door open and scanned the area behind the hotel. The pool was still near-empty, no one was walking the path to the boardwalk. Bushes and flowerbeds blocked any passage around the left side of the building, so I hustled down the sidewalk that curved around the right side. There it split off and led to either the front entrance or the parking garage below the building. Just as I rounded the corner I saw blonde hair atop a black sweatshirt enter the door to the stairwell that led into the parking garage. My heart skipped every other beat as I sprinted to the stairwell. I looked down the middle of it to try and see whoever walked below me. I saw no one. I held my breath, listening for footsteps that would've echoed off the concrete stairs. Nothing.

I checked all three levels of the parking garage, but to no avail. My chance had come and gone. I found Nolan still waiting at Alice's desk when I reentered the lobby. He hadn't moved, hadn't attempted to join me or back me up. All I said to him was that I'd meet him in our room.

He came in three minutes behind me, and the second he stepped into the room my hand was in his chest and my pistol was in his face. He gasped for breath and stuttered, asking me what was going on, begging me to put my gun away.

"You know something," I said. "You're lying to me. Tell me what's going on."

"Chris, you're going crazy!" he said. "What are you talking about?"

"Where'd you get Janice Downey's room number?"

He hesitated. "The computer, remember?"

"The computer was locked. I watched Alice lock it before we left."

He stared at me for five seconds, eyes darting around my face. "Well it wasn't locked when I got there."

"Why didn't you follow me just now when I went after her?" I said, growing frustrated at his lack of emotion. "The old woman obviously wasn't Janice Downey. Who was it?"

"How should I know?"

I didn't move. I held him against the wall with my forearm. He could've easily thrown me off had there not been a gun to his head. Something about the touch of steel to a person's forehead makes them lose all sense of physical strength.

"Nolan," I said calmly. "You're lying to me and I don't know why. Is there anything you'll tell me?"

His expression pleaded. I didn't move. "It's for your own safety," he whispered. "I promise once this is over and we're out of Virginia Beach I'll explain it to you, but if I told you now you'd just wind up getting yourself killed. Please, Chris. You know I wouldn't do anything to hurt you. Please just trust me this time and let's finish what we came here to do."

For a few more seconds I held him there, then released. I was embarrassed at having held my best friend at gunpoint. Tossing it to the bed, I mumbled, "Don't tell your mom I held a gun on you. She won't let us hang out anymore."

The pistol felt cold and uncomfortable on my bare back. In past combat situations, I was always able to dress appropriately–pants, a jacket, and so on. But going out onto the Virginia Beach boardwalk in an outfit like that would immediately arouse suspicion, not to mention cause a heat stroke. So I wore swim trunks and threw a light sweatshirt on. I wore no t-shirt underneath, trying to stay somewhat cool, but I had to wear a sweatshirt in order to hide the Compact 9mm tucked in the waistband against my back. My stomach trembled as I checked my watch: a quarter till one. Nolan and I looked up at each other. I offered a handshake, which he pulled into a hug.

"I got your back," he whispered.

I stuffed the cash into a backpack that we were to trade off, and we made our way to the stairs. Five floors was a decent trip on stairs, but we didn't want to risk being held up in an elevator. Alice wasn't working reception today, which was a relief. The last thing I wanted was to get hung up in a conversation with the most dull woman I'd ever met. We also didn't want to arrive on the pier too early, so we took our time walking along the boardwalk, stopping and pointing at any random object, store, person, trying to sell our nonchalant stroll. The sun was high, crowds were large, it would've been a gorgeous day for beach-going, had we not been busy trading off intel of national security with an anonymous informant. The situation sounded completely made up. I could've leaned over to the next person I passed and told them exactly what was going on and they would've laughed me into the ocean.

The pier was busy. Fishing rods whirred as we made our way through the crowd. The pier was long, and it took several minutes to walk the length of it. At the end, it widened out into a sharpened T shape. I glanced at the people around us as we found a spot to lean against the railing. I looked out into the water, Nolan stood with his back to it, casually scanning the crowd.

"Anything?" I asked quietly.

"Half the people here have a backpack, Chris. How am I supposed to narrow it down?"

"Does anybody look as nervous as we are? Anyone looking through the crowd like you?"

After a few seconds, he said, "I think I might've found him. Long-haired Mediterranean guy over in the other corner."

I checked my watch again. One o'clock on the dot. "Let's go." Trying as hard as possible to appear nonchalant, we crossed the end of the pier, pointing at something in the water that supposedly attracted our interest. We looked into the water for a few seconds, talking amongst ourselves, until I leaned over to the tall, brown-skinned man to my right.

"I bet you could catch a fifty-pound Yellowfin on a day like today," I said to him.

He looked at me. *"Den katalavaíno. . ."* he said. I immediately realized our mistake. This guy didn't even speak English. Even if the informant wasn't American, he would've at least recognized our code phrase. Cussing in my mind, I tried to back out of the awkward conversation. Just as Nolan and I turned away, a woman's voice came from our left.

"A fisherman's only as good as his rod."

I stopped in my tracks and turned to the source of the sentence. The woman was our height, but her wedge sandals made her taller. She looked thirty-five, maybe older. Brown hair was pulled into a ponytail, and she wore large-framed Kim Kardashian-style sunglasses.

"What was that?" I asked politely.

"I said a fisherman's only as good as his rod," she repeated, resting a backpack similar to ours on the ground against the railing and leaning on an elbow. "Wouldn't you agree?"

"You're right," I responded. "Never thought of it that way." I casually slid my backpack off my shoulder and set it in a similar position as hers, only a few feet away.

The conversation was initiated, so we simply had to mingle in smalltalk until an opportunity to leave. As we spoke, we shifted gradually left, pretending to look intently at something far out in the water. Finally, I glanced over to Nolan. "Well, it's about that time, huh?"

He nodded. "I'd say so."

"Have a nice day," I said to the woman.

"You as well."

I grabbed the backpack by the strap and slung it over my shoulder, and Nolan and I strolled back up the pier. I listened for any comments from a bystander that might've noticed I'd picked up someone else's bag, but none came. By the time we were off the pier and heading up the boardwalk to the hotel, my heartbeat was starting to slow to normal speed.

"I was *this* close to throwing up," Nolan said.

"How do you think I feel?" I said. "I was doing all the work."

"I can't believe how far off I was with that Mediterranean guy."

I chuckled. "We're just lucky that woman overheard us, or else we would've been walking around the pier all day talking about fifty-pound tuna."

We both breathed sighs of relief and gave a casual fist bump. We watched our feet as we hopped up the awkward cement steps to the back patio of the Paradise Hotel, hearts lightening, minds easing.

A moment later, as we reached the top and raised our glances, we came face to face with six black uniforms and shiny silver badges. Two pistols were pointed at each of our heads, respectively.

Gasps and shouts from the pool crowd were drowned out by orders from the police officers to lay face down on the cement. "What's going on?" Nolan demanded, hands raised.

"I said on the ground!" shouted the tallest officer.

As we reluctantly fell to our knees, two officers were on us, forcing us to the ground, a knee on the small of our backs. I felt my pistol being yanked from my waistband, which brought on a new wave of gasps from the crowd. Next, the backpack was pulled from my back, and in my peripheral vision I saw an officer slowly unzip it. Suddenly stepping back, he held it away from himself and radioed for the bomb squad.

"Bomb squad?" I yelled. "What are you talking about?"

My mind raced, my heart trembled. The pavement hurt my cheek as I watched bystanders at the pool point fearfully. Some fled, some took videos. One person didn't move. As the officer on my back wrapped cold handcuffs around my wrist, I heard him speak. "You have the right to remain silent. Anything you say can and will be held against you. . ." His voice trailed off as I stared sideways at the unmoving woman at the far end of the pool.

    She sat cross-legged on a long beach chair, tan body contrasting with a black two-piece, glistening in the sun. She removed her sunglasses and made direct eye contact with me. Even the shimmering blonde hair couldn't disguise her icy gray eyes. She gave me a cold wink as I mouthed her name.

    Blaire Devereaux.

Part VI

Vinyl Record

"We, the jury, unanimously find the defendant guilty of attempted bombing, as charged in count one of the indictment; guilty of attempted murder, as charged in count two of the indictment; guilty of attempted domestic terrorism, as charged in count three of the indictment."

The courtroom buzzed with excitement at the reading of the verdict. Cameras flashed, hundreds of pictures being taken at once. It sounded as if a flock of birds had taken off. I watched the bailiff cross the room, a tall, caramel-skinned man, who looked and behaved as if this wasn't his first rodeo. As he neared me, his size caught me off guard. He most likely could have picked up Nolan and I in each arm and carried us from the courtroom.

But he passed us and went to escort the defendant from the room. Nicole Peters was nearly level height with the bailiff in her spike heels. She looked as professional as anyone else in the room, aside from the unignorable steel handcuffs around her wrists. I rose from my seat behind the railing, as had everyone else in the courtroom, and she shot me a cold glance as she passed. Her face was drawn and pale, she looked as if she'd aged a decade since the first time I'd seen her on the pier in Virginia Beach. As she exited, my heart ached, thinking of how easily that could have been Nolan and I leaving the courtroom in cuffs.

The prosecutor, Robert Kelley, rose from his desk and offered us a handshake. "Mr. Quimby, Mr. Bragg, I greatly appreciate your testimonies today. You as well, Mr. Wexler. Justice was served in the court this time, although I can't say I'm quite satisfied."

Kelley's comment referred to the second suspect in the attempted bombing of the Paradise Hotel in Virginia Beach, four and a half months ago. Nicole Peters, who had–unbeknownst to us–handed off the bomb to Nolan and I, was the only suspect to be convicted thus far. Lance McGuire, Agent Wexler's Supervisory Special Agent, was believed by many to have played a significant role in the attempt. But while he hadn't left enough traces to find himself facing a judge, he had been discharged from his position, and released from employment by the FBI entirely. A number of reasons had been cited by the Bureau, ranging from carelessness in operation planning, to a more sinister possibility: suspected conspiracy to commit domestic terrorism.

Nolan and I had spent one confused and betrayed night in jail the night of the incident, and had been picked up by Wexler the next day and released into FBI custody. Things had moved fast, from the identification and apprehension of Peters, the charges against us being dropped, then to the firing of McGuire. Wexler had worked his hardest to gather enough evidence to warrant an arrest of his SSA, but that man had dusted his closet clean, as Wexler said.

Peters had been questioned again and again about McGuire's involvement, even offered a chance for a lighter sentence, but she claimed she had no idea who was involved. That had only raised suspicions higher. In a circumstance like that, Wexler said, "I don't know" translates to "I'm afraid to say". The case was far from settled, that was clear. It had been easy to convict Peters, the trial process only taking a few months, but with an unknown motive and no known accomplices, the case seemed to be at a standstill for now.

For all Nolan and I cared, it could stay that way forever, as long as we never had to see the inside of the Virginia Supreme Court again.

We stepped carefully down the few steps out of the courthouse, a fresh glaze having covered the cement. The first week of January had been especially cold, although I preferred the freezing temperatures rather than the usual forty-some degrees, not cold enough to turn rain to snow, so instead of a white Christmas we'd had an icy mist Christmas, which is far less romantic and more so depressing. We'd also been in Richmond for the past four days and had had no chance to celebrate my birthday, which fell on the day after New Years, but Nolan had promised a good old-fashioned "banger" when we got home, which I was hardly looking forward to.

To add to the holiday depression was the still absence of the particular woman who'd started the year-long avalanche that led to me testifying in court against a domestic terrorist. I found it rather rude when I considered it, the way Blaire Devereaux had thrown the stick into the spokes of my life, made me fall brain-numbingly in love with her, and disappeared. Since the time I'd seen her at the pool when we were arrested, there'd been nothing. Nolan had admitted to speaking to her that week, when she'd forced him to lie to me to throw me off her scent. All she'd told him was that it was a matter of our safety, and that if I didn't let off, we'd all wind up dead. So after that week and throughout the process of the attempted bombing investigation, I'd held still, knowing if she wanted to find me, she would. But lately, months passing with no word and seasonal affectiveness lowering my morale, I was beginning to lose hope.

Special Agent Phineas Wexler shook our hands as we parted ways at the parking garage, saying, "I appreciate all you've done boys. I suppose I'll see you around."

I slid into Nolan's Audi, saying, "With all due respect, Agent Wexler, I hope not."

It was nearing ten o'clock when we pulled into the driveway of my family's estate on the outskirts of Dixon. It being Thursday, I told Nolan to just drop me at the door, go home and get some decent sleep for the first time in about a week. I promised him we'd celebrate my birthday the following evening, then told him goodnight.

On my way inside I peered in the garage to make sure my car was tucked away safe and sound. I drove the classic Mustang very little in the winter months. It was common sense not to drive the salty and slushy roads with such an antique. Not to mention the convertible top was very unhandy against unkind weather.

After a welcome home from my parents, I descended into the basement lounge. I spent more time here than my own bedroom. It was a liveable apartment, really. A kitchenette, living area, bathroom and spare bedroom. It was the only part of the mansion that didn't make me feel as if I should be wearing a suit.

There was an odd surrealism in my mood that often occurred after an endeavor like the one we'd been working on in the past few months. For weeks at a time life would move a hundred miles an hour; life or death situations, matters of national security, affairs with law enforcement. Then it would stop. I was still human, leaves still grew and fell to the ground, life around me still functioned the way it had before. It was times like these, after forgetting about everything but the situation at hand, when I felt what John Koenig called *sonder*, "the realization that each random passerby is living a life as vivid and complex as your own". It's a hard thing to wrap your head around, so oftentimes I tried not to.

The thing to finally shake me out of my philosophical trance was the vinyl record lying on the counter. It was brand new, *The Essential Townes Van Zandt*. On the cover a message was scribbled. I squinted to read it.

Happy Birthday
- B

I flipped through the rolodex of my mind to try to discern who may have dropped off the gift. My mind seemed to go numb, trying to think but not being able to. I tried to read the note again, but my eyes couldn't focus. My heart slowed down, my hands became moist. I blinked, staring and wondering, trying with all my mental strength to think of anyone with the initial–anyone *else*. The moment felt so long, and the voice that followed sounded so distant I wondered if I really heard it.

"Sorry I didn't have time to wrap it."

No wonder every light had been off when I came down. The knuckles of my left hand turned white as I gripped the edge of the granite countertop. The silence in the room was a deafening ringing in my ears. I tried to remain conscious, tried not to fall to the ground in a heap of sobs. I knew the voice but refused to believe it.

My first attempt at words failed, but I breathed deeply and tried once more.

"Townes Van Zandt. How'd you know?"

"Because I know you." The voice was slightly clearer this time.

"I know you too," I answered. "Well enough to know I might get a hole in my chest if I turn around."

"Why would I do that?"

"There's a lot of things you've done that I haven't found a reason for. On second thought, I suppose I would already be whacked if that was your plan."

"I'd say you're safe this time, Quimby."

It took a moment to release my grip on the counter, suck in any tears that had nearly escaped, and turn to face the dark living room. My heart trembled as I made out the dark figure on the far sofa. I watched her hand reach to the end table to her left, pull the chain of the lamp, and illuminate her face.

I smiled.

Blaire smiled back.

"I see you've got a little blonde left," I commented. Her hair was cut at her shoulders, trying to speed up the removal of the color, but a few inches of the light hue remained. Otherwise, she looked the same as she had six months ago

"I could tell you liked it," she replied. "The way you couldn't stop staring while a police officer smashed your face into the ground."

"I've got you to thank for that," I said, slowly making my way into the living room. "Never thought of you as someone to call the cops on your best friend."

"It was either call the cops or watch you and Nolan blow up half of Virginia Beach. So, you're welcome."

My knees were so weak I was afraid I'd pass out, but I made it to the sofa and sat across from her. As if I was trying to gain the trust of a wild animal, I slid my trembling open palm across the cushion toward her. Eyes glistening with tears in the dim light, she laid her hand on mine, and only now was I sure she was real.

"Miss Devereaux," I said. "I believe we've got some things to talk about."

She sighed and held up a finger, stood, and walked to the kitchen. Taking the vinyl, she crossed the room to the record player. I watched her the whole way, every step taken perfectly, every movement swift and elegant. So many times before I'd stared at her this way. It all felt perfectly familiar in my mind.

She removed the James Taylor record currently seated on the turntable. Sliding it into the sleeve, she looked at me.

"You're such a hippy, Chris."

Placing the new record on the platter, she gently dropped the needle and turned it to a low volume. As the melody quietly began, she seated herself next to me, brought her knees to her chest, and rested her chin on them. It was a few more moments before she spoke. Her voice was so gentle, so broken through unsteady breaths.

"They threatened you. They told me there was a plan in place, and if I remained near you, you'd be killed, Nolan would be killed. If I tried to go after them, you'd be killed, Nolan would be killed. If I made any contact with you, you'd be killed, Nolan would be killed."

I raised an eyebrow. "Seems like you're breaking rule number one right now."

"The plan is over. They failed."

"What plan?" I asked. "The bomb?"

She wiped her face and spoke clearer. "Yes. They wanted to make it look like some sort of domestic terrorism. A bomb from a random 'organization in Central America' would easily be shrugged off as some sort of terrorism, and it almost did. If you hadn't gotten arrested, the bomb would've gone off, and you both would've been a million little rich pieces all over the place, and no one would've known the difference. But you were the only ones able to identify Peters before she could disappear. Terrible planning on their part too, because a caucasian woman was obviously a red flag, when she was supposed to have been from the 'organization in Central America'."

"But what was the plan to begin with?" I asked. "Blow up the Paradise Hotel?"

"You were the plan," she answered. "Nolan was the plan, and Wexler was the plan. You were scheduled to meet Wexler the next day, right?"

My jaw fell open as I came to realization. "They wanted all three of us."

"And they didn't want anyone to do any digging, hence the 'Central American informant'."

"Who is 'they'?" I asked.

"McGuire."

"I knew it."

"No, you didn't."

"Well," I stuttered. "I assumed it."

"McGuire was connected to Statham at the CIA somehow. After we put Statham away, the target went from just Wexler to all three of you."

"Why didn't they want you?" I asked bluntly.

She sighed. "Quite a few times they contacted me again, telling me they were interested in my 'skill set', implying that if we were to work out a deal, you and Nolan wouldn't be harmed. They wanted to use me, I guess. But I declined, ignored them altogether. I guess if I would've accepted, you may not have been in danger at all."

"If you'd have accepted," I said. "I still never would have seen you again. I would've rather been 'a million little rich pieces' than that."

She stared at me, processing my affectionate comment, then went on. "I was still clueless as to what their 'plan' was, and didn't pick up on it until that week in Virginia Beach."

I rolled my eyes. "Just so you know, I was on to you that week."

She shrugged. "Didn't get me, though."

"You cheated," I accused. "Making Nolan lie to me–I almost shot him, by the way. Not to mention the random old woman who said she was Janice Downey. What was that about?"

"Some lady I found in the next room over. Told her I was hiding from an ex-boyfriend. She played the part perfectly."

I went back to the situation at hand. "So, McGuire is still on the loose, right? What makes you think it's safe to come here now?"

"McGuire disappeared, didn't you hear? Dropped off the face of the earth. My guess is he made a run for it, skipped the country before the FBI dug up the real truth." She paused. "To be honest, I couldn't handle it anymore. I was looking for an excuse to come back."

"Couldn't handle what?"

She breathed heavily. "All of it. Hiding from you, from them, being afraid. . .and not being here with you."

The painful lump in my throat nearly burst. I put a hand on her cheek, and as I did, felt warm tears wet my palm. "I'm sorry," she hissed through sobs. "I didn't want to leave, you know I didn't."

"I know," I said, pulling her near me, letting her rest her head between my collar and jaw. The lump went away, and for some reason, I no longer felt like crying. For the first time in a long time, I was the comforter, not the sufferer. I held her tightly, the way I so desperately wanted to do for half a year, the way I had begun to believe I'd never do again.

Behind me, Townes Van Zandt sang a lullaby.

Friday morning was ice cold, a quick open-and-shut of the basement window told me it would be too cold to have my coffee on the front porch as I normally did. Blaire was not on the sofa where I'd left her the night before, which led me to wonder if it had all been a dream. I spent a minute rummaging around the room looking for some sort of proof that she'd been there. The vinyl still lay at the turntable where it had been, the cover was still signed "- *B*", and the sofa still smelled like her. The single backpack that had accompanied her still lay on the floor, and I had a notion of its probable contents, that of which she wouldn't have left without. For a moment I was concerned as to where she'd run off to, but I was confident she'd come back.

The worry was brief, for as I came up out of the basement to the kitchen, I found her sitting at the island, drinking coffee with my mother. This was extremely out of the ordinary for her, I knew she hated coffee, almost as much as she hated chit-chat.

My mother seemed nearly as happy at Blaire's return as I had been. I wondered what story Blaire had fabricated for her disappearance. My mother knew plenty about a lot of our escapades, and was slowly coming to accept the lifestyle that I had been somewhat forced into, but I didn't exactly divulge every threat against my life to her.

"Henry's already at the office," my mother said. "But I'm sure he'll be very happy to see you, Blaire. You know, he hasn't even opened your room to guests since you've been gone. I guess he was just waiting for you to come home."

This was news to me. I hadn't been to the Dixon Quimby Suites since Blaire's disappearance, and hadn't realized my father's devotion to her return. We talked very little, my father and I. Not that he didn't love and support me, I was living off his success, for goodness sake, but we were very different. My older brother Jared was the businessman of the family, and he was set to take over the company as soon as my father felt like retiring, although Henry Quimby would probably have a stroke the day he wasn't allowed to go to work. My easy trust-fund life was beginning to appear as a hindrance to my future. I was two-thirds of a year out of high school with no career path and no further education. Sure, I'd had a few outstanding circumstances that most graduates don't typically have, such as being arrested on suspicion of domestic terrorism, but I was still beginning to feel as if I had no real purpose in this world.

Although a large portion of my purpose had come home last night and fallen asleep on my shoulder.

Blaire no longer had a vehicle, she told me. She'd sold it during her temporary falling off the face of the earth. I'd never wondered about Blaire's financial situation, nor did I dare ask. She was humiliated enough at living rent-free in my father's hotel.

The Mustang rumbled and growled as it rolled out of the garage, angry at the cold. Despite the freezing air, there'd been no precipitation for the past few days, so the roads were dry, and the car took every turn and shift with grace, as she always had.

I parked outside The Grind, the coffee shop that Nolan and I used to frequent during high school. Life had caught up with us since then. Nolan now had classes at the Virginia School of Law three days out of the week, not to mention the time we'd spent in the last four months working with Wexler and other law enforcement and attorneys in the Nicole Peters case. At this point, I knew it was foolish to expect our endeavors with the FBI and every criminal we'd had an altercation with to go away and never return, but I was at least hoping for a breath of fresh air, for a while at least.

Jennifer Poole, Nolan's girlfriend of more than a year now, still worked at The Grind, where we'd first met her and Nolan had outshined me to win her affection. She was getting anxious, Nolan told me, to find a better, more "purposeful" job. I didn't blame her. She lived in a one-bedroom apartment on the second floor of a Main Street shop, her family lived several hours away, so her boyfriend and her occupation were the only things she spent time on. Like the rest of us, she'd been caught up in many of our recent episodes, not allowing her to give all her attention to a serious job. I told Nolan I'd help in any way I could, and had asked my father about an office job at the Quimby Suites Headquarters in Dixon. Nothing was available at the moment, he said, but as soon as there was, we'd be the first to know.

Nolan sat at a stool at the end of the counter, bothering Jennifer as she mixed coffee. He waved as he saw me enter, and froze at the sight of who'd walked in behind me, mouthing a few unrepeatable words of surprise. Jennifer shrieked with excitement and shouted out that she was on break.

Blaire offered a hug to her as she ran over, which surprised me, but Jennifer probably would've hugged her whether or not she offered, which Blaire knew. Nolan seemed awkward and couldn't decide what to say to her. They had almost as complicated a relationship as she and I had. The very beginning of our complicated chain of events had been started by Blaire being ordered to kidnap Nolan. They trusted each other and worked together, but often butted heads in the heat of the moment. Nolan had actually been the only one to speak to her during her disappearance, when she'd forced him to lie in order to get me off her scent.

After we'd made our way to the corner booth, knowing they were as anxious to learn what had happened to her as I'd been, Blaire wasted no time in giving the same details of the past several months that she'd given me. Nolan didn't move once, while Jennifer did the opposite, having exaggerated reactions to every point of the story.

I sat in the corner, head against my fist, smiling, sipping coffee. The feeling was so surreal, to be in the same place the four of us had sat so many months ago. I had changed so much in the past year it nearly hurt my heart to think about. I didn't consider myself much of a people person. Although I enjoyed going out and didn't mind a crowd, it was usually difficult and uncomfortable to be personal with someone, to have an in-depth conversation. I'd been accused of being rude and short with people, which was unintentional, I was simply just bad at making conversation with someone who I wasn't interested in talking to. But this group that I sat amongst at this booth, I could've sat with the rest of my life and never spoke to anyone else again.

Nolan made eye contact with me, noticing my pleased expression, and smiled the way a father smiles after giving his son a puppy, just happy to see me happy. He'd seen me at my worst after losing Blaire, and had taken care of me and kept me above water. I owed the world to him. If he hadn't been there I may have taken a turn down some dark roads and never found my way home.

The sunlight glaring through the glass front wall of the coffee shop was temporarily blocked by an extra large man entering. Peeking over the top of the booth to see this giant, I made eye contact with him, and he pointed at me with an excited expression.

Gabriel McDowell rushed to our booth to say hello. "Thought that was your car outside. Been a while, huh? Hey, Blaire! Nice to see you're back in town." He spoke as if to himself, hurriedly skipping through pleasantries. It was odd to see him outside of his cramped two-bedroom apartment, not hunched over a computer. We'd met in high school, he was a few classes ahead of me, but he'd become essential in many of our past exploits as he was a genius with most things in the field of technology. He was currently earning a Bachelor's degree in Information Technology at the University of Virginia, but in my opinion he was bound for greater things than your average IT guy. He was large, not overweight but not very fit. His sandy blonde hair was unkempt, and he cared too little to shave. He was friendly overall, but didn't seem like someone to go out of their way to make conversation with people he hadn't spoken to in months.

He soon made it clear that he hadn't just stopped by to say hello.

"You know," he said in a lower tone. "I've actually got something serious going on that I need your help with. Life or death, to be honest."

Jennifer excused herself, her break was over, and we invited Gabe to sit with us, asking him to explain.

He hesitated, then finally, lowering his voice, he said, "Someone is trying to kill me."

No one spoke, just stared at him, making sure we heard him right.

"Someone is trying to kill you?" I whispered.

He nodded.

Taking the opportunity to put on my best Sherlock Holmes, I spoke the way he would in a situation such as this. Leaning back, I gestured with my hand. "Pray, disclose the facts of your case so that I may shine some light upon them."

Blaire glared at me for joking around in a serious situation. Just like old times, she hadn't spoken in ten minutes but made her presence known by letting me know how stupid I acted at any given time. I apologized and told him to go on.

He was soft spoken to begin with, and the tall booth helped to hold in his words as he began. "Well, over the past week, there have been three different instances where my life has been threatened. You can say I'm stupid for thinking this way, but to me it seemed pretty obvious that someone is out to get me, for whatever reason I have no idea. I even talked to the police about it, but they tell me I'm just paranoid and that these are all coincidences or I'm blowing the situations out of proportion. So much for *"protect and serve"*.

"First, on Sunday, New Years Day, I was walking on the sidewalk, a block from my apartment complex. My dad and I had walked from my place down to that cheap Chinese restaurant on Third Street that never gets your order right. They were the only place open."

"Love that place," Nolan commented.

"Me too," I agreed.

Blaire kicked my ankle and I shut up once more.

"Anyway," Gabe went on. "We're walking back to my apartment, when a car behind us swerves off the road, up onto the curb and tries to run us over. The only reason we heard them and got out of the way was because their bumper scraped on the curb when they jumped it with their right wheel. We jumped away and the car bounced back onto the road and sped off. And before you ask, just like the police did, I didn't read the license plate. Nobody in real life thinks fast enough to memorize a license plate after they almost get killed. But I did recognize the car from when we'd been walking *to* the restaurant. They had driven slowly when they passed us, and when we looked at them, they sped off. They had obviously been looking at us for some reason. Anyway, it was a dark blue SUV. I think it was a Hyundai, but it might've been a Subaru."

"Definitely seems intentional," I said. "If it was just a random car, they could've possibly lost control and went onto the curb, but the fact that you saw them driving strange earlier makes it seem like they knew you."

"But," Gabe said. "It's still possible that they were impaired or just stupid, which is why I didn't think about it for too long. But then on Tuesday, something else happened. I had college classes all day, my first day back from winter break. So my dad picked up groceries for me, and when he got to my place around noon, a police officer was at my front door. My landlord said someone had been snooping around my apartment, and he even watched him jiggle my doorknob and try to pull my window open, so he called the police. The guy disappeared before the officer got there, and the only description the landlord could give was that he was an average height caucasian male, slightly overweight, not helpful whatsoever."

Blaire still hadn't spoken, but I could see her mind churning as she stared at him, chin on her fists. This second story made the first instance seem much more substantial. Deeply interested now, neither Nolan nor I made a comment. Just nodded, waiting for him to go on.

"So after one restless night in my apartment, I asked my dad if I could stay at his place Wednesday night, just to get some decent sleep. His stupid roommate works a night shift, so she wasn't around to harass me. Anyway, that night as I'm trying to sleep on his couch, obviously still shook up from the first few days of the week, I'm all paranoid, seeing shadows and whatnot like a child afraid of monsters. My dad has one of those fancy security doorbell systems, and sometime around midnight, the alarm goes off. I was still awake in the living room, not far from the front door, so I got to the front window within a few seconds and saw someone running away from the house. My dad's neighborhood doesn't have streetlights, so I didn't see him after he was out of the driveway.

"On Thursday I tried the police, they pretty much told me where to stick it, so now I'm trying you. I know how often you guys deal with stuff like this, and I know you're just coming off of that court case in Richmond–very cool, by the way–and, let's be honest, you owe me one after all the not-very-legal stuff I've pulled for you guys. If you really don't want to get involved, I understand, it's risky business, but if you can help in any way, I would appreciate it."

My mind was racing, and I could tell Nolan's incredible brain was struggling to contain all the information as well. Gabe had a point, he had done a lot for us in the past and we hadn't shown him enough appreciation. I tried to come up with an answer, knowing he waited for one. I looked at Blaire, afraid that she would balk at the potential conflict after just arriving home. I read her glance like a book, all the reassurance I needed.

"We'll do it."

Bob Teller, manager of Dixon's Quimby Suites, lit up at the sight of Blaire as we entered the lobby. He greeted her excitedly, telling her how he'd missed seeing her around, and assuring her that her suite was just as it had been when she left. She shyly thanked him and tried to get away from the conversation without being rude. He hurriedly retrieved her room key from where he'd kept it in his desk and we eventually escaped his friendliness.

In the elevator, I asked, "What happened to your car?" She'd driven a blue Mazda sedan for the majority of her stint in Dixon the first time.

"Sold it," she said. "It was getting expensive living in hotels and having no job. Not to mention it was another way for you or McGuire to keep track of me."

Blaire's suite was, indeed, exactly the way she'd left it. I cussed myself in my mind for not having recalled how terrible a scene it was. I heard her breath skip at the sight of it. In the living area, several empty liquor bottles from the mini bar littered the floor, an opened laptop with a smashed screen lay on the couch, cabinet doors hung open. I couldn't believe none of the staff had even come in to clean it in six and a half months.

I apologized frantically, asking if she wanted to let the cleaning crew take care of it before she moved back in. She pushed me aside, whispering, "No, I'm okay."

The bedroom was worse. The bed was messily unmade, more bottles were scattered throughout, the whole room smelled of alcohol. Her phone lay broken in the corner, where I'd thrown it out of rage upon discovering her disappearance.

Blaire sat gingerly on the edge of the bed as I silently cleaned up, tossing things into the trash can, draining the bathtub that still held old water and a floating mini whiskey bottle. I stopped as she began to speak.

"It was an encrypted email," she said. "Untraceable, too. The message was so formal, so much like any average email aside from the actual words. I spent an hour trying to figure out where it came from. It wasn't until months later that I learned it had been McGuire and his people. Eventually I gave up, stumbled around this place all night, trying to think of what to do. I don't know what compelled me to drink all night, I hardly ever touched alcohol. I took a drunk bath, as if that was going to help, thought about drowning myself right there. I wanted to stay so badly, but every time I considered it I thought of my mother. Back when Neil Trace threatened me if I didn't work for him, and I called his bluff, and just like that she was dead. I knew better than to do that to you."

She didn't cry this time, as if she'd come to terms with all that had happened. It was reassuring to me, because if Blaire was no longer concerned, I felt little reason that I should be. The whole idea of Lance McGuire suddenly "disappearing" still didn't sit right with me, but Blaire seemed to not dwell on it, so I tried not to either.

I sat down next to her. "It's all over now, right?"

She laid her head on my shoulder, something so rare yet the feeling was so familiar. "Yeah. All over."

I was about to ask how she felt about helping Gabe when she spoke again.

"Remember at Howard Statham's house?"

My heart sped up. "Yeah, which part?"

"When he hit me over the head with his gun, held it on me and tried to take me with him." She touched a small, nearly faded scar above her eyebrow.

"Yeah," I said. "I remember. Still can't believe he got the drop on you."

"Do you know why?" she asked, looking at me.

"Why?"

"I was thinking about you, and about earlier that night."

I knew she could feel the heartbeat in my chest. I could feel it in my throat. "Hasn't a day gone by when I didn't think about it," I said softly.

"Are you thinking about it now?"

The smell of liquor was suddenly drowned out by the scent of Blaire's soft black and blonde hair as it grazed my face. As she kissed me, I began to wonder if the girl who I'd fallen so unconsciously in love with had begun to feel the same.

Crazier things have happened.

Nolan and I awaited Gabe in the weight room on the second floor of my garage, where much of our more dire business took place. We decided to meet here rather than his apartment, just to be cautious of anyone that may have been keeping an eye on his place.

I hadn't spoken to Nolan alone since we'd made the deal with Gabe at The Grind. He was quiet now, scrolling through his phone, chin on his fist. Not that he was ever overly talkative. He and I spent a lot of time sitting in each other's silence, satisfied with being in the same room, not finding it essential to fill empty space. But now it seemed necessary.

"Something wrong?" I asked.

He shrugged.

"What?" I prodded.

He rubbed his forehead and sighed before speaking. "I'm just a little hesitant to be getting into all of this. Twenty-four hours ago we were sitting in the courtroom in Richmond and now we're already mixed up in this."

"I know," I agreed. "Seems like stuff just piles on. Have you ever even heard of any kind of murder conspiracy in Dixon? The last thing I remember was when that homeowner got shot in a break-in. That was big news in fifth grade."

"Makes you wonder," he said sluggishly.

"Wonder what?"

"Well lately it just seems like a given that we're going to get caught up in something like this. It just makes me wonder if this has anything to do with us, not just Gabe. Seems like quite a coincidence."

"Well, either way," I said. "We owe him a good deal for everything he's done for us, and if he's convinced someone is really after him, the least we can do is look into it."

"No, the least we could do is nothing, because we're tired of risking our lives for other people."

I looked over at him, he stared at the floor.

"You don't have to be a part of this if you don't want to," I said.

"Of course I do," he said. "We owe him, like you said, but that doesn't mean I have to be excited about it. I don't totally enjoy all this the way you do, Chris. Remember, I didn't have a very glamorous introduction into this lifestyle."

"I know you didn't," I said. "Neither did I, but I've learned to live with it and keep up."

"Not just live with it," he said. "You've embraced it. You love it, whether you admit it or not. You get excited every time something like this comes up, just like you did this morning. Every time you get into one of your self-destructive slumps, another life or death situation comes along and just like that you're raring to go. I can't always live that life Chris, I've got something to live for. I've got a career in law ahead of me, that's what excites me. I've got Jennifer, and I'm tired of having to tell her that I can't come over tonight because I have to gun down a criminal. Don't you realize how ridiculous of a sentence that is?"

"I'm sorry," I said sarcastically. "I'm not 'like' you. You have a real life ahead of you, and things to live for. I obviously don't have things to live for, is that what you mean?"

"You know that's not what I meant, don't put words in my mouth." He was on his feet now. At first I remained where I was, but he walked as he spoke, and I couldn't remain seated as he stood directly in front of me. "Just try to understand what I'm saying without taking offense to it."

"Tell me how you feel without making me look like a loser in the process," I shot back.

The side door of the garage opened and shut below us, ending our dispute. I hadn't been in a brawl with Nolan in years for any reason besides fun, but I was ready to before Gabe showed up. Even as we talked to him, asked him questions, brain-stormed plans, I couldn't get out of my mind that Nolan didn't want to be a part of this. The distance between us now felt greater than one side of the room to the other.

Friday evening brought snow, the first of the season in our part of Virginia. As I walked from the house down to the garage, I stopped and stood among it as the wet flakes fell onto the fibers of my sherpa-lined jacket. The sky was dark, not a star to be seen, and I lost myself in it as

I stood in the stillness. I often grew afraid at the sight of the sky above me, as odd as it sounds. It amazed me, how vast and endless it was. When I stared directly into the darkness, losing my perspective of up and down, it felt as though I could jump right into the heavens and fall forever. The longer I stared, the harder it was to keep my balance.

Just as I felt as though I'd begun to levitate, the yellow lanterns at the garage flicked on, as they did every evening at eight o'clock, bringing me back down. I drove my father's spare car this evening, afraid to take my ragtop out in this weather. He'd also put his pride and joy away for the winter, the '72 Oldsmobile Cutlass he'd bought and restored himself. My love for classic cars was hereditary, the Mustang I called mine had been his, which he'd given to me as a birthday present a few years prior. I didn't like to disclose that fact to people, it only boosted my reputation as a spoiled trust fund baby. Someday, I told myself, I'd repay him for all he'd given me and done for me. But how do you repay the man who has everything, all of which he'd earned off his own back?

That concern faded, as it usually did, as I pulled under the *porte cochère* to pick up Blaire. I could see into the foyer, she wasn't waiting there for me. I felt a too-familiar knot in my stomach as I entered, praying that history hadn't repeated itself. The thought had crossed my mind earlier, that kissing her could've frightened her, but it had been her who'd instigated it, and she'd acted alright when I'd left a few moments later. A guest looked at me peculiarly as I nervously tapped the elevator button again and again. It was still on the fifth floor, the meter said, so I hurried up the stairwell instead.

I was only working myself up. The longer I thought, the more I was sure she was gone again. I had to make an effort not to sprint down the hall to her door. I knocked loudly, she didn't answer. I waited five seconds, which in my mind had been a minute and a half. I knocked again, calling her name. Five more seconds passed, I jiggled the doorknob. I was afraid I'd broken the lock when the handle suddenly turned and the door fell open. I nearly stumbled into Blaire, having had my ear to the door.

"What is wrong with you?" she hissed angrily. "I'm trying to get dressed, can you keep your pants on?"

I stuttered, embarrassed. "You're always early–you used to wait in the lobby–I just worried."

"Afraid I'm gonna run out on you again?" she asked with a devious smirk. "Maybe I just want to look nice to go out for your birthday."

She left me waiting in the living room as she returned to her bedroom. "What is it?" I asked jokingly. "Couldn't decide what shade of black to wear?" I heard a faint "shut up" through the wall.

After a few minutes she emerged from the bedroom. As if I wasn't already smitten enough from her coquettish comments, her entrancing appearance now left me searching for breath. Much of her wardrobe had remained in the room at her urgent departure, waiting for her return. The dark houndstooth overcoat still found a way to compliment her figure, and the turtleneck underneath made her look all the more elegant.

"Instead of staring," she said in her usual tone. "You could try: 'You look nice, Blaire'."

I held the door for her, repeating with a smile, "You look nice, Blaire."

"Thank you, kind sir," she replied sarcastically. She kissed my cheek, something I hadn't imagined her capable of, and we made our way to the car.

The original schedule for the evening was to spend a few hours at a restaurant before initiating the plan we'd made with Gabe, but as we walked out the lobby doors and I held the passenger door for Blaire, the itinerary changed dramatically. Three unmarked cruisers with police light bars pulled into the parking lot of the hotel. At first I was curious, but Blaire's curse beside me let me know that we were the persons of interest.

"Get in the car," she hissed. "Now."

I did so.

"Do they know this car?" she asked. "Will they expect you to be driving it?"

"Probably not," I said. "It's my dad's spare, it hardly gets driven, especially not by me."

"Then drive casually–around the building and out the back exit, not past them."

As we reached the street and the police remained behind us, I barraged her with questions, most of which could be summarized as, "What the hell is going on?"

"I'll explain later, just get us out of here," was all she responded with.

"Explain now," I said. "Why would they be interested in you? You're just a regular person, remember?"

Before she responded, headlights swung quickly into my rear view mirror, then another set, then another. I remained at a lawful speed, until I realized my followers were catching up quickly. I could tell they didn't want to queue any action before I did as we both casually picked up speed. I tried to hold the distance between us and they tried to close it. Finally, the first set of flashing lights, followed by two more.

Before I could ask, Blaire answered. "Go."

I did. The Mercedes sped up to seventy in a second, and we raced past the last street light onto the only state highway running through Dixon. "What do you want me to do?" I questioned Blaire. "I can't lose them."

"You're going to have to," she said. "I don't care if you have to drive through a cornfield, I'm not giving myself up until I talk to–" She cut off.

"Who?" I asked. "Who do you have to talk to, and about what? Why would you have to give yourself up? What do they want?" Ignoring me again, she demanded my phone. I refused. She gave me a cruel look, a warning I knew too well, but I held my ground. "Tell me who you have to talk to."

She punched me square in the face, making me swerve, and before I recovered, she was already dialing on my cell phone. She hid the screen and turned the volume down, all I could do was fume and trust her to get whatever this mess was under control. Behind me, lights still flashed, but I knew these roads better than they did, and my car could take the hilly turns better than theirs. The roads were wet from the snow, but it wasn't cold enough for the asphalt to be slick. Either way, I was thankful now not to be driving the Mustang.

Blaire spoke minimally, still trying to hide the situation from me. Every time I demanded an answer, she told me to shut up. She told this secret partner that the FBI was after us, no we don't know what agents, yes we can lose them. She was silent for thirty seconds as her acquaintance apparently spoke. Finally she ended with an "okay" and hung up.

I was now too focused on the task at hand than questioning her, she wouldn't answer anyway. I was taking turns at sixty miles an hour and hitting ninety on straight stretches. I wanted to make sure I was completely out of sight before turning onto another road. I knew which one I wanted, it was coming up in another half mile. It was Nolan's old road, where he'd lived until middle school. I'd spent more time there than my own home during those summers, back when the only dread in our life was when August came around. At the bottom of a hill, at a moment I knew none of the chasers had eyes on us, I hit the brakes. The wet roads helped me glide instead of skid, so I left no tire tracks. Swerving onto the little county road, I shut off the lights and trusted my memory and a faint white line to keep me on the asphalt. The road was lined with trees, and between the starless sky and jet black paint of the car, we were virtually invisible.

  Blaire watched behind me as the FBI cars blew past the road we'd turned onto. I didn't turn the lights back on until there was no risk of them seeing our glow. Switching them back on, I made several more turns onto smaller and curvier roads, and drove another four miles in the opposite direction, until we came into the community of Freeport. It was really no town at all, just a buffer between Dixon and the larger surrounding towns. The only road through the little settlement held a gas station, a church, and a grocery store. I chose the church parking lot as it was the least illuminated and wrapped around the back of the building, where I stopped the car and killed the lights once more.

  "Out with it." I said. She raised her hands as she prepared to tell me to calm down, and I grabbed her wrist. She looked at me in bewilderment, never having been caught off guard by me this way. My confrontation held less weight than usual since I had no gun to point at her, which was becoming a bad habit of mine. "Tell me what's going on or I'll turn you in myself."

  She raised an eyebrow but didn't speak.

"Does it have something to do with McGuire?" I asked.

"Why would it? McGuire's gone, remember? Disappeared."

"When? When did McGuire disappear? How did you find out about it? Why didn't I find out about it when I spoke to Wexler and the prosecutor a few hours before you told me? I'm not an idiot, Blaire. You had something to do with it. I want to know what's going on. If the next word out of your mouth involves anything besides McGuire, I swear I'll throw you out of this car and go home."

She stared back at me, her wrist still in my grasp. Her nostrils flared like a wild horse as I held her in this standstill. It wasn't anger in her eyes like it usually was, just a blank, cool stare, like her physical form had paused as her mind raced. Finally, she leaned forward and those ice-cold gray eyes narrowed.

"Yes, I had something to do with it, I had everything to do with it. He was on the ropes, he was losing, and I ended it. I wanted it over. McGuire was all they had left, so I severed it before he could add another head to the snake. Maybe I'll explain it better to you sometime, or someone else will, but all you need to know is I did it for you, just like I've done everything else. I was tired of watching it get drug out, hoping that you or the Feds would put them all away. I ended it myself, so I could come home to you, so I could know that you wouldn't get shot if you stepped outside with me. I did it because I couldn't stand following you around, watching you suffer for months and months because you needed me as badly as I needed you, because you loved me as much as I loved you. So if the next words out of *your* mouth aren't 'thank you', I'll throw *you* out of the car and go home." She ended her admission with a piercing smirk.

"Thank you," was all I could manage.

"You're welcome. Now let's make our way back and get ready to head to Gabe's apartment."

"You're still worried about the plan with Gabe?" I asked incredulously. "The FBI is still scouring the country for you."

"Help is on the way," she explained.

"Who is 'help'?" I asked. "Who is this secret partner?"

"I'm not at liberty to disclose that, you'll probably find out soon enough. But we made the deal with Gabe, we have to follow through. We'll be out of sight at his place anyway, no one else knows our plans. Just drive, I'll call Nolan." So I warily pulled away from the church and worked my way along the most untraceable route to Dixon I could find, all the while only thinking of Blaire's last statement.

You loved me as much as I loved you.

Gabe's apartment was on the second and top level of a long brick complex. Every apartment was identical, he told us: two dank bedrooms, a kitchen not wide enough for two people, a bathroom, and a living area big enough for a single couch, which all added up to roughly six hundred square feet, or so the lease said.

We met in the parking lot of the Chinese restaurant down the street from the complex. Blaire and I had snuck the car back to my house and been picked up by Nolan. If the FBI happened to be cruising the streets and recognized our vehicle, it wouldn't take long to completely ruin the task at hand. We'd developed the plan earlier and we now went over it again to fill in Blaire, and to make sure we were all on the same page.

Nolan set out on foot towards the apartment, while Blaire and Gabe parked in Nolan's car–unrecognizable to the FBI and to whoever may be attempting to harm Gabe–across the street from the complex, with a direct view to the front door. Someone had to keep an eye on Gabe in case his attacker was onto us, while also keeping a look out for whoever may come toward the apartment.

Although I was four inches shorter than Gabe, I was nearer his size than Nolan was, so I was delegated to "play" him. The cold night justified my layers of clothes and hat that hid my appearance as I parked Gabe's car in his parking spot, and walked up the metal stairwell to the balcony of the second level. The complex was set up similarly to a motel, every door facing out, which is what gave anyone nearby a view of Gabe's front door.

I was trembling as I unlocked the door, partially from adrenaline, and partially from cold, but mostly out of pure fear as to what trap may be set inside. My left hand was on the pistol inside my jacket as my right hand turned the doorknob and pushed it open. I was still alive as I faced the seemingly empty apartment. Still alive as I stepped inside and shut the door behind me. Still alive as I frantically–but cautiously–searched the place, ready to shoot the first thing that moved. I went through every closet, cabinet, nook and cranny, but found nothing to warrant any suspicion.

The longer I'd thought on the situation, the more I was beginning to believe we were blowing it out of proportion. There really was no concrete evidence to say that Gabe McDowell's life was in danger, at least not at the hands of another human being. When we asked what he thought may be the motive behind it, the only thing he could come up with was his part in our escapades, the work he'd done behind the scenes for us. We had learned very little about possible suspects. He said the only people he had regular contact with were his mother, his sister, his father, and his father's roommate, whom he was too ashamed to call his girlfriend. That subject, Gabe had said, was just another can of worms that had no use being opened.

As I took my position in waiting, I wondered how sensible these lengths we were going to were. Even if Gabe *was* in some sort of danger, what were the chances that his assailant would make a move tonight while we happened to be waiting for them? It seemed to me that we had much more serious matters at hand with the FBI than some wild goose chase for a would-be murderer. Still, I stood in the corner of the front wall, where in the case that the door would be opened, I would be hidden behind it, and would have the drop on whoever entered.

An hour passed, and nothing. There was little communication between us, aside from a check-up text every fifteen minutes or so. Blaire had ditched most of her equipment and utilities during her fall from the face of the earth, so we no longer had any of her high-end espionage technology. Just a good old-fashioned cell phone and Ruger Compact.

I wished I had a moment to talk to Nolan, apologize for my temper earlier in the day, and explain all that had gone on since then. He currently sat among the line of hedges along the edge of the parking lot, a few spaces down from Gabe's car, the closest he could get to the apartment without raising a red flag to whoever tried to reach it. I felt guilty, putting him in harm's way once again. Whatever he had been trying to say earlier, he was right. He had a very bright future ahead of him, not to mention his life currently. I told myself now that the next time something of this nature came up, because I knew it would eventually, I would do my best to leave Nolan out of it. He was my best friend, I loved him as much if not more than my own brother, and I would rather him be safe than risk his life just to support me.

My watch read 12:02 when the rapid buzzing in my pocket gave me a near-heart attack. I answered the call from Blaire on the burner phone Gabe had acquired for her. "What?"

"Find anything suspicious?" she asked.

"No, nothing. Did you hear anything from Nolan?"

"Just that he hadn't seen anything either. Only one car has pulled into the complex since you did, and we watched them go into their apartment on the first floor. Gabe is starting to wonder if he's overreacting about this and he says he doesn't want to waste our time since we have a bit of a predicament on our own hands. I told him we'd give it another hour, and if it's still dry, we'll hang it up for the night and just keep an eye on him for a while. Sound good to you?"

It sounded great to me, I was tired of standing alone in the corner of the dark, empty apartment. I tried to hide my relief as I responded. "That'll work. Did you tell Nolan or should I?"

She didn't respond. I heard mumbling, probably from Gabe.

"Blaire?" I said. "You still there?"

"Yes, sorry, shut up. Another car pulled in, they're parking next to Gabe's car. . .looks like a woman. . .she's carrying something with both hands. . .it's all wrapped up, I can't tell what it is. Looks like she's going upstairs."

As I began to panic, Nolan called, so I hung up on Blaire and answered.

"Yeah?"

"Chris, some woman just parked next to you and she's coming up the stairwell. She's carrying something–"

"Yes, I know," I hissed. "What is she carrying?"

"I couldn't tell, she's got it half hidden in her coat and wrapped up. Seems decent-sized, she's carrying it with both arms. She's up to the second floor. . .she stopped at your door!"

I hung up and stood in waiting. Both hands shaking on my gun, I listened as the locked doorknob shook, followed by a knock. What kind of murderer knocks on the door to be let inside? Eventually, I heard keys and the knob jiggled as it was unlocked. Who could possibly have a key to Gabe's apartment? I cussed myself now for not having asked that question in advance.

My heart pounded in my chest so powerfully I worried the assailant would hear it. Finally, the door creaked open, and I watched the back of the short woman as she entered, then closed the door behind her.

"Gabe, are you here?"

"Don't move."

She did, in fact, move. She jumped, whirled, and screamed. She nearly dropped what she'd been carrying, which turned out to not be a bomb, firearm, or other tool of assassination, but a bundled up, red-faced infant, who also now screamed. Together, the two of them could've drowned out any shot that I may have wildly fired, but luckily, I held my composure and waited for at least one of them to shut up.

"Who are you?" I asked.

"Who are you?" she asked, sobbing and cowering, covering the baby.

"I asked you first."

"I'm Daisy," she cried.

I knew the name, and now realized the girl was indeed no more than sixteen. "Gabe's sister, Daisy?"

"Yes, Gabe's sister!"

"So, Daisy, Gabe's sister, are you interested in murdering Gabe tonight or know anyone who is?" Her next exclamation seemed too colorful to say around the baby, but in hindsight, he was still screaming with every ounce of his small being. I took it all simply as a "no".

"So what are you doing here?" I asked, just as Nolan burst through the door, igniting a second round of screams from Daisy McDowell and the unidentified baby. I also nearly blew his head off in surprise.

"Relax," I told him. "It's Gabe's sister."

"Nolan Bragg?" asked the girl, squinting in recognition.

"Um, no."

She now looked at me and pointed. "Chris Quimby. You guys graduated from Dixon last year. What are you doing?"

I ignored her and continued questioning. "Why are you here?"

"Gabe called me and said he was sick, and asked if I could bring him some Tylenol and NyQuil." She pulled both medications from her pocket.

"Who is this?" Nolan asked, gesturing to the infant, still wailing. "You're not old enough to have a kid."

"Of course this isn't my kid. This is my brother, Henry."

"Brother?" I asked, confused.

"Well, half brother," she explained. "The product of my deadbeat dad's affair with his so-called 'roommate', Allison, and now I'm stuck taking care of him while she works her night shift at *Jocelyn's*. Not like I have a choice, my mom moved all the way up to Charlottesville simply out of hatred for my dad–"

"Wait," I interrupted her rant. "*Gabe* called *you*? When?"

"Like twenty minutes ago. I got the stuff out of the medicine cabinet at my dad's house, bundled up Henry, and drove over here. Where the hell is Gabe?"

I grew suspicious, and a phone call brought Gabe and Blaire up to the apartment. As soon as he entered the door I had him against the wall. He may have been twice my size, but he was completely non confrontational and it was easy to catch him off guard. He had the build of a linebacker but the attitude of a placekicker. I accusingly questioned him about the apparent call bringing his sister here.

"I have no idea what you're talking about!" he exclaimed. He seemed just as surprised to see Daisy as I'd been, and Blaire backed up his alibi, saying he hadn't called anyone as long as she'd been in the car with him.

But the recent call on Daisy's phone was from Gabe's number.

"That's impossible," he said. "You had to have been able to tell it wasn't my voice."

"Well," Daisy defended. "The voice was all deep and scratchy. I figured you must've been pretty sick."

"It could've been one of those 'spoof' numbers," Nolan said. "There's apps you can download to make calls from a different phone number. Me and Chris used to–never mind." He didn't continue the tale of our past harmless misdemeanors.

But why would someone want to get Daisy to Gabe's apartment? Was Daisy's life also at risk and the assailant wanted the two of them together? Pacing the room, my mind began to work, and for a moment I thought of the scene backwards. Perhaps the call wasn't made to get Daisy *to* Gabe's apartment, but instead to get her *out* of her father's house. From there I thought of why she'd been there: the baby, the roommate, the affair, the father. . .the sidewalk, the groceries, the alarm. . .

"Oh my gosh," I hissed, staring at Nolan, then Blaire, then Gabe. "Your father."

"What about my father?" Gabe stared blankly.

"It's him. It's not you, it's him." I rambled for the next three minutes, trying as hard as I could to release every ounce of realization that was flooding into my mind, like trying to pour out a glass that sat under a faucet.

Gabe's father, Steve, was beginning to seem like a very disliked person, especially by the female members of the estranged McDowell family. I assumed the timeline was as follows: first came the affair with Allison in which she'd become pregnant with Henry, at which point the McDowells split, Gabe's mother moved to Charlottesville, and Steve and Allison moved in together. From the sound of it, Steve McDowell had much more reason to be on a chopping block than his son.

Next I recalled Gabe's account of the past week, the three instances in which he'd felt his life had been in jeopardy. "The walk with your dad from the Chinese restaurant when the car almost hit you," I said aloud. "Do you remember which of you was walking nearest the road?" Gabe stared in thought, but said he didn't remember. "What if the car was waiting for him to walk on the outside? That's why they drove past you the first time, because you were in the way, but on the way back, your father was the one in position to be hit."

Everyone in the room, aside from Henry, I suppose, began to come to the same conclusion I'd drawn, but I went on. "The guy that tried to break into your apartment wasn't setting a trap for you, Gabe, but for the person who was headed to your apartment with groceries:

your dad. He would've gotten there before you, and would've been the victim of whatever the intruder had gone there to do."

Nolan blurted out the third part of the recollection as he put the final piece together in his mind. "And the person that set off the alarm at your father's house wasn't there for you."

"He was there for him," Gabe finished.

"Let's go," Blaire said, and led the way out the door. Gabe told Daisy to stay at the apartment where it was safe, and announced he'd lead the way to his father's house.

My heart pounded through my chest, a cold sweat ran through my upper body, and adrenaline shook my extremities. It felt familiar, just like all the times before, except one thing was different in the back of my mind, the same thing I'd argued about with Nolan hours before. I felt fear now, because I had more to lose than I had before. She sat quietly in the backseat, and as I turned and made eye contact with her, I could tell she was thinking the same thing.

The scene at Steve McDowell's house could be read like a book when we arrived. As the four of us came to the front porch, we found the doorbell camera ripped from its mount, but the alarm still sounded. The front door was kicked open, the jamb splintered and broken. Apparently, the attacker was making this their final attempt, no matter the circumstance.

Blaire and I cleared the dining and living room as Nolan and Gabe hurried up the stairs from which came desperate shouts and swears. Gabe, inexperienced and fueled by emotion, burst through the half-opened bedroom door unarmed, and was lucky to not have his head blown off.

"*Mom!*" I heard him scream. I was witnessing the scene mostly through sound as I was still at the bottom of the stairs. Aside from Gabe's exclamation, I heard one from a woman, and another from a man whom I decided was Steve after he called Gabe by name. Nolan entered the room behind him, gun aimed, but as we reached the top of the steps behind him, I saw him take a blow from the shoulder of a black-clad man and fall to the floor. A lamp fell and shattered, and a fourth voice entered the scene.

"Everyone against the wall and drop your guns!" the voice shouted. Blaire and I immediately stuck to the wall outside the bedroom, knowing our presence was still unknown. I tried to paint a picture of the scene in my mind. The man who'd hit Nolan must've been the partner of Gabe's mother, who I knew was also in the room. Steve McDowell was most likely being held at gunpoint already, and now Gabe and Nolan had joined him.

In movies, dialogue in action scenes are often well-scripted, thought out, and extravagant, while in real life it is simply a mixture of shouts, curses, and screams. This sequence seemed to last at least a few minutes, while in reality, it was hardly thirty seconds. Blaire grabbed me by the shirt and whispered, "On my cue, kick the door open and take them down." She shoved me to the door that now stood slightly ajar, ten feet from where she stood.

With no further warning, she fired through the wall and leapt away. I heard the gunman's indistinct shout as a barrage of bullets peppered the area where she'd been standing. In the moment that he was distracted, I kicked open the bedroom door. The half second it took for the shooter to redirect his aim was a half second too long. My bullet hit him in the right shoulder and he fell to the ground with a scream. Nolan had crossed the room with two lunges and knocked Gabe's mother against the wall. Her pistol fell from hands it had no place being in, and she fell to the ground in a sob, a broken wife blinded by hatred.

Somehow, one of the wild shots made by Mrs. McDowell's partner managed to graze Blaire's thigh, but she assured me she was alright. I knew in the moment she wouldn't appreciate the irony of her being shot in the leg through a wall, so I kept it to myself.

As police arrived and took over the scene, Nolan, Blaire, and I sat on the front steps. Leaning to Blaire's ear, I said, "I suppose our friends from this evening will be the next to show up once they find out we're here."

She checked her watch. "No worries. Help is on the way."

I still had yet to learn who "help" was.

My watch read 2:00 a.m. when three black cruisers made a line down Steve McDowell's driveway. A pair of agents emerged from each, but remained near their vehicles, as if waiting for someone. One paced the driveway on the phone, not speaking much, but nodding and offering occasional "yes sir"s as if taking an earful. Ten minutes later, a blacked out Suburban parked at the bottom of the driveway, and a single man emerged. As he made his way into view, there was no mistaking who it was.

Blaire let out a deep sigh next to me. "There he is."

Phineas Wexler scowled at his agents and led the way to greet us at the front porch.

"Mr. Bragg, Mr. Quimby, Miss Devereaux," he said. "It appears you've had yourselves quite an eventful evening."

"Just helping out a friend," I said.

"As I've heard. I wouldn't call it a most traditional strategy, although I cannot say the job isn't done. I would, however, recommend inviting law enforcement into the matter next time."

"He tried," Nolan said. "They thought he was full of it. Lousy police force around here, if you ask me."

"Ah, incompetent law enforcement–a brilliant segway into the reason for my visit." He gestured to the six agents behind him. "It appears the members of my team paid you a visit earlier this evening, which turned into a sort of cat and mouse game. Do you recall?" We nodded. He turned to the agent that had been on the phone earlier. "Agent Withers, please explain the reason for your bombardment this evening."

The man stepped forward meekly. "Well sir, Lance McGuire was confirmed missing a day ago, and a search of his home suggested foul play. When we heard of Miss Devereaux's reappearance in Dixon–"

"You decided to summon the troops and raid the home she'd just moved back into," Wexler cut him off. "You remember I've been promoted to your SSA, don't you? But did you care to run it past me, get my approval?"

". . .No."

"No, you did not. A simple query as to my opinion on the matter would've shut it down completely. A few minutes of research would show you that Blaire Devereaux has not been within a hundred miles of Washington D.C. or Lance McGuire in a year at minimum."

I stood in amazement at Wexler's rant as he continued to tell off his subordinates and throw any suspicion from Blaire into the wind. Much of this was new information to Nolan, as we hadn't completely filled him in on what had transpired earlier, so he was as transfixed as I.

Finally, Wexler turned back to us. "I apologize, Miss Devereaux, for this ransacking of your domestic life, especially at a moment that could have prevented you from carrying out your life-saving feat this evening. Please forgive my agents for the inconvenience, I assure you they will not go unpunished. Goodnight."

With that, Wexler returned to his car, as did his agents, tails between their legs.

"So Wexler was your partner in all this?" Nolan asked Blaire in a whisper. "How did that happen?" I was wondering the same thing.

"We both stood plenty to gain from McGuire's disappearance," she explained. "For Wexler, every day that monster was on the streets was another day he knew he could be assassinated. As for me, well, I'm sure I've made it clear by now." She laid her head on my shoulder and closed her eyes. Quietly she said, "I'd like to go home now."

Gabe walked us to Nolan's car, thanking us up and down. "I don't know what may have happened tonight without you all, I really appreciate it."

"Let's just hope one of these days we'll be able to sit down together without any of our lives being in danger," I said.

"I'm sure we will," he said. As he walked back to the house, he casually threw over his shoulder a comment that would linger in my mind for several days. "You really impressed me, Chris. You should do this for a living."

I shifted down as I took the off-ramp off of I-95. My head was clear for the first time in months, a decision so quickly made by my heart that my brain hadn't even had time to question it. The only pondering that had been done was on whether or not to involve those closest to me. But even that had not lasted long.

Nolan, my best friend, whom I loved more than I did myself, was well on his way to a successful career. It was something he was passionate about, and more importantly, something that the world needed. Even after everything this cruel world had thrown him into, everything that had left both physical and psychological scars, he still felt he owed it something. Nolan's heart was better than many, and if anyone could brighten what little good was left in the world, he could. That was why I knew he was better off left on his path.

I'd questioned Blaire outright whether or not she wanted to be involved in my next step, and she'd given the answer that I'd been hoping for. She was the love of my life, and was beginning to show me that I may be that of hers, and the only dream she'd ever had was to live a normal, civilized, boring life. One where she can wake up in the morning and not worry if it was the last time. One where she can walk downtown and smile at the person passing by, and not have to watch them go in fear that they may have a bead on the back of her head. One where I can pick her up and take her out to dinner without having to watch out for the next ambush. That was why I left her home that morning, eating pancakes on the balcony.

I drove alone into the driveway of Phineas Wexler's country home. How easily I'd made this decision, how I hadn't realized until Gabe said it that every piece of the puzzle had fallen directly into place. How I'd finally understood that these things didn't happen to me out of coincidence, they happened because it was who I was. People try to kill each other every day, crime runs the world, but I had never noticed until I'd been the one involved. A bird doesn't wait to fly until it falls out of the tree, it flies because it's a bird and it's meant to do so. I had fallen out the tree enough times now to realize that I was supposed to be flying.

So when Wexler invited me into his study and asked what brought me to Springfield, I wasted no time. "Well, as a matter of fact, it deals with the subject of my last visit here. If you remember, you'd made a proposition to Nolan, Blaire, and I."

He nodded. "I recall."

"While today it's only me," I said. "I'm wondering, does that offer still stand?"

Phineas Wexler smiled. "Mr. Quimby, I'm glad you asked."

Made in the USA
Columbia, SC
24 March 2023

cab65c23-e1a7-4b7a-918c-355612306cd2R01